# Whispers Before Death

## Death Agents Book One

G. L. Didaleusky

Published by Rogue Phoenix Press, LLP


ISBN: 978-1-62420-443-2

Credits
Cover Design: Design by Ms G
Editor: Deborah C. Day

# Dedication

To my wife, Holly. Thank you for your love, patience and advise.

# Prologue

The students in Ms. Maddox's eleventh-grade world history class sat at their desks looking down and reading a handout assignment. On the wall to the right of the classroom door hung a wall clock. The wall clock's large hand sat on eleven and the small hand was on twelve. In five minutes, the school bell would blare its piercing ring, ending the fourth period. One of her students, Allen Murdock, who sat in the front row, peered up at her. His eyebrows raised as far as they could, displaying the upper whites of his eyes; his mouth gaping. Fear stared back at her.

A few seconds later, Murdock's lips moved up and down, uttering a faint whisper—no one could hear but him. He then gently laid his forehead on the top of his desk.

Ms. Maddox walked over to his desk and tapped his shoulder. "Aren't you feeling good, Allen?"

He didn't answer her.

His head flopped to the right, resting the right side of his face on top of the desk. Wide-opened emerald-colored eyes appeared to gaze toward the desk next to him. Drool spilled out from the right side of his mouth. His chest ceased movement. A previously energetic teenager sat lifeless in his chair.

~ * ~

The noise threshold of the high school cafeteria, filled to near capacity, neared the decibels of a rock concert. How anyone could hear their fellow student sitting across from them at the long rectangular tables seemed impossible. With their iPads playing piercing music—and not Beethoven or other classical orchestrated renditions—these students in the future would more than likely be wearing hearing aids.

"Can you believe it?" said Cindy. "Paul asking Mary to the senior prom and not you. What a jerk. And I thought you and Paul were good friends."

"I thought we were too," said Pam, sitting across from Cindy at the crowded high school cafeteria table.

"I'm sure this is for the best. I have a feeling he would've ignored you at the prom anyway."

A lanky, pimple-faced boy walked up to Cindy from behind. "Hi, Cindy."

She turned and looked up. "Hey, Aaron. What's going on?"

"Not much."

Cindy turned back toward Pam: whose head now lay on top of crossed arms. Reaching over the table, she flicked her middle finger on top of Pam's head. She didn't flinch. "Come on girl. You can't be tired. The lunch bell's going to ring in a few minutes." She flicked her finger again.

Pam still didn't move.

She reached across the table, lifting Pam's head off her arms. Dead eyes stared back at her.

Cindy's scream silenced the noisy high school cafeteria.

# Chapter One

Michael Bennett, a family practice physician, pulled his car in next to his wife's SUV in the garage of their two-story colonial house at five thirty-five p.m. A few moments later he walked into the kitchen where his wife, Crystal, stood next to the stove. Sitting at the kitchen table were his two teenage children. "Hi, everyone."

"Hi, Daddy," said Carla, his thirteen-year-old daughter.

"Hey, Dad," said Matthew, his fifteen-year-old son.

Michael walked over and kissed Crystal on the lips. "How's my best girl?"

"I'm good, honey. Please sit down. Supper is almost ready."

He raised his head and sniffed. "Supper sure smells good."

The phone rang on the kitchen counter. "Are you on call tonight?" asked Crystal.

"No. John's on call." He picked up the phone. "Hello." Michael listened to the caller at the other end of the line. "Yes, Randy Mitchell is a patient of mine." He listened to the caller. His shoulders slumped; his face became ashen. "What was the cause of his death?" Michael looked toward Crystal. "Oh, I see. No. He wasn't taking any medications, nor did he have any medical problems. Thank you for calling me."

"Who were you talking to?"

"A forensic investigator from the medical examiner's office. A patient of mine died today."

"Oh, one of your older patients?"

"No. He was sixteen years old."

"Did he die in a car accident?" Carla asked.

"No. His mother got home from shopping around three o'clock and found her son sitting in front of his bedroom computer with his head resting on the desk. He was dead."

"Holy shit!"

"Matthew, don't swear," said Crystal.

"Sorry, Mom. But two kids today died at school. One was found in the classroom sitting at his desk with his head resting on his arms. The other one, a girl, was in the cafeteria sitting at a table with friends. They said she was talking with her girlfriend then laid her head down on her arms and died. They both died around noon."

In the twenty years as a doctor, Michael couldn't remember three teenagers dying in different settings with a similar presentation: heads peacefully resting on top of their arms or desks. Were they friends who ingested something in a suicide pack? A drug screen and an autopsy would answer his speculation. His sister was a Marion County Sheriff's detective. She might know something about these deaths, or she might know if the teenagers knew each other. He'd give her a call after supper.

"What do you think these kids could've died from?" asked Crystal, taking the meatloaf out from the oven and placing it on the kitchen table onto a large hot pad.

Michael told her what he thought about the teenagers' deaths. "I'll call Janet after supper. She may know something."

During supper, no one further discussed the teenagers' deaths. One scenario of these deaths crossed Michael's mind. Some type of virus, bacteria or even a devastating fungal infection could've caused these deaths. And were these three deaths the beginning stages of a contagious biological entity? Although, there should've been warning signs such as fever, headache, pain, or neurological manifestations. Did any of these teenagers have any of those medical signs before they suddenly died? There was one problem with this scenario: it would've been impossible for these victims to die about the same time, including the Mitchell boy, who probably also died near noon today. The teenagers being part of a suicide pack was a more logical scenario to Michael.

After supper, Michael called his sister, Janet, from the bedroom, where there could be privacy from his children. His kids would blab any of the latest information about the deaths of their fellow students to their friends at school. "Hi, Janet. How are you doing?"

"Doing okay. I'm sure you're calling about all these deaths occurring a couple minutes before noon today. Am I right?"

"Yeah, you're right. You always get right to the point." He was eleven months older than Janet. They were close growing up. As the big brother, he had protected her in elementary and middle school, and up to her junior year in high school from any potential bullies. Although, his little sister could handle herself with her cocky attitude of: *If you don't like me or what I think, that's your problem.* "So, are the three teenagers' deaths related? Like a suicide pack?"

There was momentary silence. "You know I can't tell you anything over the phone even if I knew the answer. Unless I was authorized by the sheriff' department's news media liaison. But there are more deaths than the three teenagers."

"What are you talking about? More people died today?"

"Don't you listen to the news? Five others died under mysterious circumstances in Ocala today. They all died around twelve o'clock noon."

"Was this a mass suicide pack? Like a cult? How could eight people all die around the same time unless it was a premeditated act by all of them?" Michael had no other explanation.

"I can't say one way or the other."

"Can you tell me this? Have you been assigned to the investigation? I'm sure this isn't restrictive information."

"You are persistent, Big Brother." She chuckled. "Yes. I'm investigating one of these deaths. The fact is, I'm at the home of the boy who died sitting at his bedroom desk. He was homeschooled. A few minutes ago, the medical examiner left with the deceased. The ME's investigator told me she'd talked to you earlier on the phone about the boy's medical status. You told her the boy didn't have any medical problems or any indications of drug abuse."

"Yes, I did tell her these facts. I guess I'm now part of your investigation." His sister couldn't say too much on the phone about the deaths of the teenagers. They couldn't be sure who might be listening in on their conversation. This was the twenty-first century, the age of the government's stealthy listening tactics of *speak no evil* against the US government or its citizens or non-citizens. There was no assurance of privacy when talking with someone by phone or any other means of communication in the world of electronic surveillance today.

"Sort of. I'd say indirectly and superficially, Big Brother. I gotta get going. Talk to you soon. Bye."

Crystal walked into the bedroom. "What did your sister have to say about the three teenagers' deaths?"

"Nothing. Other than she's the lead detective in one of the investigations, a patient of mine, Randy Mitchell. Janet couldn't say too much on the phone since she's in the middle of the investigation at the Mitchells' house. I can't imagine what Randy's parents are feeling now." He reached over, gently grabbed Crystal's hand and kissed the back of it. "We'd be devastated if it was one of our kids."

~ * ~

Janet Bennett put her cell phone into a holder on her belt then turned to her partner, Detective Bill Matters, who stood next to Randy Mitchell's bedroom dresser writing something into a small notebook. "We need to check for any suicide note and anything related to suicide, cults, or anything pertinent to him suddenly dying."

"You're right," Bill said, as he walked over to the desk. "I'll examine his computer since it's already on."

"Good. I'll look around the room for any evidence pointing to why or how the Mitchell boy died."

Matters' five-foot, ten-inch overweight frame sat at the desk chair. "I think I need to go on a diet," he muttered as he squeezed into the desk chair. His body didn't have any room to spare. He played halfback for the Tennessee Volunteers' college football team twenty years ago. Of course, he gained about thirty pounds since the last time he carried the ball through an opening in the offensive frontline.

Janet opened all the dresser drawers, looked under the bed and between the mattress and box springs of the young Mitchell boy's room for drugs, drug paraphernalia, or a suicide note. Nothing was found. "Did you find anything, Bill?"

"Nope. Not a thing. No mention of how to kill yourself without leaving a trace of evidence or material relating to dying or suicide in the computer search engines' history files."

Janet picked up Mitchell's cell phone lying next to the computer and checked it for recent messages. "The last person he'd talked with was Derrick Olsen at 11:58 this morning. It's around the time the other teenagers died. This could be the break we've been looking for." Janet called him.

"Hey, man," said Derrick. "Why did you hang up on me?"

"This is Detective Bennett from the Marion County Sheriff's Office. Are you Derrick Olsen?"

"Yeah. Why are you on Randy's cell phone?"

Janet couldn't tell him about his friend. It would be against police procedures when dealing with a minor. "Your friend Randy can't come to the phone. Did you talk with him this morning?"

"Yeah, detective. It was around noon. We were talking, then he suddenly stopped talking. I thought maybe his mom was coming, so he hung up on me. Is he all right? Did he get into trouble?"

"I can't discuss this with you. Can you tell me if he said anything unusual before he stopped talking with you?"

"No." A short pause, "He did whisper something. But I couldn't make out what he said. Then the phone went dead."

"Thank you, young man." Janet then put the cell phone in an evidence bag. She told Bill what the victim's friend had said.

"We'll have Randy Mitchell's computer analyzed for any hidden and relevant information by our computer forensic department. Also, his cell phone." Bill turned off the desktop computer.

They left the bedroom, talked with the parents briefly and walked to their car parked in the street. The Crime Scene Investigation team was finishing up, gathering possible pertinent evidence, including Randy Mitchell's computer and cell phone.

Janet pulled out of the Mitchell's driveway. "I don't ever remember deaths like these before," said Detective Matters.

"Because there's never been eight deaths occurring in the same manner, at different crime scenes, and happening around the same time."

Janet parked their unmarked car in the designated area of the Marion County Sheriff's Office Major Crime Unit. She'd been a detective for twelve years, the last five years with the Major Crime Unit. In all her years in law enforcement she'd never encountered so many unexplained deaths at once. Her brother might be right about a mass suicide. The toxicology report on all these victims would answer the question of suicide. If the deaths pointed toward self-induced then the next logical step in this investigation would lead to the organization or group initiating these deaths.

Janet and Bill walked into their office, a large room accommodating eight desks with space to spare, including a large coffee maker in the corner of the room. All the detectives of the major crime unit occupied the room. They chatted on a serious tone with one another. Their faces were solemn, not displaying any signs of jovialness. Most mornings and afternoons, at least one or two detectives joked around with one another.

She talked with the other detectives about their investigations on the deaths of their victims. Eight victims had mysteriously died. Ages ranging from fifteen to seventy-five. One had died in her car while stopped at a stop sign; three were at work; three died at home; and two died at school. There weren't any signs of trauma on any of the bodies. This was all the information the detectives had on their deaths so far.

Their boss, Captain Robins, walked into the room with two men in their thirties. The two strangers wore identical dark-grey suits. Janet didn't recognize them but assumed they were federal law enforcement, likely FBI by the stoic stature and attire. Robins gestured for them to come over.

"Detective Bennett and Matters," said the captain, "these are Special Agents Williams and Carpenter from the FBI."

Janet's assumption of whom the two unidentified men represented was right on. She had the innate ability to quickly assess a situation or person and come up with an accurate observation a good percentage of the time. They wouldn't be involved unless federal law was broken by these deaths. She nodded to each of them. "I assume some federal law statute was broken due to eight people dying at two minutes to noon today?"

"Yes. Correct," Carpenter answered. "One of the victims was in the witness protection program. And he was going to testify against a major drug dealer in New York next month."

Janet's legs felt rubbery as an arctic blast of frigid air seemed to wrap around her spine. The face of the dead fifteen-year-old sitting at his bedroom desk flashed across her mind. "Why kill seven innocent people in order to kill a person in hiding from an organized crime syndicate? It doesn't make any sense to me. Or it was a coincidence the informant was included in these mysterious deaths?"

"It may be a coincidence, detective." Agent Williams answered. "Or it may be a monstrous act by criminals or a psychopath. Either one doesn't have any empathy toward human life."

"Whatever the reason for these deaths, a criminal element was involved by all indications."

Both the agents nodded.

"But what's more intriguing with these deaths...what could've caused these people to die around the same moment in time?" Janet asked.

"Just as you and your detectives, we don't have an answer yet either."

Janet glanced away. She visualized an electronic timer of some kind inside the victims' bodies switched to the off position at 11:58 this morning.

~ * ~

Michael walked out the bedroom with his wife, Crystal. As they walked into the living room a TV news anchor stated: *It has been confirmed, eight people, including three children, had died at exactly 11:58 this morning. According to reliable sources these deaths don't appear be a suicide pack. There hasn't been any medical cause of their deaths. Sources aren't excluding this was a terrorist act....*

A cold chill streaked from the back of Michael's neck to every muscle in his face, as if he had stuck his head into an opened freezer. His first assumption regarding the deaths in Ocala was that they all died due to a suicide pack. But this assumption had now lost credibility. "From what the news reporter said we're not dealing with suicide deaths in Ocala. I'm going to call Janet back and see if she can stop by the house after she gets off work. She may know more than what was reported by the news media."

Around eight o'clock, the front doorbell rang. He suspected it had to be Janet, since her sister told him she'd be over in about two hours. During the two hours waiting for his sister, he had searched the internet for the latest information on these deaths and, if any logical theory of how everyone could have suddenly died a couple minutes before noon today. Of course, there were the usual explanations: aliens from outer space had something to do with these deaths. Or all these victims had taken capsules at exactly 11:58 in the morning. Each of the victims had been brainwashed and programmed to take the capsules at the same time. There weren't any medically feasible explanations for their deaths, so far. Of course, an autopsy would be done to determine a cause of the mysterious deaths. Toxicology would determine if any substances were ingested.

"Hi, Sis. Glad you were able to stop by."

She frowned and contorted her lips as a grumpy face peered back at him. "I had to come over, otherwise you'd be calling me throughout the night with questions about all of these suspicious deaths."

"You sure know me. Can't help it. It's my inquisitive nature. You're graced with the same genetic trait in your body as do I. It's why you became a detective and I became a doctor."

Janet grinned. "Yeah. A Sherlock and Dr. Watson combo."

Michael sat at the kitchen table with Janet as she discussed the findings in the deaths of the three teenagers, something she couldn't say over the phone. Crystal watched TV in the living room. His children were in their bedrooms doing what teenagers do; communicating with friends on their electronic devices—an iPhone—and wouldn't be listening in on their parents and aunt's conversation. Young people and a growing number of middle-aged and older people were becoming addicted to their iPhones, iPads, tablets, laptops, desktop computers or a combination of them. Landline phones were becoming obsolete to all the generations, especially anyone born in the twenty-first century. If Carla or Matthew weren't talking to their friends, music from their electronic devices would be blaring out the latest song or tune into their ear buds.

Janet told Michael about the FBI's involvement.

"Does the FBI have any idea what had caused these deaths?"

"No. Not a clue. At least, this is what the agents said. Working with them in the past, they don't always give you full disclosure of information. It's a territorial thing. They like to be in charge. Their philosophy is, 'what latest information is ours and what information you get is ours,' if you know what I mean?"

"It's like what Crystal told me after we got married."

"What did she tell you?"

"What's mine is mine. And what's yours is mine." He chuckled. *Of course, she was kidding me.* He and Crystal had a good relationship and shared everything with one another. They didn't have any secrets between them. "It's not a one-sided marriage, as you already know."

Janet nodded, frowned. "You had to rub it in? Since you know my ex basically cared about himself, creating a one-sided marriage."

Michael's shoulders slumped, as he glanced away. "I'm really sorry, Sis. I didn't mean to bring up—"

"There's nothing to be sorry about, big brother," she interrupted. "My marriage to him wasn't your fault."

He raised his shoulders, nodded and sighed. She had divorced Rick about a year ago. Thank God his sister didn't have any kids with him. For sure, he wouldn't have given financial or emotional support to a family. Janet stated it right, *he cared about himself and no one else.*

"You told me before I married him, ten years ago, he wasn't the right guy for me. Of course, I didn't listen to you. And I let my emotions blind me for what he was…a selfish asshole." She got up from her chair, went to the kitchen counter and poured another cup of coffee from the coffee pot. The coffee was made by her sister-in-law earlier. She then turned around and added, "What was even worse, several years passed before I realized who and what I'd married. Toward the end of my marriage to him, I finally admitted to myself that I'd made a mistake in marrying him. I have a tough time even mentioning his name. Instead I refer to my ex as 'him' rather than Rick."

"I'm sure you'll find the right guy."

"Hum. Maybe."

"You're pretty and smart." Janet stood five-foot nine-inches tall with short, blonde hair. Her size twelve slacks with a belt containing her holstered nine-millimeter gun and a pair of handcuffs fit snugly around a slim waistline. A size twelve, grey sports coat fit comfortably on her, covering her handcuffs and weapon. Michael snickered to himself. *Unfortunately, she's probably intimidating to most men, either before or after they find out she's a sheriff detective.*

Janet smirked. "I've heard this line ten years ago and look where it got me. If you weren't my brother, I'd take your compliment about me as an ominous statement and prompting me to walk away from you and not look back."

After about an hour of discussion, Michael and Janet concluded the deaths of all these people occurring exactly at 11:58 in the morning was an act of terrorism by its definition: The use of violence to instill panic as a means of achieving some type of goal. If this scenario turned out to be true of why all these people had died—even though no group had come forward and claimed responsibility—then what was their goal or reason for this evil act? Who were the perpetrators behind this horrendous act? And another important question: How did they achieve killing eight people in different areas of Ocala at the same time? Michael suggested there had to be a network of malevolent militants using a chemical or device directed at their victims. The logistics of delivering their deadly outcome was monumental. Yet these possible unknown terrorists completed this evil act flawlessly. Michael and Janet dismissed the idea of one psychopath responsible for this heinous act, it would've been logistically impossible.

"These deaths were deliberate, instigated by evilness," Janet said.

"I agree." Michael got up, put their empty coffee cups into the dishwasher and turned off the coffee pot. He turned around and rubbed his chin as an ominous possibility flashed across his mind.

"You look as if you stepped on an explosive device ready to explode, big brother."

"What if these deaths today were only the beginning? And possibly many more people will perish in the near future at another selected time."

The thought of this possibility frightened them.

## Chapter Two

Janet woke up to her alarm clock buzzing. She rolled over in bed, half awake and glanced at six-thirty flashing its red numbers back at her. She fumbled for the off button and turned off the aggravating sound. She had left her brother's house around ten-thirty last night and didn't fall asleep until about midnight. Her last conscious thought before falling asleep asked: *Would the people in forensics find the cause of all these mysterious deaths?* The same question crossed her mind this morning as she sat up at the side of the bed.

The morning light filtered through the mini-blind and the bedroom's white sheer curtain. She would call Barry Sullivan, the head of the forensic department, as soon as she got to work. The two of them had a good working relationship, bouncing off crime scene information to each other beyond the standard police and crime scene investigation department's protocol. There wasn't any amorous attraction between them. They were more like first cousins—mutual friends at work. She grinned. *Although he's good looking and a bachelor at thirty-three.* She got up, walked to the bathroom and took a shower.

Janet parked her car in a designated space and went to the Forensic Lab.

"Hi, Barry. How ya doing?" He sat at a long, hospital-white counter staring into a microscope.

He turned around on a swivel chair. "Hey. No complaints." He reached into his lab coat and removed his eyeglasses, putting them on. "I know what you're going to ask me. No. There isn't any explanation for the deaths of these victims. The medical examiner's preliminary report on the eight autopsies so far is *Undetermined Deaths*. We're still waiting on toxicology results. They should be done sometime today according to the ME."

"You're psychic as usual, Barry. You always seem to know what I'm about to ask you."

"Part of my job description, Ma'am." He paused, wrinkling his forehead. "Or was my job description 'psycho' instead of psychic? I always get those two mixed up."

They both laughed.

Almost every time she'd come to the lab to talk with Barry, he'd make a funny comment about something. She loved his witty humor. "Anyway, I was hoping you'd have some information on the cause of these deaths."

"So were we. There weren't any track marks indicating IV drug use on any of the victims. And the ME didn't find any abnormalities in their bodies. There were a few people in the news media reporting a possibility of electronic implants in the victims' bodies causing their deaths." Barry shook his head. "Can you believe that? It's something you'd see in a TV science fiction series or something in a Hollywood movie. Not in the real world."

"I can believe it. The news media is anxious to know the cause of these deaths. And when someone in the media conjectured a possible means for these mysterious deaths, news reporters clung onto this implanted electronic device theory for sensational news, to increase TV and radio ratings."

He snickered. "Isn't that the truth."

"Talk to you later, Barry. Let me know if you get any more information on these deaths."

"You got it, kiddo."

Janet grinned. Barry had been calling her "kiddo" right after they became work friends. It was a term of endearment, like "baby girl" used between two team members on a popular TV crime series.

She left the lab and headed toward her office in the adjacent building connected by a common hallway. When she got to her office most of the other detectives were at their desks; some of them sat or stood drinking coffee and conversing with other detectives while others sat by themselves reading—a typical early morning in the Major Crime Division. She glanced across her desk to an adjacent desk with an empty desk chair where her partner, Bill Matters, normally sat. He was running late for work, as usual. Bill on many occasions would stop for coffee and get into a conversation with someone. It was one of his common reasons for showing up to work later than most of the other detectives.

Janet sat down and checked the voice mail on her telephone for any messages. On previous death cases under her investigation she'd have numerous messages, most of them worthless without any merit. But not this time. There weren't any messages in the voice mailbox. Where were the calls from the crackpots wanting their fifteen minutes of fame, and from those wanting to confess to these tragic crimes? It seemed people from all walks of life, sane to mentally unstable, were afraid of the deadly events yesterday, afraid they may be the next victims. In the annals of crime or in the news media's time vault of tragic stories, Janet hadn't ever confronted similar deaths of this magnitude or scope. She and everyone involved in these apparent homicides were facing a challenge never encountered before.

Janet reached down, opened the file drawer in her desk and pulled out the file on her dead teenager. She stared at the file and sighed. *What a shame. He was so young.* Her thoughts flashed back to Jeffery Stone, the first teenage homicide she'd investigated about five years ago during her first month with the Major Crime Division. At the homicide scene, the victim sat behind the steering wheel of his car with a bullet hole in the side of his head. A jealous girlfriend had decided to take matters into her own hands, a hand holding a loaded gun, missing one bullet from its chamber. Her present homicide had no apparent trauma. And so far, no motive for her victim's death.

"Good morning," said Bill walking up to his desk with a smile.

"Why do you look so cheerful?" Her partner on most occasions had a stoic appearance, morning, noon and night. His serious-minded demeanor could be compared to the head boss on *Criminal Minds*. In addition, Bill had five children ranging between the ages of seven and sixteen. Janet didn't have any children. Although, she could imagine the mental stress dwelling in the mind of Bill. Each day putting himself in harm's way as a detective, hoping he would come home safely to his wife and kids. Bill and many detectives with a family knew there could be a phone call to their wife, husband or significant other from someone in the Sheriff's Department, stating their companion had been shot or killed in the line of duty. Therefore, the seriousness and danger incorporated around detective work produced a serious demeanor in those individuals involved.

"I stopped at a convenience store for a cup of coffee and decided to buy a lottery scratch off. I rarely play the lottery. I can't remember the last time I bought a scratch off. All I can say is an unknown force made me purchase it. I scratched it off, and low and behold I won five hundred dollars!"

"Aren't you a lucky duck? As they say to players in the lottery world, 'play a hunch, win a bunch.'" Janet played the lottery twice a week with the same lucky numbers. She started playing right after she turned eighteen. She had never won any significant amount of money, but still she continued to play the same numbers every time. A dream for a dollar, she'd say to herself. Her brother told her it was a waste of money. Janet told him on several occasions during her investigations luck and hunches sometimes played a role in solving the crime. Of course, hard evidence normally led to an arrest of a perpetrator and the eventual conviction in a court of law.

A grin appeared on Detective Matters. "My hunch paid off. Even though you're the one who plays hunches, at least in our investigations."

Janet's desk telephone rang. A sudden fear engulfed her entire body, as if she had jumped into a swimming pool filled with ice cubes. Since she was a child, she'd experience this reaction without warning. The frigid sensation occurred before an ominous or auspicious event or situation, including phone calls. No rhyme or reason explained why at times this feeling of an arctic blast overwhelmed her. Someone many years ago told Janet her subconscious mind had psychic powers tuned into important future happenings. For a few seconds her body trembled, her smile disappeared, replaced with a grimace. All signs of her premonition. She glanced at Bill. His jovial expression changed to a solemn one. Her partner recognized her foreboding appearance.

Janet reached for the phone and picked it up. "This is Detective Bennett. Can I help you?"

"No," said a man with a soft voice, "but I can help you."

Janet was taken aback by the comment. "What do you mean by that?" She heard a deep sigh at the other end of the line from the caller. Was he one of these crackpots she'd hear from during a high-profile crime? "Are you still there?"

"Yes. You may find what I'm about to tell you as strange or crazy…but believe me, Detective Bennett, it's real. It has to do with all the people in Ocala dying yesterday a couple minutes before noon. Can we meet…so I can talk to you face to face? I'd rather not discuss it over the telephone."

"You can come to the sheriff's office. We can talk here."

"I'd rather meet somewhere else than there. If you don't mind?"

Janet frowned. *Now why does this person on the phone want to meet me somewhere else other than here at the sheriff's office? And why doesn't he want to discuss whatever information he has on these deaths over the phone?* This was beginning to sound like a cloak and dagger situation you'd see in a James Bond movie. "Okay. But I'll at least need your name."

"My name is Simon Woods. You already have my phone number on your caller ID sitting on your desk to your right, next to the little statue of a green frog."

Janet glanced down at the frog, then stood and looked around the room, making sure her caller wasn't standing somewhere in the room.

"What's wrong?" Matters asked, frowning.

She moved the phone down to her side, so the caller couldn't hear. "I'll explain it to you in a minute." How did he know what was on her desk, unless he'd been here before? Janet said to the caller, "How did you—"

Simon Woods interrupted, "I've never been to the sheriff's office, and I've never seen a photograph of your desk. When we meet, I'll explain everything to you."

"Let's meet at Northgate Diner at the intersection of Old Jacksonville Road and Thirty-Fifth Street in about forty minutes. Do you know where it is?"

"Not exactly. But it shouldn't be a problem finding it. I'll be wearing a University of Florida Gator cap."

Janet put the receiver down. "We may have a lead on these deaths."

"Do you want me to go with you?"

"Not necessary, Bill. I can handle this possible lead by myself. You can finish the paper work on Randy Mitchell. Also, you can check with the other detectives of any other leads on these deaths."

His furrowed forehead lowered his bushy eyebrows. "How come I'm assigned to desk duty? I thought I was the senior partner here."

"Someone has to do it. And since the guy called me, it seemed logical I go meet with him." She grinned. "You're still the senior partner. I'd never take that away from you."

"At least I still have some prestigious recognition with you."

She explained to Bill what Simon Woods had said, including the frog on her desk. They concluded someone must've told him about it. There wasn't any other feasible answer. And as far as why the caller didn't want to talk on the phone, there were many scenarios to explain why. He didn't want to be seen going into a law enforcement building because he was involved in a street gang. Several occasions in the past, unscrupulous people with information about a criminal case had requested a meeting outside, in secluded or public locations. They weren't even sure Simon Woods was the caller's real name. At the restaurant, in less than an hour from now, Janet would ask him these questions and other questions regarding the mysterious deaths yesterday morning.

Janet pulled into the parking lot of the restaurant. She had already obtained information on a Simon Woods. He should be a forty-five-year-old Caucasian male without any felony charges. DMV didn't have any record of him having any driving violations. The guy was apparently a model citizen. He lived in a house situated in a low crime, middle-class part of Ocala. Woods worked as a roofer. He was married with a son and daughter in their twenties, if in fact, he was whom he claimed to be.

Janet opened the restaurant's door and walked inside, not knowing if Woods was already there, waiting for her.

# Chapter Three

Northgate Diner was filled with patrons as she walked inside and stood at the entranceway. There were a couple of tables and booths available to sit at. Chatter created a vibrating mixture of voices throughout the room, making it difficult to make out what was being said in any of the conversations. It was an ideal environment to talk with someone at a booth or table and not be easily overheard or understood. Most restaurants were relatively quiet where conversations can be heard by someone sitting at a table or booth within a short distance from you. Besides being the ideal place to talk with someone, the food was great and inexpensive. She glanced around the room to see if any male was sitting alone wearing a Gator's baseball cap. None. Everyone sat with at least one other person. A booth in the corner to her left was unoccupied. She sat down and ordered a glass of orange juice, along with a half order of biscuits and gravy. If Simon didn't show up at least she'd have a breakfast. She glanced down at her watch. About forty minutes had passed since she talked to the mystery man who had vital information about the eight deaths yesterday.

The entrance door to the restaurant opened. A couple in their sixties walked in and waved to another couple sitting at a table across the room.

Ten minutes had passed, and Janet had eaten half of her biscuits and gravy. The door opened again. A sudden chill engulfed her entire body as she stared toward the door. A man in his early thirties wearing a University of Florida Gator cap walked in and stopped. He glanced around the room, then stopped when he peered to his left at her. Janet nodded, acknowledging he had found her. *This wasn't the Simon Woods on the DMV picture.* She had experienced two psychic chills toward him, once when he called her and now. Was this a premonition of evilness or good fortune toward her?

Or was it something else?

"Sorry. I'm a little late," he said as he sat across from her at the booth.

He was clean shaven with a medium build. His chestnut-brown hair nudged through the bottom of his cap. Deep blue eyes peered back at her. He was good looking. "No problem. I'm glad you found the restaurant. Would you like breakfast, a cup of coffee or something else to drink?"

"No thanks, I'm fine. I already ate. And I don't drink coffee. Caffeine makes my heart race."

Janet pushed the plate with her remaining biscuits and gravy to the right. She glanced at his left hand. He didn't have a wedding band. His nails and cuticles were well-manicured. She speculated he didn't do any type of manual labor. He had a confident posture with shoulders back, chest forward and a neck erect with a straightforward positioned head. All these physical features complemented his stoic expression. He wore his watch on his right wrist, indicating he was left-handed. A two-inch figure of a scorpion was positioned in the upper-left corner of his navy-blue pullover shirt, possibly representing his Horoscope sign. She had also noticed when he was walking up to the table that he wore light-gray slacks and a pair of white tennis shoes. "In that case, tell me why you wanted to talk with me."

He chuckled. "You sure get to the point."

Janet had been told this statement many times ever since she was a child. Family, friends, acquaintances, people she worked with at the sheriff's department, all had remarked about her brashness. She believed why beat around the bush with trivial talk, it was a waste of time and effort. Someone once told her she must've been made from the same mold as the detective on the old TV program *Dragnet*, who'd say before interviewing a female witness or victim: *"Just the facts, Ma'am,"* or "*Sir*" to a male. "That's my job as a detective, Mr. Woods."

"Can't dispute your comment." The raised corners of his mouth expressing pleasantry dropped. He sighed, as he leaned forward. Clearing his throat, he continued: "What I'm about to tell you may sound a little crazy, like someone released or escaped from a mental ward in a psychiatric hospital. I've never been diagnosed or treated for any mental disorder. I can assure you I'm sane and rational as you are. The deaths yesterday—"

The front door opened and in walked a man about the size of a grizzly bear talking loudly in a deep raspy voice to a small-built man behind him. It seemed everyone in the restaurant turned to see who was talking, including Janet and Simon. The interruption gave her time to think about what Woods was about to tell her. She was skeptical in the manner how he introduced the word "crazy" regarding the information he was about to tell her. Was this guy going to tell her another one of those far-fetched explanations of a crime she'd heard many times before in past criminal cases? At least she had breakfast. All wasn't lost this morning, other than her time. She turned her attention toward Simon. "What about the deaths yesterday?"

"I was about to say, more people will die this morning at 11:58, the same way those other eight people died yesterday."

"How do you know this? Do you have something to do with their deaths?"

"I have nothing to do with their deaths. This morning before I called you at your office, I had a visual premonition of other people dying at 11:58."

"What do you mean you saw them dying? That doesn't make any sense."

"I've been having these visions of things happening in the future. And at times I'll get visions of objects and surroundings when talking with someone. Like talking with you this morning on the phone. A vision of a frog statue on your desk appeared. I knew it was your desk because your name on a silver nameplate sat next to the frog. These visions I get can occur at any time night or day. I'm sure, Detective Bennett, these visions I get all sounds crazy to you. But it's the truth."

Janet gazed into Simon's eyes and saw sincerity, sanity—not the eyes of a deranged individual; even though his declaration sounded like something out of a science fiction novel. She had to admit to herself, he did know about the frog on her desk and her silver nameplate. She can't ever remember having her picture taken in front of her desk. Besides, she bought the frog a couple weeks ago from a novelty shop at the mall. She couldn't be skeptical of Simon's declaration of his psychic powers since she sometimes experienced a chill overwhelming her entire body moments before an encounter with a person, phone call or an event. She wasn't sure why she experienced this feeling toward Simon. He didn't seem to be dangerous or evil. His pronouncement of having a gift of visual premonitions wasn't unheard of in the world of psychic phenomena. Although it could be a curse if it interfered with everyday living, preventing him from performing normal daily tasks. "I believe you."

"You do?" He sighed, leaned back against the back of the cushioned booth, and touched the tips of his fingers with the tips of fingers of the other hand. "Most people I tell about my visions shake their head in disbelief and laugh. You did neither."

Janet explained to him about her unpredicted psychic episodes of feeling a frigid burst engulf her body since she was a teenager. "I guess we're both somewhat clairvoyants in the world of psychic phenomenon."

Simon grinned. "You're right…we are."

"How long have you had these visual premonitions?"

Before he could answer, a waitress in her early fifties with reddish hair walked up to the booth and looked down at Simon. "What can I get for you, darling?"

"A glass of ice water. Thank you."

"You don't want anything to eat? We have a breakfast special this morning on our stuffed French toast with a choice of fruit topping. A young man like you needs to fuel his body for a workday."

"Your breakfast special really sounds great to me, Missy. But I already ate. Maybe next time."

The waitress turned to Janet. "You need anything else, sweetie?"

"No. I'm fine." The waitress placed Janet's bill on the table and left. "So how long have you had these premonitions?"

"Since I was around thirteen years old. At first the visions in my mind occurred couple times a month, then once I got in my twenties, they appeared about once a week. Now I get them at least once or twice a day. The visions last several seconds, such as this morning. Seven people suddenly died in my foreshadowing vision. The visions can be compared to speeding up a DVD movie three times."

*If Simon had this psychic power, he might know what caused those eight deaths yesterday*. "Do you have any idea what may have caused their deaths yesterday morning and now this morning?"

"No. I see the moment they die, not what caused their deaths. I didn't have a vision of yesterdays' deaths. I was in Atlanta, Georgia. I can only see deaths occurring in approximately a fifty-mile radius around me."

"So, you're not from Ocala?"

"No. I live near Atlanta." He paused. "One thing about these victims in my vision, they were all saying something before losing consciousness and dying."

A chill streaked up Janet's spine, not the warning sensation she'll get periodically. No. The chill was the body's normal reaction to an unexpected profound statement. There was no way Simon could have known these victims whispered something before they died yesterday morning. This detail of the eight deaths yesterday hadn't been told to the news media. It seemed to confirm Simon's declaration of his clairvoyance. "You're right about three of the victims—the teenagers—they whispered something before they died according to witnesses. There's two ways to know what these unfortunate teens were whispering before they died, standing or sitting next to them in a quiet environment, or if you were a lip reader. And what would be the odds of a lip reader being present with one of these victims when they whispered something inaudible to them before they suddenly died? Too bad you're not a lip reader."

Simon nodded, then grinned. "I'm not, detective. Otherwise, I'd know what they were saying this morning. I guess I could take a course in lip-reading. That would be feasible if we were assured there'd be daily deaths at 11:58 for the next three hundred and sixty-five days."

"God, I hope not." What if these deaths were the beginning of a perpetual occurrence of people suddenly dying two minutes before noon? If what Simon said was true about other people dying later this morning, there could be mass hysteria for the residence of Marion County and the city of Ocala. And how could she or anyone else prevent this from happening without knowing the reason and cause for these mysterious deaths? She thought a moment then asked, "During these visions, can you see where the people are, such as driving a car, sitting behind a desk or any other surroundings?"

Before Simon could answer, the waitress walked up to the booth and placed a glass of ice water in front of him. He looked up at the waitress. "Thank you." He then turned his attention toward Janet. "Yes, to answer your question. It's like I'm facing them a couple of feet away. I see what's behind them and a foot or two beside them. For instance, this morning, a vision of two teenagers dying appeared. One was an Asian girl sitting in a car and the other, a Caucasian girl sitting on what looked like a bleacher in a gym. A full bearded middle-aged black man driving a car with no one in the back seat, to mention a few of the victims." Simon closed his eyes. "A white male in his forties with a tattooed tear drop on his left cheek. He was riding a motorcycle without a helmet. There was an elderly black woman sitting on a lounge chair. Next to her was a table clock displaying 11:58. And finally, a man in his sixties painting a wall with a roller. All these people—"

"This could be helpful," interrupted Janet. "Not exactly sure how this will help us." *Now did I just recruit Simon as a consultant in the investigation, since I used "us" in my statement to him?*

"Did you recruit me for this investigation?"

"No. I meant everyone in my department who are involved in these deaths." Janet needed to be more careful when talking with Simon. He obviously listened attentively and picked up every word she had said. "Although, I can use you as an unofficial member of the investigative team." *Simon could be an asset to this investigation*. "The hours are long, and the pay is gratitude…no money."

His forehead furrowed as he grinned. "I've never been offered such a great proposition like this before. Do I get to carry a gun?"

Janet smiled. "How about a gun that shoots water?"

They both laughed. Several patrons in the restaurant turned their attention toward the two of them, apparently trying to figure out why they were laughing. Several seconds passed before the customers went back to their own conversations after the laughter stopped.

"I don't think a water gun will intimidate a criminal," Simon said, as he reached for his glass of water and sipped a drink through a straw.

Janet couldn't believe she made a joke about a serious situation of eight people mysteriously dying yesterday at exactly two minutes to noon. And now according to Simon more people will die today at the exact time as yesterday's victims. A psychic wasn't the normal type of informant she'd used before in the past. But she couldn't dismiss the details of the future victims whispering before dying. Either he was the perpetrator in those deaths yesterday, or in fact, he had accurate psychic powers. Her gut feelings told her it was the latter. But why did she experience her premonition chill before he walked into the restaurant? Simon may not have had anything to do with her premonition feeling. Maybe something else was about to happen to her shortly? She chased these questions from her mind and focused on Simon's visual premonitions, and the water gun. "All seriousness, I can't issue you a gun."

"The fact is, Detective Bennett, I already carry a gun. I have a concealed weapon permit to go with it."

Janet was taken aback by his comment, as she slid back against the back cushion of the booth, raised her eyebrows and peered into Simon's deep blue eyes. "Why do you have a concealed weapon?"

Simon reached into the inside of his jacket. What was he going to show Janet? She inhaled deeply, apparently not sure what to expect from a man she only met a little while ago.

~ * ~

Simon pulled out a wallet, flipped it open, displaying an official looking ID badge with his name. Above his name in bold, gold letters stated: FEDERAL MEDICAL INVESTIGATOR.

"I've never heard of this organization."

"I'm sure you haven't, Detective Bennett. It's a newly formed department of the CDC in Atlanta, Georgia. The department isn't connected to the CDC's normal medical investigative team. We're a covert group of three individuals with a special gift not recognized by the factual and traditional thinking of the federal, state or local medical communities."

"So, you're saying there are other people with your type of premonitions in your organization?"

"No. Not like mine. Two other people make up our group. Each with different abilities. Frank Littlefield, a computer analyst, has a keen sense of smell enabling him to distinguish the various scents a person had encountered in the recent past, such as drinking a diet Coke, touching motor oil, a rubber product and using isopropyl. In other words, he can surmise a person had drunk a soda recently, opened the hood of his car to check or change the motor oil, changed a car tire, and the perp was probably a diabetic. He can also follow the scent of where a person had recently come from. Frank has the super scent of a dog."

"Amazing."

"Our last agent, Jean Cliftwood, a physical therapist, has the uncanny ability to visualize a yellow glow—one that no one else can see—around a person who may possibly die or be seriously injured in the next twenty-four hours. She can't foresee what the person will experience or encounter, such as a heart attack, an accident or a victim of murder. The glow is a foreshadowing of possible death or serious bodily injury."

"Can she stop a person from dying or being injured?"

"Yes and no. For example, a few weeks ago in a restaurant late in the afternoon Jean overheard a man with the yellow glow scheduled to trim a tree on a hoist called a cherry picker the following morning. She convinced him not to go to work. She predicted the tree trimmer would've had a catastrophic injury or a life-ending accident while trimming a tree. Two days later, he trimmed trees without an incident."

"In other words, she can change the fate of a person."

"Yes. To some degree."

The three FMI agents must be prepared to be called in all hours of day and night to investigate strange medical occurrences throughout the United States. They might be gone a few days to a few weeks. Simon, Frank or Jean normally didn't walk into a county health department or a sheriff's, state or local police department and announce they were investigating an unusual medical case. Simon and his cohorts tried to keep a low profile. They were on the fringe of being a clandestine government agency. The investigative team decided to pick out a detective, medical examiner, or someone from the ME investigative team and confide with them about the eight deaths all occurring two minutes to noon yesterday. After doing thorough profiles on several candidates, they chose Janet. They were pretty sure she'd be open minded about the agents' special talents. The agents carried a concealed weapon due to the dangerous situations they put themselves into during their medical investigations. Simon explained these facts to Janet.

Janet sighed. "I've never heard of anything like this before. It sounds like something out of a science fiction novel." She intertwined her fingers in a fist and brought out her index fingers, placing them against her chin. "So why did you and your team choose me?"

Simon drank some of his water. "I can understand your skepticism, but it's the truth. As for why we chose you, you answered this question earlier regarding your ESP. A premonition feeling about something good or bad happening a few seconds or minutes before it occurs. You can't always distinguish which outcome will occur. I'd say you probably had this premonition before I walked into the restaurant. Am I right?" Simon was guessing. Although according to her team, Janet would have a forlorn expression prior to an unforeseen event, such as turning a corner while driving, answering a phone call or a door opening. Earlier he noticed this expression as he approached the booth.

"I did." She frowned, as she sat back and folded her arms in a defiant manner. "So, you pried into my professional and personal life? Is that what you're saying, federal agent man?"

Now he did it. Antagonized a sheriff's detective, a person he and his other agents were depending on to assist them in their investigation. He needed to get her cooperation. "Not entirely true, Detective Bennett. All of us were extremely impressed by your investigative prowess. As for any personal information, we obtain a minimal level of data. Our goal is to confide in a competent person such as you to help in our investigation into the cause of the mysterious deaths occurring yesterday. And unfortunately, those deaths yesterday will happen again this morning if my vision turns out to be accurate."

Janet uncrossed her arms, placing her palm-down hands on the table. A grin momentarily appeared followed by a look of concern. "Thank you for your confidence in me. I'll be glad to help you and your colleagues. But I think I should let my captain know I'll be helping your team."

Simon sighed. He hadn't intimated her. "Our medical director in Atlanta will be contacting him this morning. As far as everyone else in your department, you can tell them you're working with CDC in these deaths.

Which of course is somewhat the truth. And we'd appreciate you not telling anyone of our special abilities. Not everyone in your department may have the same view as you do. From my limited experience it is best to keep our abilities known to a few people outside our FMI team. The news media doesn't have any knowledge of the Federal Medical Investigators…at least not yet."

"No problem."

"By the way, that includes not telling your brother, Michael."

Janet shook her head. "I thought you only knew a little of my personal information."

"Your brother is part of the little personal information we have on you. And since he's a medical doctor, I'm sure you already talked with him about the eight deaths yesterday."

"Huh," she grumbled, followed by a frown. "Do you have a tap on my phone? I wouldn't be surprised Big Brother is listening in on my phone conversations."

"No. We don't have your phone tapped, Detective Bennett. I assumed you talked with him about the deaths. It was a logical assumption to me. That's all."

"A logical assumption?" She thought a moment. "I guess you're right. I'd think the same thing. To answer your request about my brother, I won't mention you or your organization, Federal Medical Investigators."

"I'd appreciate it." Simon's cell phone rang. The ring mimicked the Star Wars' theme music. He glanced down at the caller ID. It was Frank Littlefield. Simon answered on the second ring. "Hey, Frank."

"Can you talk?"

"I'm sitting here in the restaurant with Detective Bennett."

"Did she say yes?"

"Affirmative."

"Good. The reason I called was to let you know Jean and I talked with District Five's medical examiner. He was cooperative about those mysterious deaths yesterday. Of course, I didn't tell him about our special abilities. The preliminary autopsies on four of the eight victims yesterday didn't show any cause for their sudden deaths. They'll be doing the other four autopsies this morning. They're waiting for the drug screen results on all the victims. Did you learn anything from the detective?"

"No. Although, we haven't formally discussed the deaths yet. I thought we'd all meet back at the hotel in about forty-five minutes."

"We'll see you there."

Simon put his cell phone back into the holder attached to his belt. "We're going meet at the hotel in about forty-five minutes and discuss these deaths, and the deaths that'll probably occur this morning a couple minutes before noon. Do you think you'll be able to join me and meet the rest of the FMI agents?"

"I don't see a problem, since it has to do with those unexplained deaths yesterday. And besides, you already said Captain Robins will be notified about your group assisting in the investigation."

"True. Looking forward to working with you." Simon gave her the hotel room number.

"Do you have any idea what could've caused these mysterious deaths yesterday in Ocala?"

"Not yet. We're as baffled as you and everyone else. The possibility of mass suicide is highly unlikely, if not impossible. The eight of them would've had to take a poison at the exact time. And for the chemical agent to cause their deaths at precisely two minutes to noon would be statistically infeasible. No. There has to be some other explanation for the deaths yesterday, something not seen in the annuals of medicine."

"You said earlier this was a newly-formed department. What other investigations have you and your team done?"

Simon snickered to himself. The detective questioned him like he was suspect in an unsolved case. "This will be the team's third investigation. Our prior investigations weren't in any medical journals or textbooks either. The first case the team investigated was the unexplained deaths of an entire family of six people. Father, mother, two sons and two daughters. Police and the county medical examiner couldn't find a cause of their deaths. Me and my team found a genetic link to their deaths. All the family members had a congenital aberration in a specific gene in their chromosome makeup. The family was visiting a cavern in Pennsylvania and was exposed to a common mold not normally harmful to humans. But due to this family's genetic aberration, the mold was fatal to them. The second case—"

"You don't have to tell me," interrupted Janet. "I have a few things to take care of before I meet you at the hotel."

"No problem. I do have a tendency sometimes with rambling."

Janet slid to her left from the bench seat and stood, followed by Simon. She picked up her receipt from the table. "Nice meeting you, Dr. Woods. I'll see you and your agents at the hotel."

"Looking forward to it."

She walked toward the other end of restaurant to pay her bill.

Simon left the restaurant. As he walked toward his car, he sensed someone was staring at him. He glanced around the nearly filled parking lot. He didn't see anyone peering at him.

Across the parking lot to the right of Simon sat a dark-blue paneled van with its engine running. Dark-tinted windows prevented anyone from seeing inside the van.

## Chapter Four

Janet opened her desk drawer and removed a folder with her notes about the death of the boy she and her partner had investigated yesterday. There were also photos of the crime scene taken by the forensic investigators. She had already talked with her captain, who had gotten the call from the CDC, or at least that was what he was told from the person on the other end of the line. Janet was still apprehensive about her stealthy participation with the Federal Medical Investigators. Although it sounded like they were proficient in solving difficult medical mysteries. Simon Woods was good-looking with a pleasant mannerism. But she thought the same way when she first met her ex-husband, and he turned out to be an asshole with good looks. Her brother told her over the years about falling for a single man: don't judge a book by its nice-looking cover, you need to read a few chapters to determine if the story and main character are worthy of your time to continue reading. If she had taken heed to her brother's philosophy of men, she would've thrown her ex-husband's book, along with him, into a fire pit.

"Hey, partner, I hear you'll be helping the CDC with these deaths." Detective Bill Matters said as he walked up to her.

*Word travels fast.* How was she going to explain to him that he wasn't part of the ESP team, a name she coined in her mind to describe the FMI agents? "I'm advising them about any information we gather on these deaths. I'm their liaison. No big thing."

His perky smile was replaced by a saddened expression. "Oh. Okay." He sighed. "What's on our agenda for today?"

Janet closed the desk drawer, holding the file in her left hand. "I have a meeting with the CDC in a little while." She wanted to tell him more but had agreed to keep FMI a secret. It wasn't like her to deceive Bill. They had a good working relationship. She didn't want to jeopardize it, but for now she didn't have a choice. "I'll give you a call after I get out of the meeting."

"Talk with you then."

Janet knocked on room 122 of the Holiday Inn Hotel. She wasn't having an ominous premonition. A few seconds later, the door opened. A man of medium build, at least six-foot three inches and in his late twenties with stoic facial features greeted her.

"My name is—"

"I know who you are, Detective Janet Bennett. Please come in. We've been waiting for you." He spoke with deep baritone voice, a voice resembling a county singer or a radio personality's deep thundering voice.

"Thank you…Mr. Frank Littlefield."

A smirk appeared, as if acknowledging "touché" to his greeting of her. He breathed in deeply, then said, "Biscuits and gravy…and orange juice."

Janet glanced down at her blouse and blazer. No remnants from her meal at the restaurant. "That's what I had for breakfast this morning. Doctor Woods told me you had a keen sense of smell."

"I do. It can sometimes be a nuisance."

A woman in her mid-thirties with short, black hair, wearing a white blouse and jeans sat at the end of a king-size bed. Her feet dangled several inches from the carpeted floor. Janet assumed the woman was Jean Cliftwood. And she was probably close to five-foot tall.

Janet didn't see Simon Woods in the room.

"Simon will be back shortly," said Jean. "I sure you know my name."

"Ms. Jean Cliftwood, or should I say Nurse Cliftwood."

"Call me Jean. Ms. Cliftwood or Nurse Cliftwood sounds so formal." She looked up at Frank. "You can call him whatever you like," she said with a hint sarcasm.

"Thanks. I love you, too," Frank said frowning. He turned to Janet and displayed a slight smile. "You can call me Frank."

"Both of you can call me Janet."

Jean slid off the bed, stood on the floor and faced Janet. "Now that we got our greetings done, we'll being getting down to business soon. I'm anxious to know what's causing these deaths here in Ocala."

The entrance door to the room opened. Janet and Frank turned around and saw Simon walk through the doorway. He was carrying a flat cardboard container with three cardboard cups with lids. "Detective. Glad to see you made it. I'm sure you already got to know Frank and Jean."

"Yes. Like Jean said, we're anxious to get this investigation underway." She glanced at her watch. It was almost ten o'clock. In about two hours other people in Ocala were going to suddenly die unless somehow the four of them can determine what caused the previous deaths.

Simon passed out three cups of coffee. He handed Janet a cup. "I believe you take your coffee with a small amount of milk, no sugar."

"Yes. Thank you." How did he know what she took in her coffee? At the restaurant earlier she drank orange juice. It was apparent to her this group knew more about her than what Simon had stated earlier.

Frank brought out a laptop computer, opened it and placed it on a small round table to the right of the room's drapes. "Here's what we know so far about these deaths."

On the screen in a large font it read:

EIGHT DEATHS OCCURRED AT 11:58 A.M.
THE VICTIMS HAVE NO COMMON CONNECTION
DEATHS APPEAR TO BE RANDOM
DEATHS OCCURRED AT DIFFERENT LOCATIONS
NO SPECIFIC AGE
NO SPECIFIC GENDER
VICTIMS HAD NO UNUSUAL MARKINGS OR PHYSICAL ANOMOLIES
CAUSE OF DEATH IS UNDETERMINED

Simon glanced at everyone in the room. "Is there anything else that needs to be added to this list?"

"There's one thing missing," answered Janet. "Three of the victims, the teenagers, whispered something prior to suddenly dying. None of us knows what the victims had whispered."

"What about the other victims?" Jean asked. "Did they whisper something?

"I don't know."

"We should ask the other detectives if their victims had dying whispers."

"Once I get back to the station, I'll ask the other detectives."

Simon nodded. "If someone heard what was whispered, it could be relevant to their deaths. Can you call them now on your cell phone?"

"I can."

Janet called the detectives. Three of the remaining five victims had whispered something, but witnesses couldn't make out what they had said before they collapsed. The other two victims weren't close enough for anyone to hear if they had whispered something before dying.

Frank sat at the desk and added: SIX VICTIMS WHISPERED SOMETHING BEFORE DYING to their list of known facts into the computer. "We now have nine known facts about these mysterious deaths."

Janet turned toward Simon Woods. She glanced down at her watch. "And if your vision comes true, we'll have more deaths in less than two hours from now."

"Unfortunately, yes."

"You said you saw a Caucasian girl in her teens wearing gym shorts and a white pullover shirt sitting on an indoor bleacher. I'd guess she'd likely be a public high school student sitting on a bleacher in gym class, since the private and Christian academy students wear distinct uniforms and gym clothes. Jean is the only person in this room who can possibly know who the next victims are going to be. She can't be at all three high schools in Ocala at the same time. I'll go with her to the first high school, Vanguard. I'll call the principal and have him round up the students scheduled to be in the gym around noon and have them sit on the bleachers in the gym. And if Jean glances at the student and sees no one displaying a yellow glow, we'll rush over to Forest High School. There Simon will have put sitting on the gym's bleachers the female students scheduled to be in the gym near noon. If the girl isn't present, we'll rush to West Port High School where Frank will be stationed and arranging the potential students to be in the gym. Once we find our student, we'll all converge at the school. I'm not exactly sure what we'll be able to do to prevent her from suddenly dying."

"True," Simon said. "But we may be close enough to hear what she whispers before dying."

The three members of the FMI agreed with Janet's proposal regarding the sequence of the three high schools. Janet downloaded each of their cell phone numbers into her cell phone's address section.

Everyone put the address of the three high schools along with the name of the principal into their phone's GPS. They'll tell the principal there was evidence regarding the deaths of the students yesterday and that they needed to see the female students scheduled for gym class between eleven and noon this morning. They couldn't tell the principal the truth since it would cause potential panic.

Janet pulled out of the Holiday Inn's parking lot with Jean Cliftwood sitting in the passenger's seat. "How long have you experienced these yellow glows around people?"

"They first started about a year ago. At first, I thought something was wrong with my eyes. I went to an ophthalmologist and he didn't find anything wrong with my eyes. He wasn't sure why I was seeing this yellow glow around some people. He even did a brain scan with negative results. I didn't realize the significance or meaning behind them until it affected me personally. I was talking with my Aunt Betsy and saw the glow. The next day she died unexpectedly of a heart attack. After a month, I'd paired the vision with death. The CDC came to my home. Somehow, they knew of my powers and recruited me for the FMI. They made an offer I couldn't refuse. Since I'm single without children, the challenge enticed me. We're still in the infant stage of our organization."

"You must feel uneasy when you see the yellow glow around someone, knowing they'll likely be dead or seriously injured in the next twenty-four hours. I'd be a nervous wreck."

"Yes. It does create anxiety in me, but thank God, I don't see the yellow glow often. It is a Godsend and a curse at the same time. I used to avoid crowded places like the malls or shopping centers before I joined the FMI. Now it's an asset in our investigations into strange and mysterious illnesses and deaths."

"What do you mean it's an asset?"

"When we're investigating a suspicious medical event, I'll know how many people may be affected by its deadly effects. In those cases, the doctors can treat those people before the organism or medical condition causes harm to their bodies, if possible."

"In other words, if you see the yellow glow around me, I should have a thorough medical evaluation for any potential problem that may kill me. Like a blocked artery in my heart."

"Yes. But on the other hand, you may be killed in the line-of-duty or serious injured in an accident. I have no way to know which one your demise or bodily injury would be."

Jean's foresight, of predicting death or serious bodily harm in someone in the next twenty-four hours could potentially prevent a subway disaster. If she happened to be taking a subway train and saw most of the people in the car had yellow glows around them, it could be surmised there would be a subway accident involving all these people in the next twenty-four hours. It would also hold true if she was at an airport, bus terminal, passenger boat or a vast number of scenarios. She'd have to be in the right place at the right time. The odds of it happening would be astronomical, thought Janet.

Ten minutes later, Janet stopped her car on the circle driveway in front of Vanguard High School. She glanced at her watch. It was ten-nineteen. They got out of the car and hurried to the front door. She rang the doorbell. A male asked, "Can I help you?" His voice came from an intercom speaker next to the door.

"Yes. I'm Detective Bennett from the sheriff's department. I need to talk to the principal, Ronald Simpson." Janet displayed her badge to a small camera above her to the right of the double doors. "My associate, Jean Cliftwood, is with me."

A buzz rang out from the door. Janet reached to her right and pulled the door open. They walked inside to large enclosed vestibule and briefly stopped. The vestibule could accommodate at least twenty people. Scanners were positioned in the area to detect weapons and illicit drugs. The inside door opened allowing Janet and Jean to enter the school. Since the several incidences of school shootings the past few decades, all schools throughout the United States had instituted locked schools with security cameras and intercoms at the entrances to schools and other vulnerable sites around the school. It deterred an outsider or a disgruntled student with harmful intent from entering school premises. Since implementing this type of security, there hadn't been a school shooting.

They headed for the principal's office, which was about twenty feet to their right along a long corridor. Janet had earlier on the phone explained to the principal their reason for the visit. He seemed satisfied with her explanation. Simpson escorted them to the gym. The third-hour gym class was sitting on the bleachers with their street clothes. He left after introducing them to the gym teacher. Janet asked the teacher if all the students where here and no one was in the bathroom, locker room or any other place in the school. All the students were accounted for stated the teacher. While Janet talked with the teacher, Jean walked from left to right in front of the bleacher, scanning the students for anyone with a yellow glow encompassing them. A moment later, she turned toward Janet and shook her head in a negative gesture. Janet nodded. The detective thanked the gym teacher. She and Jean left the gym and hurried toward the school's front door.

Janet called Simon. She told him they were leaving Vanguard High School and heading to his school. She glanced at her watch: 10:42 a.m. She sped away from the school. A block away, she put on the police warning siren, flashing headlights and sped toward Forest High School.

Janet stopped her police vehicle at the front entrance of the high school. Simon stood in front of the gym class students, who were standing at the bottom of the concrete stairs. *Smart thinking* thought Janet as she got out of the car. Jean quickly got out of the car and walked up to the students. They were standing in horizontal line at the bottom of the steps. She had to be within ten feet of the person for her to visualize a yellow glow. Jean stood in front of the student to her far right. She then proceeded to walk hurriedly to her left. A minute later, she stood in front of the last gym class student. Jean turned toward Simon and Janet. "She's not here." No one presented with the yellow, death glow.

Janet glanced at her watch. It was 11:23. They had thirty-five minutes to get to West Port High School and identify the next victim before 11:58.

The gym class teacher, who was standing behind the students, escorted her class back into the school. Simon got into the backseat of Janet's car; Jean sat in the front seat. Simon called Frank Littlefield on his cell phone and told him that they were on their way to him, and for him to have the students lined up in front of the school. "How long will it take you to get to the high school?"

"About twenty minutes," she said peering down at the GPS on the front of her car's dashboard. The time of arrival on the GPS read 11:42 a.m. Janet had downloaded the addresses of all three high schools in the GPS earlier. *They'll have sixteen minutes to identify the gym class student, who's scheduled to die at 11:58.* "It should give us plenty of time. Barring any delays or unexpected circumstances." She sped away, putting on the car's siren two blocks from the high school.

Simon leaned forward. "I'm still not sure what we're going to do once we find the girl. Are we going to tell her that she may only have a few minutes to live? If we tell her this grim news, she'll likely freak out and scream or cry hysterically. I'd thought we might ask her if she took any medications or street drugs in the past twenty-four hours. Like most teenagers on drugs, she'll deny taking anything. Unless we see needle marks on her arms there wouldn't be any way to know if she had taken any drugs, besides doing urine, blood or hair test on her. Which of course would be postmortem. And if she did, depending on the amount taken, it wouldn't necessarily mean it was the cause of her death. One of the most relevant things to the deaths would be what she whispered prior to her suddenly dying. It appeared to be the common denominator connecting some of the deaths yesterday."

Janet glanced in the rearview mirror at Simon. "I agree with everything you said."

"And it pretty much supports Frank's evaluation of the victims yesterday," Jean said. "There wasn't any common smell on the eight victims, eliminating a common denominator."

"It still amazes me, the three of you having these paranormal gifts," Janet added to their conversation.

The traffic light ahead turned green. Luck was on their side. If they had to stop for a red light, it would've taken over a minute for the traffic light to change back to a green signal. Janet knew the timing on most of the traffic lights in Ocala. A chill engulfed her. She glanced to her left at the stopped vehicles.

Simon peered out the rear passenger window to his right. "Look out," he shouted as they entered halfway into the intersection and beneath the traffic light.

A speeding black pickup truck was about to crash into them.

# Chapter Five

The pickup truck rammed the rear passenger panel, near the taillight, causing their car to spin three hundred and sixty degrees. The front driver and passenger airbags burst out from the dashboard pressing against Janet and Jean. Both were wearing seat belts. Simon's body lunged toward the impact area but was secured in his seatbelt behind Janet, preventing him from flying to his right and crashing into the passenger rear door.

A whirling sensation twirled in Simon's head as if he sat in a salt and pepper shaker ride in an amusement park. Their car stopped after spinning two times. The impact had shattered the passenger right-side window and the rear window, spewing tiny pieces of glass over the back seat and all over him. Simon peered at Jean. The airbag had now partially deflated after the crash. She was conscious, as she looked around in front of her, then to her left and right. Simon couldn't see over the front seat where Janet sat behind the steering wheel. "Is everyone all right?"

"I'm okay," Jean answered as she rubbed her forehead, then her nose. "Other than feeling like I've been in a boxing match with George Foreman…and I lost."

"Me, too," said Janet. "Just shaken up a little. What the hell hit us?"

"A pickup truck," answered Simon, as he unlatched his life-saving seatbelt. Any physical sign he felt was a slight soreness around his waist. No dizziness or visual problems. "Before you guys get out the car, let me check you over." He opened the driver side back door and stepped out of the car. Their driver side wheels of the car were up against a curb. Simon quickly scanned the area around him. No pickup truck. A hit and run accident flashed through his mind. He looked up at the poles supporting the traffic light and saw traffic cameras. Several vehicles had stopped, and its driver and/or passengers hurriedly walked toward their car, some of them yelling "Is everybody okay?"

"We're all fine," answered Simon.

"I called 911 and told them there was an accident with possible injuries," stated one of the bystanders.

Jean got out of the car, walked to the back of the car and peered down at the damaged rear panel. Janet also got of the car, walked over to Simon and stood next to him. In the distance, Simon heard the piercing, rhythmic sound of an emergency vehicle. "I assume, you and Jean don't have any problems. I would've liked to examine you and Jean before the two of you got out of the car."

"Where's the vehicle that hit us?" Janet asked as she looked around.

"Whoever it was drove off." He looked toward Jean. "What does the damage look like? Do you think we can still drive the car?"

"It should be drivable. The rear wheel appears okay."

Janet gave a middle-aged male bystander her business card and told him to tell the police and EMS no one was injured in their car and they had an emergency to go to. Other than broken windows and a crushed in rear passenger side car panel, the car ran fine. They had lost over ten minutes due to this accident. The time of arrival on the GPS showed 11:52 a.m. This gave them about six minutes to identify the female gym student before she suddenly died. Simon called Frank, told him what had happened and to make sure he had the girl's gym class waiting on the front steps of the school to expedite Jean's identification of the female gym student.

"We should have enough time to find the girl," Simon said optimistically.

So far, Janet had gone through three traffic light and two stop signs with caution, making sure the traffic in all directions at each intersection saw and heard the emergency siren and lights before she went through the intersection. Janet still couldn't understand how the pickup truck could've ran a red light when the traffic light had changed ten seconds earlier. The speed limit for the truck was thirty-five miles an hour, not that the driver was going the speed limit. She had her siren blaring and the emergency lights were flashing. The truck couldn't have hit her car in a better location than the back-passenger side panel near the taillight. It resembled a Pit maneuver used by law enforcement. She had practiced this maneuver during a training session for the Sheriff department a few years ago. *Were we lucky? Or was this accident intentional?* Janet passed on her scenario and her two questions about the accident to Simon and Jean.

Simon said, "You make good points about the accident. It's understandable you'd be thinking about the accident, since your mind was trained as a detective. But right now, we should concentrate on identifying the girl at the school."

"Yeah. You're right," Janet agreed. *Simon must think I don't care about the gym student's likely death. I can't help it, I'm suspicious about almost everything I don't completely understand.* She glanced at the GPS. Time of Arrival: 11:55. *Three minutes to identify the girl.* Janet announced, "The high school is three blocks away, on our right."

Two minutes later, West Port High School came into view. "I hope Frank has the students out in front of the school?" Simon said.

"What's going on?" Janet asked.

In front of them students were exiting the school and forming pockets of several separate groups on the front lawn and sidewalk. Janet rolled her window down. The pulsating sound of a fire alarm surrounded the school. Was the school having a fire drill? Or was there an actual fire inside the school? The groups of students began to merge together, forming one large conglomeration of the high school's student body.

Janet stopped the car in front of the school. Everyone quickly got out of the car. The deafening sound of kids talking to one another and on their cell phones along with the fire alarm's high-pitched reverberation made it almost impossible for the three of them to talk with one another.

Simon shouted, "I don't see Frank. He's got to be somewhere in this mass of students." He glanced down at his watch. A chill engulfed him. "We've got less than a minute to find him and the gym class."

"I see him," said Janet, pointing to her right in front of the school. He was standing on the upper steps of the school entrance waving his arms. It was difficult to determine if the gym class students were with him. Janet glanced down at her watch: 11:57:28. Less than thirty seconds before the Reaper of Death appears and takes away an unsuspecting teenage girl. Janet along with Simon and Jean pushed their way through the collage of teenagers. There was no way they could silence the high school students so they could hear the whisper of death from one of their fellow students. The three of them kept yelling, "Move. Let us through." Most of the teenagers moved aside, a few were defiant and stood their ground.

Janet, Simon and Jean made it to the upper landing in front of the school.

"There she is," Jean shouted as she peered and pointed to the group of students to her left.

"Which one?" Janet asked. The other two FMI agents focused their attention on the group of students, not knowing which student was about to suddenly take her last breath.

"The one in the middle with long blond hair and a green sweat band around her head. She's wearing a white gym shirt," Jean answered.

The girl must've sensed she was being stared at, as she peered at the three of them. Her lips moved apparently saying something to them. Janet couldn't make out what she was saying. The girl then seemed to lose all muscle control as her body collapsed to the concrete, landing like a porcelain doll. Students around the fallen girl stared down at her motionless body. Janet and the three FMI agents rushed over to the fallen student.

Simon kneeled next to the student; leaned down, placing his left ear near her mouth for breath sounds and looking down at her chest for any movement, as he placed the tips of right index and middle finger on the left side of her neck, checking for a carotid pulse. "No vital signs," Simon said, looking up at Janet. "We need to start CPR now. Call 911."

For the next fifteen minutes, CPR was performed. EMS arrived and started advanced cardiac life support. After another fifteen minutes, the student, Melody Richards, continued not to have any vital signs, including dilated and unreactive pupils, indicating no brain function. The paramedics pronounced her dead at 12:35. They put her onto a gurney, placed her into the EMS vehicle and drove away.

It turned out the fire alarm was a hoax. A deliberate act by someone inside the school. The students went back to their assigned classes prior to Ms. Richards' body being placed inside the paramedic's vehicle. Janet stood with the three FMI agents near her car. She turned toward Simon.

"Your vision of the gym student dying was obviously true."

Simon nodded. "Unfortunately, it was."

"I called my office when the paramedics arrived," said Janet. "The sheriff's dispatcher told me there were four other victims dying before noon today. A Caucasian man losing control of his motorcycle and crashing into a parked car. A black woman sitting in a lounge chair inside a bank, waiting to talk with a banker. An oriental teenager sitting at a lunch table in a restaurant. And a male real estate agent sitting at his office desk." Janet briefly peered down at the ground and sighed. She then looked back at Simon. "Again, the victims were from all walks of life and ages. And I'm assuming the guy on the motorcycle lost consciousness before he crashed, at least according to your vision this morning. As you can guess, the captain assigned me to Melody Richards death since we were here when she died."

"We all observed the student saying something to us before dying," said Simon. "And after talking with the students who were standing next to her, no one heard what she said before collapsing. So, we're right back to where we were regarding these deaths. Hopefully, some of the witnesses at those other sudden deaths heard what the victims were saying before dying."

"Except for the guy on the motorcycle," Janet added.

"Maybe there were other victims," added Jean, "and their bodies haven't been discovered yet?"

"True, there could be other victims," Janet answered as she removed car keys out of her pocket. "There may be other mysterious deaths we don't yet know about." She thought a moment, then looked at Simon. "Don't you think it was somewhat coincidental?"

"What's that?"

"First, we're in a hit-and-run accident, then we encounter a false fire alarm here at the school. Both incidences hindered us from getting to the gym student, Melody Richards. I believe someone is trying to prevent us from finding out the cause of these mysterious deaths. What do you think?"

Everyone nodded. Simon answered: "I think your assumption has validity. All we have to do now is find the driver of the black pickup truck with a dent on his front bumper and the person who set off the fire alarm."

"I can help regarding the fire alarm," Frank said. "If I can smell the fire alarm box in the school, the person who touched it may have left a scent. A scent I may be able to follow and locate the responsible culprit."

"Great idea," Janet said, as she put her car keys back into her pocket. In any other normal police investigation, this wouldn't have been an option.

The four of them walked into the school. Beyond the entranceway to their right, a security guard stood next to an arched metal detector. The four of them showed their badges. "The principal's office is the first door to your left," said the security officer as he pointed up the hallway. "It's a shame about the student dying on the front steps. I wonder if she had been taking drugs?"

"Not sure," answered Janet. The thought of all these deaths were caused by a drug would make her investigation much easier. Unfortunately, the probability of a drug causing their demise, is between nil and not possible.

They stood in Principal Edward Perkins' office. Perkins asked Janet how they knew a gym class student would be a victim of sudden death. Janet explained to the principal they got an anonymous call about a female student in the fourth-period gym class who may have information about the high school student deaths yesterday. It was a coincidence they happened to be there when the student died. She omitted some of the facts, of course. The principal seemed satisfied with Janet's explanation. She then asked him where the activated fire alarm was located. He escorted them to a hallway at the far end of the school. The box hung on a wall at the beginning of a hallway leading to the science classrooms. The hallway was empty except for them. The principal got a call on his cell phone to return to his office. He left the four of them in front of the pulled fire alarm.

Frank got close to the box and began sniffing, especially the pulled down red handle. He nodded. "I got something." He turned to his left and slowly walked down the science hallway. After passing two classroom doors, he stopped at the third door and looked up. Above the door was a plaque with the name: Mr. Markham. "The scent stops here."

"Whoever pulled the fire alarm is or was in this room," said Janet.

"Definitely. I agree," Simon said.

"Everyone stays here," Janet said. "Here's my plan. I'll go in and introduce myself and tell the teacher I need to ask the students a few questions about the death of the student earlier." She glanced down at her watch. "The fifth-hour science class will end in less than ten minutes. After the students leave the classroom, I'll have Frank come in and locate the desk of the fourth-hour student responsible for pulling the fire alarm. How does that sound?"

"Your plan definitely works for me," answered Frank. Simon and Jean also agreed by nodding.

Janet knocked and entered the classroom. The teacher agreed to her request. After she stood in front of the class asking the students questions for a few minutes, the sixth-hour bell rang. None of the students knew anything about who had pulled the fire alarm.

Janet asked Mr. Markham if her associates could come into the room because she needed to talk with them.

"No problem, Detective Bennett. I'll keep my next class in the hallway until you're done talking."

"Thanks. We'll need a minute or two." The last student and Mr. Markham walked out of the room and into the hallway. Markham had to leave the room anyway; teachers were required to stand outside their classroom door and monitor the students in the hallway between periods. Janet waved to Simon standing outside the door.

The three FMI agents walked into the room. Frank immediately started to check out each desk, bending down and taking a deep sniff, until he came to where the student responsible for pulling the fire alarm sat. Frank had stated earlier at the hotel room everyone had a unique odor, a distinctive smell. Everyone had their own DNA smell.

Janet peered at the classroom door to see if anyone was looking at Frank's peculiar action. No one in the hallway stared back at them.

Frank spent less than thirty seconds to find the unique smell coming from the perpetrator's desk and chair. "We have our perp. There's no doubt in my mind…or should say, smell."

Janet went out into the hallway asked the teacher, Mr. Markham, if he'd come back into the room for a moment. Markham came in and stood by his desk.

Janet walked over and stood next to the perp's desk. "Can you tell us who sits at this desk during the fourth-period?" She pointed down at the desk.

He thought a moment, then answered: "Caleb Johnson. Why do you ask?"

"He may know something about the girl who died this morning." Janet had to lie. It was part of detective procedures when trying to obtain information.

"Was he here during fourth-hour?"

"Yes. Although, he was called to the principal's office a few minutes before the period ended."

Janet didn't remember seeing any students in the principal's office, other than the female student assistant.

Markham glanced down at his watch, then toward the entrance door to the room. "Sixth-hour will be starting in about a minute."

"We won't hold you up," said Janet. "Thanks for your help."

"Glad to help."

The four of them walked out of the room and hurried down the hallway toward the principal's office.

They walked into Principal Perkins' office. Janet glanced around the room. No Caleb. A female student stood next to a table separating a stack of papers. Janet asked the secretary, "I understand from Mr. Markham that student Caleb Johnson was called to this office toward the end of the fourth-period. We'd like to talk with him, if we could. Can you tell us what class he's in now?"

A perplexed expression crossed the secretary's face. "Caleb wasn't called to this office. I know this because Principal Perkins and I are the only people authorized to use the PA system. Plus, I take all the incoming calls and messages. Are you sure you got the right student?"

*There must be logical explanation to this.* "I'm sure Mr. Markham said Caleb was called to the principal's office."

"I'll page the student to come to the office," said the secretary. She got up from her desk chair, walked over to a short counter on the other side of the room, reached down to a microphone and announced: CALEB JOHNSON. PLEASE COME TO THE PRINCIPAL'S OFFICE.

They waited for at least five minutes. No Caleb. The secretary looked up his class schedule. He should be in his English class, which was less than a minute from the principal's office. She sent a student assistant to see if he was in the class. A few minutes later, the student returned and stated, Caleb never showed up for his English class. This left one scenario: Caleb Johnson, a senior, left school without permission. According to his school records, he never had a disciplinary action recorded against him the past year. He transferred from a high school in Nevada last year. He also had a good attendance record.

Was his action of setting off the fire alarm a prank? Or was there a more sinister reason? These questions were discussed by Janet and the three FMI agents as they walked out of the school building. Simon assigned tasks for Frank and Jean. Frank would go back to the hotel room and search the internet for information on today's victims. Jean would go back to the coroner's office, regarding the victims dying today at 11:58, and find out if there was any more information on yesterday's suspicious deaths. Janet and Simon would drive to Caleb Johnson's house. When they got to the bottom of the stairs, Frank and Jean headed for his car parked at the far-right circle drive in front of the school. Janet and Simon walked straight ahead to her car.

"We need to find this young man," said Janet, "and question him about this incident. We can't tell anyone how we know it was him. If we're questioned by someone, including my captain, I'll tell him I have an anonymous source that saw Caleb Johnson pull the fire alarm lever." Janet was normally an honest and truthful detective, but under these circumstances, working with three individuals with paranormal powers, lying was a necessary exception.

The fire marshal, Roger Simmons, pulled up behind Janet's car. He got out of his car and walked up to Janet. They'd known each other professionally for about five years. She had investigated arson deaths along with him on a few cases. She introduced Simon as an investigator for the CDC. They were here to investigate the deaths of people in Ocala the past two days and the high school student here at the high school during the false alarm incident. She told Roger the girl may have had an undiagnosed heart condition, causing her to suddenly die. But of course, an autopsy would have to be done to determine the cause of death. The fire marshal agreed.

"I have to get something out of the trunk of my car. Talk to you later." He left and walked back to his car.

"There are a lot of unanswered questions," said Simon. "First, was the accident with the pickup truck done on purpose or was it an unfortunate crash at the intersection? Second, we need to investigate the other deaths occurring this morning at 11:58. Third, talk with the high school student, Caleb Johnson regarding why he set off the fire alarm."

A local news station paneled van with a satellite dish sitting on top of the roof pulled up in front of them.

"We don't need to talk with any news reporters," Janet said as she retrieved her cars keys from her jacket pocket. "Simon, get into the car."

But before she could open her driver side car door, a female reporter in her late twenties shouted, "Detective Bennett, can you tell me about what had happened here at the high school regarding a student's death at the time of a fire alarm scare?"

"No comment at this time. The investigation is still ongoing."

"Who's the man in your car?"

Janet got into the car, ignoring her last comment. *Thank God the guy with her hadn't turned on his camera yet.* Janet pulled the car around the news van as the camera man aimed his camera at her car. Her car had dark tinted side and rear windows, making impossible to see her passenger. The news reporter and videographer then turned around and headed toward the fire marshal, who was walking up the front steps to the high school. A moment later, the high school was now in her rearview mirror.

A dark-blue paneled van with dark tinted windows sat in the visitors' parking area to the right of the school. Its engine was running. Next to the van was a pickup truck with a slightly dented passenger side front chrome bumper.

## Chapter Six

Simon reached out toward the center of the dashboard and put Caleb's home address into the car's GPS. They obtained the address from the high school principal's secretary. They would drive to his house and interrogate him about the fire alarm incident at school today. Simon glanced down at the arrival time on the GPS. "We'll arrive at Caleb's house in fifteen minutes."

"Hopefully we'll find out why he pulled the fire alarm."

"I agree." He was glad they had picked Janet to assist them in the investigation. Janet possessed tenacity with the willingness to change her viewpoint in these mysterious deaths in Ocala. Besides her attributes, she was good looking, a physical feature which made it more pleasant to work along with her in trying to solve the "Whispers Before Death" case. Earlier in the morning at the hotel room, Frank had come up with this descriptive name for these unexplained deaths. Everyone agreed the name suited their investigation.

The car came to a traffic light intersection. Simon's muscles throughout his body tightened up as his heart began racing, anticipating a pickup truck or any vehicle that might come speeding through the red light straight at them. *My God, do I have PTSD? No way. It's only a natural reaction following a traumatic experience. Tomorrow I'll be back to normal*. Although, Simon couldn't be sure there might be other harrowing experiences today or sometime soon. So far, he hadn't had any more psychic visions since this morning vision of Janet's office desk. He wished he'd had a vision prior to the accident with the pickup truck earlier. He knew he had no control over when a vision occurred. He wasn't like the renowned clairvoyant Edgar Casey, who went into a self-induced trance to summon visions of people and events. Simon's visions came spontaneously, without warning. Simon decided to close his eyes prior to entering a traffic light intersection.

Janet looked both ways then at Simon as they passed through an intersection. "This is the third intersection we went through, and each time you had your eyes closed. Is there something I should know?"

Simon opened his eyes and chuckled. *I don't think I can hide anything from her.* "There isn't much that gets past you…is there?"

"Only when I'm sleeping," she said with a grin.

The GPS's female voice simulator announced, "Turn left at Cyprus Street." Since downloading the address, the voice on the GPS had directed them through the streets of Ocala, telling the driver to turn right or left or continue straight ahead. It was like they had a third occupant in the car.

"We're almost there," Simon said as he glanced at the GPS arrival time display and the vehicle's clock; they were identical in time. Janet turned onto Cyprus Street. "It should be the third house on the right."

The houses on the street were mostly cinder-block ranch-style homes, a deterrent for wood-hungry termites. Some of the houses had attached one-car garages. The lawns and homes were well-maintained. It was a typical working middle-class neighborhood for the Ocala area. Simon grew up in a similar neighborhood, but instead the houses were wood-framed constructed with brick facing or aluminum/vinyl siding. A typical middle-class house built in the Northern states, where termites weren't a major concern.

Janet drove her car onto the Johnson's driveway and stopped. They got out of the car and walked up to a concrete slab positioned in front of the front door. A metal awning hung above them, protecting anyone from a rainy day. Simon pushed the doorbell. A moment later, the front door opened to a woman in her late fifties. *It's probably the grandmother*, thought Simon.

"Can I help you?" asked the woman.

"Hopefully, ma'am. I'm Detective Bennett for the Marion County Sheriff's Department and we need to talk with Caleb. Is he here?"

She frowned. "Yes, he is. Why do you need to talk with him?"

"He left school today without permission. We need to ask him a few questions about school today."

She laughed.

Simon couldn't understand why she reacted this way. It wasn't appropriate behavior. "Mrs. Johnson, this is a serious matter," he interjected.

"You must have the wrong house, detectives. Caleb doesn't go to school. He's homeschooled by me."

That didn't make any sense to Simon. This was the address given to them by the principal's secretary. Either Mrs. Johnson was trying to protect her son or grandson, or the high school was intentionally given the wrong home address for Caleb Johnson. "Can we still see Caleb?"

Mrs. Johnson turned around and shouted for him to come to the door. Several seconds passed. A young man in his early twenties came to the door in a wheelchair.

Simon recognized the congenital condition which caused Caleb to use a wheelchair. Cerebral Palsy. This wasn't the Caleb they were looking for. "I'm sorry to bother you, Mrs. Johnson. We must've been given the wrong address by the school."

"Please accept our apology," Janet added.

Once they got into the car, Simon said, "Wasn't this a waste of our time? Obviously, the school gave us the wrong address."

"There's possibly two other answers: this was the address given to the school by a different Caleb Johnson family who didn't want to divulge their real address. Or, Caleb and his family are imposters, hiding from law enforcement."

"Or they're in the Federal Witness protection program," Janet added, then shook her head in a negative gesture. "Although that wouldn't make any sense. The government would've settled them at a legitimate address, not an address where someone else lives. On the other hand, if they are a witness protection family, they may not want the school to know their real address for whatever reason."

Simon raised his eyebrows and smirked. "This sounds like detective work to me, and since you're a detective…"

"But aren't you a medical investigator? Your profession is like detective work. And don't you also carry a badge and gun?"

"Touché. You got me." Simon liked her comebacks and wit, which were attributes other people had mentioned about her. Their working relationships was becoming like a spy versus spy situation but in a congenial manner. "So, detective, what do you suggest we do next?"

"We need to get more information about Caleb Johnson or whatever his real name is. One place to start would be his locker at school. If anything, we can get fingerprints and DNA from inside his locker. This will give us his identity. But before I call the Forensic Unit and make this a major crime, I'll tell the principal they gave us the wrong home address for Caleb." She backed out of the driveway and headed for the high school.

"We still have to investigate the hit and run accident."

"I've already got it covered. I had talked with my partner, Detective Matters, about our accident when I called my office about the death of Melody Richards, another 'Whispers Before Death' victim. He'll check the intersection cameras for the description of the pickup truck and identifying marks, stickers or anything unusual about the truck, including its license plate number and a picture of the driver or any passenger in the truck. I'm sorry I didn't tell you earlier."

"No problem. I was busy doing CPR on Ms. Richards. We have a lot of issues on our plate and the plate is getting a little crowded."

"Isn't that the truth," Janet said, as she stopped for a red light. "We still have to solve the 11:58 Deaths."

"I thought we called the case 'Whispers Before Death'?"

"It's my subtitle name."

Simon chuckled. *I like this woman. There hasn't been a dull moment with her.* "I'll call Frank and find out if Caleb has a social media site on the internet. Hopefully that might give us the answers we're looking for."

"Do you want to go with me?

"The way I look at it, there isn't much more I can do right now. Frank and Jean are investigating any answers or leads with these puzzling deaths, along with your partner investigating our accident with the mysterious truck. I'm sure you'll find out from other detectives in your department if these victims today whispered something prior to them suddenly dying."

"I guess you're saying you're staying with me after your dissertation?"

"Yes. I do tend to ramble a little when a simple answer would do." Simon had been told by many people over the years about his longwinded answers. Someone suggested to him that he should never take the stand as a witness in a court case. He'd have a tough time giving a short answer to an attorney.

When they walked into the principal's office, the secretary asked, "What reason did Caleb Johnson give for leaving school?"

Instead of expounding on what they had found or who they didn't find living at the address given to them by the school, Janet answered, "Caleb wasn't there." The fact was the student named Caleb Johnson going to West Port High School was an imposter. "We'd like permission to check out his locker."

Principal Perkins walked out of his office into the reception room. "Detective Bennett. What excuse did Caleb Johnson give you for leaving school without permission?" Janet repeated what she told his secretary, and added they were suspicious about Caleb possibly setting off the fire alarm.

"Why do you suspect him? Did someone see him do it?"

Again, she had to confab an answer without telling him an FMI agent used his paranormal sense of smell ability to identify the perp. "It's what our evidence is pointing toward. And we'd like to look inside his locker."

Principal Perkins walked Janet and Simon to Caleb's locker. He opened the locker and stepped aside, allowing Janet to step in front of him and block the view of the opened locker. Simon reached inconspicuously into the locker and removed a hairbrush from the top shelf of locker, sliding it into the inside pocket of his sports jacket. A perfect item to obtain a person's DNA and fingerprints. He then closed the locker.

"Thanks for your help, Mr. Perkins," Simon said, stepping around Janet.

"As soon as we hear from Caleb," Janet said, "I'll give you a call or have him call you and explain why he left school at noon today."

"I'd appreciate it. I'll do the same if I hear anything."

Janet nodded. The final school bell blared from speakers throughout the school, ending the seventh period and the end of a school day for the high school students. It would be impossible now to interview any of the students, as classrooms emptied students into the hallways. Organized chaos surrounded them. Not all was lost to find the identity of the student calling himself Caleb Johnson. The DNA from hairs embedded on the brush and fingerprints on the hairbrush's handle should give them the answer they needed. Janet thanked Mr. Perkins.

They followed the flow of students toward the front entrance of the school. Simon compared it to getting caught in an anxious crowd of people standing outside a department store on Black Friday as the doors opened. The piercing vibration of mixed male and female voices in the school's confined hallway suddenly vanished as she and Simon walked outside into the warm spring air.

Unnoticed by Janet and Simon, a dark-blue tinted van with its engine running sat in the visitor's parking area to the left of the school entrance. It was the same van in the restaurant's parking lot this morning and during the fire alarm incident, along with the death of Melody Richards.

~ * ~

"What do you think they found out inside the school? This is their second visit," asked a man in his late forties to the driver of the dark-blue van with tinted windows.

The burly looking slightly overweight man in his early thirties grunted as he stared at Janet and Simon getting into the detective's car. "Not sure, Keith. Other than they now know there's two Caleb Johnsons with the same home address. Like I said earlier, how'd they know who set off the fire alarm? Alex told us no one saw him do it."

"He did, Cary. I guess it was good detective work. What other explanation could there be?"

"I got a feeling there's something more to the three from the CDC. And how did they know a girl from a high school gym class would be a victim? They obviously didn't know her name, or that she'd be from a fourth-hour gym class. We're supposed to prevent them from uncovering the cause of these deaths."

"Do you think we have a mole amongst us?"

"What other explanation could there be?"

# Chapter Seven

Janet walked up to her desk. She had dropped Simon off at his car in Forest High School parking lot. She then handed the hairbrush to a forensic lab employee for DNA and fingerprint analysis and reported the hairbrush as evidence in Melody Richard's death. Janet didn't think it was a coincidence regarding a false fire alarm instigated by a student named Caleb Johnson, who had an incorrect home address, at the same time of the gym student's unexplained death. Somehow there was a connection between the two events. She needed to prove it, along with the help of FMI's paranormal agents.

"Hey, partner. Glad you're back," Bill Matters said as he sat at his desk. He picked up a sheet of paper from his desk. "I got the information you requested on your accident this morning. Plus, I talked with the officers of the Ocala Police Department regarding their investigation of your hit-and-run accident."

"Did they arrest the person?"

"Nope. The cameras at the intersection had malfunctioned a few minutes before the accident, then went back on a few minutes after the accident. You'd swear someone had a remote control and turned off the cameras. I'd compare it to watching a TV program. The power goes out, then goes back on in ten minutes. The officers reported a black Ford 150 pickup went through the red light as you said on the phone. No one saw who was driving due to the tinted windows and no witnesses got the license plate number. There weren't any distinguishing marks on the truck. The debris at the accident scene was glass particles from your car. No taillight or headlight glass was found from the other vehicle. Thank God, your car wasn't hit broadside. It could've been much more serious."

*I think the person hit me right where he planned.* "Yeah. You're right. It could've been worse." Janet checked the top of her desk for any phone messages. None were there.

"By the way, what did you find out about the high school girl's death this morning? And how did you happen to be at the school?"

Janet knew she couldn't tell him the complete truth. She had already thought about what she was going to tell him on her way back to the station. "CDC had received a tip that a fourth-hour gym class girl might have information about the deaths yesterday. The tip came from a male using one of those throwaway cell phones, the kind you can't trace."

"Isn't that the pits? Bring back the days of landline telephones. It made our job less complicated. When I think about it, the characters on the TV series *Star Trek* in the nineteen sixties used communicators, a version of today's cellular telephones. I thought it was an impossible way to talk, except in science fiction stories or TV shows. Never could happen in real life. Boy…was I and most people wrong. I guess I'm old fashioned when it comes to talking with people. I can do without cell phones, computers and social media. I miss the sound of the typewriter."

Janet chuckled to herself. "Think of all the phone calls you would've missed if only landline phones existed today."

"Most of the time it's people I'd rather not talk with. It's amazing we all survived in a world without cell phones, computers, and all of today's electronic devices."

"I agree, we did survive. Now that we have got all this off our chests, do you have any information about the other victims dying at 11:58 this morning?"

"There aren't any more victims than the six we know of. All of them were taken to Division Five coroner in Leesburg. Other than the guy on the motorcycle, none of the victims had obvious trauma. I did get the preliminary results on the eight victims yesterday. Normal autopsies on all of them. Toxicology reports on them were all negative for illicit drugs or any toxic levels of prescription medication."

Janet assumed the cause of death on the autopsy reports from all the victims would read *Undetermined.* Like she had said to Bill previously, possibly a microchip was planted in their brains, programmed to go on a certain day and time, 11:58 in the morning, causing their deaths. Of course, no foreign bodies were found anywhere in the victim's body. If their deaths weren't caused from a drug or a microchip planted in their body, then there had to be some other demonic way all these people died. And if their accident and the false fire alarm were done to prevent her and the FMI agents from finding out the truth about these deaths, they must be getting close to the truth. The perpetrators responsible for these deaths seemed to be focusing on Janet, Simon and his associates. They'd become the target. These assumptions were added to the other puzzling assumptions and unknowns in all these mysterious deaths the past two days. She peered at Bill. "There has to be a logical cause for all these people dying at 11:58 in the morning."

"We may be dealing with an illogical cause…something not ever seen before."

*Like Simon and the other FMI agents.* "Unless we come up with solid evidence or a clue, we're groping inside a darkened room without any source of light."

"I love your adages," Bill said with a smirk.

Janet's cell phone rang. She glanced at the LD screen. It was her brother. "Hey, Michael. Are you calling for your daily briefing?" Through the years, when she had an important case to solve and investigate, he'd call her usually once a day to inquire on her progress. She couldn't divulge any findings to him, but he still would call her.

"How'd you know? Are you telepathic?"

"I don't have to be telepathic to know you'd be calling me today. And like I've said to you the past several years—"

"You can't give out information about a pending investigation," interrupted Michael. "I have this phrase etched into my brain. I wanted to know how your day was…that's all." There was a hint of jest in his voice.

"All I can say, it wasn't one of my normal days." Of course, her reply was an understatement. She couldn't tell her brother about her association with three government agents with paranormal abilities. Or about a high school student who pulled a fire alarm, a student with likely an alias name, who incidentally vanished. "Of course, you probably heard about the high school student dying around noon today?"

"I did. Along with five other people dying at 11:58. How'd you like to come over for supper? Crystal's making her famous pot roast with potatoes and carrots. The one you can cut the meat with a plastic knife."

Janet chuckled. "You sure now how to get to me, big brother. How can I refuse such an invitation?" She knew the primary or secondary reason for his invitation to supper was for information about Ocala's mysterious deaths. Besides, she hadn't had a good home-cooked meal a quite a while. Her cooking talents included preparing Marie Callender's premade meals and eating at restaurants.

"How about six o'clock?"

She glanced at her watch. It was a quarter to five. "Six sounds good. See you then." She looked across her desk at Bill, who was writing. "I'm sure now these deaths in Ocala the past two days will make the national news stations, including all the news stations in Orlando."

"According to Captain Robins, several news media outlets, including the big ones in New York City…Fox News, CNN and all the three-letter news stations have contacted our department. We're not to talk with any news media about any of these deaths. We're to say the deaths are under investigation. Of course, you already know this from previous high-profile cases. The captain will be giving a news conference at five o'clock in the media room downstairs."

"I noticed all the news media vans in the visitor's parking lot when I came in. I'm glad we have our own secured entrance door to the building. I've already dealt with a news reporter at the high school today." Janet didn't envy the captain with reporters asking him pointed questions about fourteen unexplained deaths occurring at exactly at 11:58 in the morning on two consecutive days. There weren't any precedents to compare with in the world of unexplained deaths. "I appreciate you talking with Melody Richard's parents about the death of their daughter."

"No problem. That's what a partner's for. Right?"

Janet nodded. "You're the best partner I've ever had."

"And since I'm the only partner you ever had—"

"You know what I mean." She sighed. "I assume, you didn't learn any significant information about her."

"No. Their daughter wasn't into drugs or alcohol. She never got into any serious trouble with the school or at home. I checked out her bedroom and laptop computer. Didn't find anything connecting her with any of the other victims either yesterday or today. All these deaths seem to be random. I talked with the other detectives and they didn't find anything connecting these victims to a clandestine group or anything else."

"These sinister acts are reflecting a demonic group who randomly picks out their victims. And somehow this evilness touches its victims at a precise time."

Janet pulled up into her brother's driveway with her personal car and stopped. She had left her damaged detective vehicle at the forensic lab adjacent to the Sheriff Department's building. Since the perpetrator's truck had a chrome front bumper, there wouldn't be any paint transfer to her car for forensic analysis.

On her way to Michael's house she called Simon and told him what her partner, Bill Matters, had found out about their accident with the pickup truck. Simon said someone had somehow interfered with the cameras. It seemed likely the accident was intentional, preventing them from getting to the high school and find with the victim, Melody Richards, before she died. The student, Caleb Johnson, an obvious alias, who set off the fire alarm was involved with the people responsible for the deaths occurring at 11:58. Janet and Simon agreed Caleb could lead their investigation to the arrest of the perpetrators. They would have the results of his fingerprints and DNA tomorrow. Janet had stated the probability of a teenager having either or both test results on file was highly unlikely. Simon agreed.

She got out of the car, walked up to the front door of her brother's house and rang the doorbell. Behind her and to the right, a dark-blue van with tinted windows pulled up and parked along the curve a few houses down the street

~ * ~

"According to our records, this is Detective Bennett's brother's house she's about to go into," said Cary Gaines as he leaned forward.

"Yeah. It's probably a social visit," said Keith Nelson.

"The news conference by their captain a while ago didn't have a clue on the who, what or why regarding the deaths yesterday or this morning. And I'm sure they never will."

Cary's cell phone rang. He glanced at the caller's name: Seth. "Yes."

"Where are you?"

"We're watching Detective Bennett go into her brother's house."

"Come back in. There are things we must go over before tomorrow. I also called all the others to return to the control center."

"Yes, sir." He turned toward Keith. "We're done. Going back for a meeting with Seth and the others."

~ * ~

"Hey, Sis. Right on time. Dinner is almost ready."

Nothing was discussed regarding the six deaths this morning, other than Janet's hit-and-run accident. She sloughed it off, saying it was the hazards of being a detective. Janet hadn't mentioned she was working with FMI agents. The less she acknowledged, the less explanation she'd have to give to her brother. "Thank you for dinner, Crystal. It was great as usual."

"Thanks. I'm glad you enjoyed it."

"Let me help you clean up," Janet offered, as she stood.

"No. I appreciate the offer, Janet." Crystal peered at her two children sitting across from her.

"Carla, you clear the table. Matthew, you put everything into the dishwasher."

"I had dishwasher duty last night. It's Carla's turn."

"It's your lucky day, young man," Michael proclaimed. "You get to do it two days in a role."

Matthew huffed, displaying his dissatisfaction, then got up from the table and went into the kitchen.

"You two go into living room and relax," suggested Crystal. "I have to put away the rest of the roast in a container."

Michael sat at one end of the couch, as Janet sat at the other end. She prepared herself for the questions her brother was about to ask her. He had medical knowledge which helped her on previous cases, pointing her sometimes toward an answer in her investigation. Although, these unexplained deaths didn't have a cause of death or motive.

"Okay, sis. What's going on with all these deaths the past two days? I know you couldn't say anything over the phone earlier."

"There isn't much to say. The medical examiner didn't find any medical cause of their deaths, other than their hearts stopped beating. So far, all the autopsies haven't shown a cause of death. The drug screens are all negative. It's a medical mystery. The one clue we did find pointed to a high school student pulling the fire alarm prior to the death of a student. We were going to talk with this student, but he disappeared. We discovered after further investigation, the student is using an alias name. At least, that's what we think."

"You keep saying 'we.' Do you mean you and Detective Matters?"

*Damn. His mind picks up everything. I hate to lie to him. But I don't have a choice.* "Yeah. That's what I mean."

"What about—"

Janet's cell phone rang. She answered it on the second ring. The cell phone's caller ID displayed a phone number. No name. She didn't recognize the number. "Hello. This is Detective Bennett."

"It's Simon. We found out something about the student who pulled the fire alarm. I don't want to discuss it over the phone. Can you come to the hotel?"

She glanced at her watch. It was two minutes passed seven. "I'll be there in about fifteen minutes."

## Chapter Eight

Janet knocked on room 110's door. She had apologized to Michael, then Crystal, for her abrupt exit. She told them an informant had some information about the deaths but didn't want to talk on the phone. She was going to meet him at a designated place. This hadn't been the first time she had to leave her brother's house in a hurry due to a case she was working on. Janet knew Michael understood her position as a detective, since he had to be available to his patients by telephone when he was on call. The difference was she had to leave wherever she was and investigate a new case or an ongoing case. What she told her brother and sister-in-law was a half-truth and not a complete lie.

The hotel room door opened.

"Glad you could make it," Jean said. She moved aside so Janet could enter the room.

Frank sat in front of his computer, as Simon stood behind him peering over his shoulder at the computer screen. Janet walked up to them. "You got some information about Caleb Johnson?"

Simon turned and faced her. "Yes. But his name isn't Caleb Johnson, as we pretty much already knew. His name is Alexander Mandelson. He's wanted by Interpol for hacking into the German government. They found sophisticated computers in his Munich townhouse. They missed capturing him at his home by an hour. Somehow, he was tipped off. That was two years ago."

"Apparently he was a teenage computer prodigy?"

"He wasn't a teenager. Mandelson is twenty-two years old. He has the appearance of a teenager. According to Interpol records he's still on their most wanted list for hacking into German banks, corporations and government agencies two years ago. They don't think he was a lone wolf but affiliated with a secretive computer network. Interpol hasn't identified them yet."

Janet glanced down at the computer screen. "How were you able to discover Caleb's true identity?"

"Facial recognition," answered Frank. "I got Caleb's photo from his student file. Enhanced it. Then I scanned it into a photo recognition program."

"How did you get access to his high school file?"

"If I tell you, I'll have to kill you." Frank then laughed. "Just kidding."

Janet rolled her eyes and smirked. "Don't forget. I carry a gun, too."

"And it's bigger than mine," Frank added. "To answer your question, I hacked into the high school's computer system. I also hacked into the forensic lab's computer system for the results of Caleb's...that is, Alexander's, hairbrush analysis. The results of the DNA and fingerprints weren't in the system yet."

"I can't believe Alexander Mendelson infiltrated a high school to pull a fire alarm. There had to be another more devious reason for him pretending to be a high school student?"

"You would think so," Simon answered. "As the situation we're in with all these unexplained deaths, the intersection cameras malfunction during our hit-and-run accident and our fire alarm perp, we're only seeing the tip of the iceberg."

Janet nodded. She hadn't been on a case, Frank called Whispering Deaths, with so many twists and turns, unknowns and good guys with paranormal powers. In the distant future, if she was writing her memoirs about this case, she'd have to change the genre to fiction instead of non-fiction because no one would believe there were characters with psychic abilities trying to solve mysterious deaths. One absolute fact crossed her mind as she stood peering down at the computer screen, an unscrupulous, fanatic entity was part of their investigation now. And possibly the mysterious deaths the past two days were carried out by a terrorist group. "Maybe, Alexander caused the death of the gym student, Melody Richards, this morning? And what if all these deaths were simultaneously caused by someone near the victims? A network of terrorists."

"As I see it, anything is possible," Simon said.

Frank turned his head and looked up at Janet. "We could be dealing with something completely different. Nothing relating to terrorists. The fire alarm may have been a coincidence. Until we can interrogate our person of interest, Alexander Mendelson, we really don't know if he or the people he's working for are responsible for these deaths."

Janet now knew why Frank loved computer work. "Did anyone ever tell you that you have an analytical mind? I'd compare you to a computer's unprejudiced, nonbiased, unemotional digital circuits which deals with facts, and not conjectures."

Everyone in the room laughed, including Frank.

"You sure pegged him," Jean said. "But we still love him despite his computer-like mind."

Frank glanced at Jean. "Are you calling me a loving nerd? If you are, I take your comment as a compliment."

"Yeah. But Detective…that is, Janet, said it best. Besides, you can smell the roses before anyone else can. Or smell them long after they've been gone. I feel bad for you when an odor is putrid. I'd probably be puking my guts out if I had your sensitive nose."

"Like I've said many times before, I can blank out unpleasant or even pleasant odors when it's not relevant in a case we're investigating. Like someone cooking ribs on a barbecue grill."

Simon shook his head. "Let's get down to business, now. So far, I haven't had a vision of people dying tomorrow. This could be good. There might not be any deaths tomorrow at 11:58. Then again, whatever or whoever is causing these deaths may have changed the time or stopped the deadly rampage all together."

Janet agreed to Simon's speculation. There had been many cases in the annals of unsolved murder mysteries over the past two centuries, Jack the Ripper's murders and the Zodiac Murders being the most infamous. She didn't want Whispers Before Death added to this list. They needed a clue, a piece of evidence leading them to the cause of fourteen people dying at 11:58.

After a forty-minute discussion, they planned out tomorrow's investigation. Frank would continue to search the internet for some type of correlation between the victims. Jean would revisit the coroner's office, gathering any latest information on the victims. Janet and Simon would interview students at the high school about Caleb Johnson. They won't inform the students or high school personnel about Caleb being an imposter, a possible terrorist. Janet hoped someone might know where he truly resided. As far as Mendelson's parents, Frank had stated there was no record of their existence. They had obviously used false names when they registered their "son" at the high school.

Janet said goodnight to the FMI agents and left the hotel room. She would pick up Simon at eight o'clock tomorrow morning. They would then drive to West Port High School.

~ * ~

Cary Gaines and Keith Nelson walked out the front door of Perfect Flower Shop at eight-thirty. It was a functioning florist business, although the actual purpose of the business was to conceal a clandestine world organization on the second level of the building. A streetlight lit up the sidewalk and their van that was parked in the street. Storefronts displayed multicolored neon lights advertising products and/or services. They got into the van.

"Seth made it clear," Cary said, "we must continue to prevent the authorities from finding out the cause of all these deaths. Like he said, fear and panic are our strengths toward the eventual control of our subjects."

"One thing is good. They'll never find a trace of Alexander."

"It's amazing how The Circle can make people disappear, change their identity or physical appearance."

"His present role was compromised when he was identified by this detective and her group from CDC. Still don't know how they did it. One of the students must have seen him set off the fire alarm."

"Yeah. Seth came to the same assumption."

"I can't see why the CDC is investigating these deaths. Disease isn't causing these deaths."

"They'll eventually realize this fact and leave. We don't have to worry about them. It's Detective Bennett we must be concerned about. Our sources say she might solve these deaths. How The Circle knows this hasn't been divulged to Seth yet."

"Yeah. A real mystery. Huh?" Keith laughed.

Cary didn't respond to Keith's laughter. "We'll get a good night's sleep. I'll stop by your place about six-thirty tomorrow morning. Detective Bennett will be leaving her house around seven-thirty." He drove away from the flower shop.

# Chapter Nine

The morning sun was near the treetops, causing Janet to pull down her car's visor to block the blinding light and avoid crossing over the median line or venturing off into a ditch. She didn't get a call from Simon after leaving the hotel last night. He apparently didn't get a vision of more people suddenly dying, otherwise he would've called her. She had already called Captain Robins and told him where she'd be this morning, following up on Melody Richard's death at the high school. Janet also called her partner, Bill. He wasn't happy she'd be on her own again today. But he agreed to continue investigating her hit-and-run accident yesterday and check out if any establishments near the accident scene had video cameras on which might show the pickup truck, the driver and any passengers. He would also check the forensic lab for any additional information. If it wasn't for a possible connection between the accident and her rushing to the high school before 11:58, Janet would've had the Ocala Police Department investigate the hit-and-run incident.

Janet pulled into the Holiday Inn's parking lot around 7:50. A few minutes later, she knocked on Simon's hotel room door. The door opened. He glanced down at his watch. "Right on time."

"I like punctuality. I'm not a patient person and hate waiting. If a person shows up late for a scheduled appointment, it usually means they're not respectful toward the person."

Simon chuckled. "I'll make sure I'm not late for any of your appointments…or for dinner."

"You're a doctor. Being punctual is not a word recognized in a doctor's vocabulary. I almost always wait past my scheduled office appointment."

Simon's shoulders slumped as he shook his head and smirked. "You sure know how to hurt a guy's feelings."

"Sorry. I was only stating the facts." Janet was starting to like Simon's laidback demeanor. It didn't seem many things rattled him, or he hid his true emotions and feelings from her. She'd have to wait to see if this continued. Of course, she thought the same thing about her ex-husband, Rick Ridder, when she first met him. Calm demeanor, trustworthy and good looking. Only the last feature held true during their relationship.

Janet and Simon arrived at West Port High School's visitor's parking lot at 8:23. They got of the car and walked toward the front of the school. Unbeknownst to them, a dark-blue van drove into the parking lot and parked before Janet and Simon entered the front door of the high school.

Principal Perkins asked Janet if they knew the cause of Melody Richard's death. She told him not yet. She then got the list of Caleb's classes with the name of students in each of the classes. They crossed checked the names of students in Caleb's other classes. They chose seven names. They spent about an hour interviewing the students. None of the students knew him personally since he didn't participate in any outside social activities. He was personable and likable but never let anyone get close to him. No one knew anything about his personal life. Some the students indicated Caleb felt intellectually and maturity-wise above them. Janet could understand since he was eight years older than most of them. Of course, she didn't tell any of the students his actual age of twenty-five. When they went back to the front office, Principal Perkins told them he received a phone call from Caleb's mother, stating they had to withdraw their son from school. Her husband had accepted a job in Harrisburg, Pennsylvania and they had to leave right away. She would email the school their new address.

Janet sighed. "Do you have their phone number?" Yesterday, Frank had checked the telephone number on Caleb Johnson's high school records. It was a bogus phone number. He had also checked for Caleb Johnson and his parents on the internet. Nothing had matched. They didn't exist on the internet, DMV, or any other public record other than the real Caleb Johnson she and Simon visited yesterday. Of course, Frank did find information on an Alexander Mendelson from Berlin, Germany. But no information after Mendelson fled Germany.

"Yes. I'll get it for you," Perkins said, as he sat down on his desk chair, reached for his desk phone and checked for the Johnson's number on the recent call memory list. He wrote the number on a note pad and handed it to Janet.

She couldn't believe it: finally, a connection to the fire alarm perpetrator and his so-called parents. Janet dialed the number on her cell phone. She glanced at Simon. "Maybe we'll get some answers."

He nodded. "I sure hope so."

The phone rang three times. A recording interrupted the call. An electronic created female voice announced, "This number is not available." Janet surmised the call to the principal was from a throw-away cell phone. There was no way to trace the caller. This was becoming like a cloak and dagger case except for no knife or any other weapon causing the demise of fourteen victims. *The perpetrators have covered their tracks.* She turned toward Principal Perkins. "No answer. Give me a call if the parents call back or if there's a request for Caleb's high school records." Janet knew it was unlikely either of these two things would ever happen. Of course, she didn't let on to Perkins about her knowledge regarding Caleb and his so-called parents and that the Johnsons would likely never contact the high school again.

~ * ~

After Janet and Simon had walked into the high school, Cary Gaines got out of the van, walked over to driver side door of Janet's car and unlocked the door with a silver-colored, square remote-control device with a horizontal line oscillating rapidly up and down; the device was the size of a computer mouse. He glanced around to see if anyone was paying any attention to him. The three people in the parking lot weren't looking his way. He opened the door and slid behind the steering wheel. Reaching underneath the dashboard, he placed a black, square remote-control speaker the size of a quarter. Cary then got of the car, went back to the van and waited for Janet and Simon.

"Here they come," Keith Nelson said peering through the windshield at Janet and Simon walking out of the front entrance of the school, as he sat in the passenger-side front seat of the van.

"Now we'll be able to hear what they're saying inside the car," said Cary. "We know CDC is working with her on these deaths, which we'd expect. Our major concern is making sure the sheriff's detectives or CDC people don't get too close to the cause of these deaths."

Keith nodded as he moved his lower lip over his upper lip, then said, "We're too smart. They'll never find out."

Cary rolled his eyes and smirked responding to his partner's first comment, "We're too smart." He had acknowledged in the past to his cohorts about Keith not having too many brain cells between his ears. There was one thing going for his partner: he was loyal and trustworthy, and would do anything he was told to do, including murder. Cary had the first two traits but hadn't and never would kill someone. "Yeah, Keith. You're definitely an asset to me and to The Circle."

Keith frowned. "What do 'ya mean I'm an ass?"

"No. Not ass…asset. That's a good thing."

"Oh. Okay. Thanks."

Keith placed an ear bud into his right ear. He then reached down toward the van's console and turned on a listening device recorder.

~ * ~

Janet sat behind the steering wheel and was about to start the car. Simon reached over and touched her forearm. At the same time, he placed his index finger to his mouth in the gesture of "be quiet, don't say anything." Janet nodded, acknowledging his gesture. Simon leaned to the left, reached out with left hand until it was underneath the dashboard. A moment later he removed a listening device from under the dashboard and set it down on the console.

"Dang it. I left my medical bag in the trunk," Simon said. "I need to get something out of it."

"I'll have to come with you. My trunk release control in the car isn't working."

They stood behind the trunk. Janet fumbled with her keys, then whispered, "How did you know there was a bug in my car?"

"I had a vision of a quarter-size bugging device underneath the dashboard right after I got into the car."

She opened the trunk. They leaned forward into the trunk. "Why would someone want to listen in on my conversations?"

"Not sure. We need to go somewhere to talk without someone listening to us. I'll take pictures of the listening device on my cell phone and write down any identifying numbers and lettering on it, then have Frank find out if we can trace the device to where it was bought or manufactured."

"Great idea." She closed the trunk. "I know a place where we can talk in private and away from listening bugs."

They got back into the car. Simon snapped pictures of the listening device on his cell phone. An area on the back of the device was obliterated of any writings and/or numbers.

"I sure could go for a cup of coffee," Simon announced.

"Sounds good to me, too. We might as well, since we don't have any leads on these deaths." *This was for the benefit of whoever was listening in to our conversation.* Janet backed out of her space. She glanced around the lot for any vehicles with people sitting inside. She didn't see anyone in the immediate area. There were several vehicles near the entrance of the parking lot, including a dark-blue van with tinted windows. She slowed her car and stared through the windshield of all the vehicles, including the dark-blue van.

No one was sitting in any of the vehicles.

Unknown to Janet and Simon, Cary and Keith had scurried to the back of the van as they saw Detective Bennett drive toward them.

Janet pulled into IHOP's parking lot. She glanced into the rearview mirror to see if any vehicle was behind her. No one followed her in. When they reached the window-enclosed vestibule before entering the restaurant Janet peered at the front driveway to her left, as Simon stared at the right front driveway. No vehicle entered the parking lot. A moment later, they stood together inside waiting for a waitress to seat them. A waitress came and was about to take them to a booth to their right. Janet told her they wanted to sit in the back room at a table. A few minutes later, Janet ordered coffee and Simon decided on a large glass of orange juice.

"Was there a reason you insisted on sitting here in the back room instead at a booth up front?" Simon asked.

"When we found out someone had us under surveillance and apparently trying to obtain information on our investigation, it was important for us to be in a room where we can see who's around us. A booth has too many blind spots. Besides, I wanted to be the one who chose where we sat."

"You think the waitress is working for them?"

"You may think I'm paranoid, Simon, but after finding the listening device in my car, and after all that has happened the past two days, I've become suspicious of everything and everyone. Until we find out who's spying on us, I think it would be best to whisper pertinent information on our investigation or even write them out on a piece of paper. Any electronic communication device can be bugged or hacked into. I'm not sure if I mentioned this to you before, but with all the electronic, cellular, and landline fiber optic cables connected to different communication devices in today's world, people are vulnerable to someone listening in on their conversations."

"Like a clandestine government agency, including the NSA?"

"Or non-government groups with sinister intentions…like the ones apparently watching our every move and listening to our conversations."

Janet glanced around the room to see if anyone was staring at them. People were concentrating on their cell phones, talking with whoever they were with, or sitting alone and reading a newspaper. No eyes were upon them. She leaned forward and whispered: "What do you think about my car being bugged?"

Simon pursed his lips, leaned forward, then answered: "I thought about it on our way here. The one logical explanation I came up with was whoever planted it, was likely the same person or persons involved with our hit and run accident, the false fire alarm and the 11:58 a.m. deaths. They want to know what information we have on the unexplained deaths the past two days."

Janet rubbed her tongue on the back of her front teeth and furled her eyebrows while gazing into Simon's eyes. She then said, "If what you said is true, then there's the possibility my home phone is bugged. And I wouldn't doubt your hotel rooms are being bugged too. We're not dealing with amateurs."

"And we're not amateurs either."

"No, we're not."

"I'll call Frank and Jean and have them meet us here at the restaurant. I won't tell them you and I found a listening bug in your car. Just in case we're being listened to on our cell phones."

~ * ~

Janet had finished her first cup of coffee and was pouring her second cup and Simon had finished drinking the last of his orange juice as Frank and Jean walked up to their table and sat down.

Frank breathed deeply through his nose, then said, "Is this our breakfast meeting served with pancakes, sausage and a cup of Java?"

Jean frowned and sighed. "We had breakfast earlier this morning at the hotel. Did you forget?"

"No. This is a later-morning breakfast."

"I can't believe how much you eat in a day. You should be roly-poly like the Pillsbury doughboy."

"I burn a lot of calories every day. I need to replenish my body."

"I don't see how typing and moving the mouse on your computer can burn that many calories."

"Easy. I burn a lot of mental energy."

"Okay, you guys," Simon said, as he glanced around the room. The initial patrons who were sitting here when he and Janet walked into the back room, had left, being replaced by a young couple with two children sitting three tables away to their left and a man and woman in their sixties or early seventies sitting four tables away to his right. None of them were paying any attention toward their table. "Let's get down to why I called you here." He leaned forward and told them in a low tone of voice, making it difficult for anyone sitting a couple of tables away to hear what he was saying, about Janet's car being bugged, and what their thoughts were about it.

Simon then told Frank to check their hotel rooms for any bugging devices, including their rental cars. After flying into Ocala International Airport in their unmarked ten-passenger jet two days ago, each of them got a rental vehicle. Frank had a bugging device detector at the hotel. It was one of many specialized devices he had brought from Atlanta. Simon also stated to his team that if they obtained any pertinent information about the investigation to wait until after Frank checked for bugging devices. Simon glanced at Jean, then Frank. "Don't mention the bugging of Janet's car until you check everything out."

Frank nodded, followed by a forlorn expression. "I guess this means we're not having butter pecan pancakes topped with caramel syrup and whipped cream?"

"Not today," Simon answered, chuckling to himself. "Have either of you this morning," glancing at Jean then Frank, "gained any pertinent information in our investigation of Whispers Before Death?"

Frank and Jean shook their heads in a negative gesture. Their investigation was at standstill. Not a single clue, except for someone not wanting them to know the truth behind the 11:58 deaths. They all agreed, the deaths of fourteen people in Ocala weren't accidents, but premeditated murders. Right now, the four of them had no answer to the how and why.

The sound of a cell phone ringing at their table had everyone instantly reach for their phones, even though each of them had different rings. Janet said, "It's mine." She removed the phone from its belt carrier. She glanced down at the phone, then brought in up to her ear, "Bill. What's up?" Several seconds later, her eyebrows raised. "You found the pickup truck that hit us yesterday?"

## Chapter Ten

"Where did you find the truck?" Janet asked.

"It was found behind a vacant building off Silver Springs Boulevard this morning," Bill answered. "Ocala Police ran the license plate and registration about an hour ago. The plates were a forgery. Can you believe it? Someone had made them. The police ran the VIN number and the truck was stolen from a Ford dealership's lot in Detroit about two years ago. The fact was ten vehicles were stolen from the dealership's lot. The theft of these vehicles is still unsolved by the Detroit Police Department. But there's—"

"Can't believe we're at another dead end," Janet interrupted.

"But that's not all."

"What do you mean…that's not all?"

"I got off the phone with Detective Morse from the Detroit Police Department. I wanted to talk with the detective who was in charge of the vehicle thefts. To make a long story short, Detective Morse told me the security cameras at the dealership blacked out for thirty minutes during the theft of the vehicles. No evidence of an inside job. Also, the security guard was found dead without a determination of death. His death sounded similar to the deaths here in Ocala."

"I agree. There's too much of a coincidence between the two. I'm sure we're dealing with the same people responsible for both incidents." She sighed. "What could be the perpetrators purpose?"

"That's the million-dollar question. By the way, how's it going with your investigation of Melody Richards?"

Janet told him what had transpired at the high school with the deceased student, which was nothing significant. She still wanted to tell him about her stealthy investigation with the ESP team from the CDC, but she knew it would complicate things. Besides, knowing Bill over the past few years, he'd have to tell the other detectives about a group of mutants working on the strange deaths occurring in Ocala these past two days. She loved working with her partner but understood he'd have a tough time keeping a secret to himself. "I'll talk to you later, Bill. Thanks for the information." She put her cell phone back into the holder. Janet turned her attention to everyone at the table and told them what Detective Matters had said to her.

Simon spoke first. "I agree with the comment you made to your partner, 'what's their purpose?' We're obviously dealing with a sophisticated and evil entity. We know we're being observed and listened to by them. Let me repeat again: we'll have to be extremely cautious in what we say, not letting them know we're on to them, and making sure we don't give them any pertinent information about our investigation."

"I'm sure they haven't hacked into my computer," declared Frank. "I've inserted a failsafe computer program which immediately detects anyone trying to gain access to my computer."

Jean added, "If these perps were in Detroit two years ago, I wonder if there were any other unsolved deaths in the Detroit area?"

"You make an excellent point," Simon answered. "We have three options here. The first would be have Frank search the internet for other suspicious deaths with the diagnosis of Undetermined Death in and around Detroit during the time of the security guard's death. The second option would be for us to call the medical examiners in the counties around and in Detroit, asking them for a list of sudden deaths with the diagnosis of Undetermined Death around the time of the security guard's death. And thirdly, we go to Detroit and do our own investigation."

"If I may interject," Janet said, "It seems our investigation on the unexplained deaths here in Ocala has come to a standstill."

"I agree."

"Unless someone comes forward with information, we can only wait until the next series of deaths to occur."

"If I'm hearing what you're saying," said Simon, "you think we should go to Detroit and investigate the unexplained death of the security guard and any other similar deaths around the time of the vehicle thefts?"

"It's just a suggestion."

Simon nodded and grinned. He then turned to Frank. "Besides checking for any bugging devices, you'll need to stay in Ocala, at least for now, and continue your computer search for information about the fourteen deaths in Ocala. I also want you to go inside the truck and find any odors. Maybe the driver and/or passenger used a distinct cologne or perfume." He next turned to Jean. "Continue your investigation of victims' families. There still might be a common link between these victims."

"We'll take care of everything here," Jean said.

Janet couldn't believe Simon's response to her suggestions. She'd have to have a justified and warranted reason to take her investigations of the "11:58 Deaths" to Detroit. It was unlikely Captain Robins would let her travel to Detroit regarding the death of a security guard two years ago.

~ * ~

Three repetitive dings burst from the PA system, filling the plane's ten-passenger cabin. A deep baritone male voice from the plane's co-pilot announced: "Please fasten your seat belt. We'll be landing at Detroit International Airport shortly."

Janet turned her head to the left toward Simon, who sat in a seat on the other side of the plane's aisle and said: "I can't believe we're here." When she went to her captain yesterday afternoon with the information about a possible connection with the death of the security guard in Detroit and the deaths in Ocala, she expected him say, "No way. It would be a waste of time and taxpayers' money." Lo and behold, he gave approval to carry her investigation to the Motor City. He had based his decision on the fact the expense of plane fare would be zero since she'd be flying on a CDC government jet. And due to no leads to the fourteen deaths in Ocala, he conceded and let the investigation proceed to Detroit, hoping for a break in the Ocala's unsolved deaths.

Frank didn't find any listening devices in their cars or hotel rooms. He also checked Janet's house, including her home phone. None were found. As for identifying the listening device's manufacturer, he found the company. The problem was there were tens of thousands sold worldwide. No way to trace the purchaser.

Janet squinted. The nine o'clock morning sun shone into her eyes as she and Simon exited the plane.

~ * ~

A rental car was waiting for them on the tarmac next to the plane. After putting their luggage in the trunk of the car, Simon got behind the wheel and said, "Precinct Three of the Detroit Police Department is close to the area of the city they call Greek Town. Do you like Greek food?"

"I've eaten baklava and drunk ouzo."

"Baklava is good. But I've never acquired a taste for licorice, especially in a liqueur. How did you happen to drink ouzo?"

"I went to a Greek wedding a couple of years ago. The wedding reception served both baklava and ouzo. I shouldn't say this, but after drinking a few shot-like glasses of it, I had to call a cab to drive me home."

Simon chuckled to himself, as he started the car and drove off the tarmac. He had a similar situation with peppermint schnapps after he turned twenty-one. He was sitting at a table with friends celebrating his birthday. It was first time he had drunk this sweet-tasting alcoholic drink. After downing about ten of them, he stood and immediately collapsed to the floor. He had lost all feeling in his legs, besides being inebriated. "I can relate to your encounter with ouzo." He told her about his episode with peppermint schnapps and how he hadn't taken another sip of the liqueur ever since.

"I haven't drunk any more ouzo either. And when someone mentions the word licorice, I cringe."

Laughter erupted from them.

Simon liked Janet's laugh; it was genuine with humility. There were many attributes he liked about her. Intelligence, integrity, and good-looking. *My God, it seems like I'm profiling a woman for a dating site.* "I guess we have something in common."

"Yeah. Stay away from liqueurs. For me, a couple of beers occasionally is my limit when it comes to alcohol."

"I'm right along with you regarding consumption of alcohol."

*Now we have two things in common.*

Janet called Detective Morse and told him they'd be at the Third Precinct in about an hour. She'd called him yesterday afternoon and told him she and Simon would be flying into Detroit regarding the vehicle thefts and the suspicious death of the security guard two years ago. Detective Morse knew about the fourteen deaths in Ocala from the national news TV coverage. As Simon was listening to the conversation between Janet and the Detroit detective— Janet had put their conversation on speaker—his mind focused on the security guard's death. If it turned out his death was caused by natural causes, such as a heart attack perpetrated by sudden stress, then there wouldn't be a connection to Ocala's deaths. He'd have to talk with the pathologist who did the autopsy on the security guard.

After Janet finished talking with Detective Morse, she turned toward Simon. "I'll use the GPS on my phone to take us to the police station. The police station is on Atwater Street. I wrote down the address Detective Morse gave me yesterday."

"No need to. I know how to get there."

"Have you been to Detroit before?"

"I went to Wayne State University Medical School in Detroit. So, I'm very familiar with the different areas in the city. Good and bad. I know what areas of Detroit to visit and the areas to avoid. That's why I knew about Greek Town, which is down the street from Wayne County Jail and—"

"I believe you're familiar with the layout of Detroit," Janet interrupted, "and where we're going."

"Sorry. There I go again getting carried away with an answer."

"It's better than a boring short answer."

*Was that a compliment? Or did she just insult me?*

In about an hour they were in Detroit driving east on Woodward. They passed Wayne State University on their right. A few minutes later they were parking in the visitor's lot at the Third Precinct Police Station.

He and Janet walked up to the front desk. “I’m Detective Bennett. Detective Morse is expecting me.” The desk sergeant glanced at Simon. “Oh. This is Dr. Woods. He’s a member of our investigative team.”

“Huh.” He picked up a pen and wrote down their names and handed each of them a visitor’s ID card attached to a metal clip. They clipped the ID to their sports coat’s lapel. He then raised his left arm and pointed to his left. “Go through the door on your right. It’s the last room on the left.”

As they walked down the hallway, a vision flashed across Simon’s mind: a black man with a mustache drinking from a mug. He didn’t mention his vision to Janet.

The last door on the left was open when they walked through the doorway and into a large room with several desks scattered throughout the room. Janet asked a detective who was leaving the room. “We’re here to see Detective Morse.”

He turned around and pointed to his left, “He’s the—”

“He’s the one over there standing and holding a cup of coffee,” Simon interrupted.

“Ah…yes. You already know him?” asked the detective.

“Yes,” answered Simon. He had to lie. What was he supposed to say to the inquiring detective, “I saw him a moment ago in a vision?”

Janet interjected, “Thanks, detective.” He nodded and left the room. She glanced at Simon. “You don’t have to explain to me, visionary man.”

Simon raised his eyebrows and smirked. *I like the name, visionary man.*

Detective Morse stood about six-feet tall. He had light-black skin with short black hair and a well-trimmed mustache. He was talking with another detective. Morse turned toward Janet and Simon as they approached him. In a deep baritone voice, he declared, “Detective Bennett and Dr. Woods, I presume?”

“Yes, we are…Detective Morse,” Janet answered. She reached out and shook his hand. Simon then shook the detective’s hand.

Simon and Janet sat in chairs in front of Morse’s desk. The detective, sitting behind his desk stated: “I pulled the two-year-old evidence file on the Ford dealership vehicle heist." He reached to his right into a rectangular plastic container on his desk and removed several files. He laid them on the desk in front of him. "Like I said on the phone yesterday, the case is still open and unsolved. There wasn't any physical evidence at the crime scene. We went over the area of the missing vehicles with a fine-tooth comb. Not a shred of evidence was found. Like I stated before, the security cameras weren't working during the theft. None of the vehicles, which included pickup trucks, vans and SUVs, had turned up until your call yesterday. That is… the call from your partner, Detective Matters. Anyway, we suspect it was a well-organized vehicle theft ring involved with the stolen Ford vehicles. Plus, the death of the security guard at the Ford dealership during the vehicle thefts was determined to be from a heart attack. His death didn't point toward any foul play."

Simon wasn't convinced the security guard's death occurred due to stress and anxiety. He wanted to know if any other unexplained deaths in the Detroit Metropolitan area had happened the day of the vehicle thefts. The first place to start would be the county coroner's office. But first, he and Janet needed to review Walter Osborn's police file. "We appreciate your cooperation in our investigation."

"No problem. I'm glad to help. You'll also be assisting us in this cold case. You can go through these police files on Mr. Osborn in our lunchroom. It's where we go to get away from the noise in here and eat. It'll be ideal for examining files. There are food and drink vending machines in the lunchroom also."

"Thanks, Detective Morse."

Simon and Janet picked up the files and followed Morse to the lunchroom. After he left, they sat across from each other at a four-chair square table and went through the files, hoping to find a minute piece of evidence overlooked by the Detroit detectives.

About thirty minutes later, Simon reached over the table and touched Janet's arm. "I found something very interesting."

"What did you find?"

"The security camera's recorder was in a secured room inside the dealership. Even though the outside cameras directed at the new vehicle lot went blank for thirty minutes during the vehicle theft, all the other cameras functioned without any interruption, including a camera pointed at the room containing the video recorders. So, no one interfered with the recorder. Detective Morse stated in his investigation report the video recorder had an unexplained technical glitch."

"Quite a coincidence…don't you think? Like we said on the plane, 'a coincidence when the camera at the intersection happened to go blank during our traffic accident.' There are genuine coincidences, such as bumping into a person you were thinking about a few minutes before or thinking about ordering a pizza sitting on the couch then a few seconds later the TV shows a Hungry Howie Pizza commercial. Those are true coincidences. I don't think we're dealing with a coincidence here."

Simon agreed with Janet's perspective of happenstance. The intersection and security cameras had been tampered with, a deliberate criminal act by someone. It was a mystery how the cameras were manipulated.

They went back reviewing the files. Twenty minutes later, Janet exclaimed, "Oh my God. I can't believe this."

"What is it?" He leaned forward and stared down at the file in front of Janet. "What did you find?"

Janet turned the file a hundred and eighty degrees, sliding the file toward Simon. "Read the last paragraph."

Simon began reading notes taken by Detective Morse: *Interviewed Caleb Johnson, electronic technician at the dealership….*

## Chapter Eleven

"I suppose there could be several Caleb Johnsons in the United States," Janet said as she retrieved the file from Simon. "This is uncanny, though. A high school student used this name and now a person working at a Ford dealership as an electronic technician had the same name. We need to interview this guy named Caleb Johnson."

"I agree. Shouldn't we call the dealership first and make sure a different Caleb Johnson works there and not our perp in Ocala? Since Frank found the student using the name Caleb Johnson in Ocala was Alexander Mandelson, he may be the same person who worked for the Ford dealership? If he was, it would correlate with him disappearing from Germany two years ago."

"You're sounding like a sheriff's detective."

"Thanks. I'll take your comment as a compliment. Like I said yesterday, we both have investigative minds: mine leans toward medical facts and yours toward criminal evidence."

Janet called the Ford dealership. The general manager stated Caleb Johnson quit about two months after the theft of the ten vehicles. She asked the manager to describe him. He had identical features of the student who pulled the fire alarm two days ago at the high school. Simon and Janet agreed it was obviously the same person. Simon suggested they go to Wayne County Coroner's office and ask questions about the security guard's death. Janet agreed, since they were at a standstill with the theft of the vehicles, other than learning that Alexander Mandelson was directly or indirectly involved with the computer glitch and the death of the security guard. Then two years later Mandelson became involved with the high school's false fire alarm and the death of Melody Richards.

They thanked Detective Morse, not telling him what they had found out about Caleb Johnson, and left the police station. Simon and Janet felt it best not to get him involved in a potentially dangerous situation with a clandestine and evil group or organization. Besides, the fewer people who knew about it, the better chance for Janet and the ESP team from CDC to solve these horrendous deaths.

Simon drove out of the police parking lot and turned right onto Atwater Street. A late model, medium-blue Ford SUV, with two male occupants, started its engine. The SUV slowly made its way out of the police visitor's parking lot, turning right. Were they following Simon and Janet, or was it a coincidence they left the police station nearly together?

Simon sighed to himself, unaware of a Ford SUV a few car lengths behind him and Janet. Being in Detroit brought back numerous memories when he was a medical student at Wayne State University Medical School. "I got an idea. Since it's almost lunch time, why don't I take you to a Greek restaurant? It's a few minutes away."

"Sure. I'd like that."

Simon turned left onto St. Antoine Street. The medium-blue SUV also turned left. A few minutes later, Simon parked on the second level of a parking structure near Monroe Street, the main street for Greek Town. They got out of the car and walked over to an elevator. Janet pushed the down arrow button to the right of the elevator. The elevator door opened and the two of them stepped inside. As the door was closing Simon saw a medium-blue SUV pull up into a parking space next to his car. When the elevator got to the ground level and they got out, Simon stopped and said: "I saw something odd a moment ago, after we got into the elevator on the second level."

"What did you see?"

"We parked the car with several open parking spaces on both sides of us. As the elevator door was closing an SUV parked right next to our car."

"Huh. What make vehicle was it?"

He closed his eyes trying to visualize the vehicle. A cold electrical-like pulse bolted up his spine to the back of his neck, as he opened his eyes. "A Ford. Maybe two years old. Are you thinking what

I'm thinking?"

"I'm sure I am. It's one of the stolen vehicles. There were two SUVs reported stolen from the Ford dealership. Or it's a coincidence."

"Since we're near a casino, I'd bet on it being one of the stolen vehicles. Plus, why would someone want to park next to us unless they were going to do something to our car. Like plant a listening device under the dash…or even worse."

"An explosive device comes to mind."

"Should we call Detective Morse?"

"Let's not draw any conclusions until we get all the facts. Let's take the elevator back up to the second floor."

Simon pushed the up-arrow button. The elevator door opened right away. They stepped inside the elevator. Simon glanced down to his right and saw Janet remove her Glock from its holster, as the elevator moved upward toward the second level of the parking structure. His thoughts conjured up different scenarios, and what they would find when the elevator door opened. His car sitting there alone with no SUV in sight. Or a SUV present and someone under his car planting a bomb to detonate once he started the car. Or possibly someone in the car positioning a listening device under the dashboard. He sighed deeply, trying to calm himself as the elevator stopped.

The elevator door opened.

"Oh my God," shouted Simon. "Where's my car?"

Janet replaced her Glock back into the shoulder holster. "I believe we're victims of a car theft."

A sigh of relief overtook Simon, as the alternative would mean the clandestine group responsible for the stealthy events occurring two years ago and the past few days weren't involved with his car being stolen. He couldn't be a hundred percent positive it wasn't the same people.

~ * ~

Janet called Detective Morse and informed him about their car theft. According to the detective, their make and model car was at the top of list for most stolen car in the Detroit Metropolitan area. Morse told her their car would be taken apart bolt by bolt with each part sold on the black market. It would be unlikely the car would be recovered. She gave him the description of the Ford SUV without the license plate number. Neither her or Simon saw any of the letters or numbers. Morse sent a patrol car to pick them up and brought them back to the police station, where Simon gave an officer all the information on his stolen rental car. He called the rental company and gave them the bad news. About an hour later, a rental car was delivered to them at the police station. Before ordering another vehicle, he was given a list of most stolen vehicles by Detective Morse. Simon picked out a car not on the list. There was no guarantee their new car wouldn't be stolen. It was about one o'clock when they left and headed for Greek Town.

Janet looked out the front passenger window of the car at a vender on the sidewalk selling what looked like sandwiches and sodas. "Hopefully…we won't run into another problem?"

"We deserve a calm and rewarding day."

"Amen. I'm looking forward going to what you call Greek Town."

Simon parked the rental car on the first level of the enclosed parking structure. Janet looked behind a few times until they reached the street. A few minutes later, they came to Monroe Street. She stopped and gazed up at a building a block or two away which probably stood several stories tall.

"That's Wayne County Jail," Simon said in a matter-of-fact tone. "There's another building across the street from it which also holds inmates. A tunnel runs from one building to the other."

"How do you know so much about the jail? Were you a—"

"No. I wasn't an unwilling guest of the sheriff's department. I did a month rotation in their medical department when I was a medical student. I could probably write a book on the incarcerated patients at the county jail. I was there during the month of December and—"

"Thanks. I was only wondering," Janet interrupted. *Simon usually never gives a simple answer to a question.*

"There I go again, rambling. Anyway, to our left is Greek Town." He extended his arm to the left pointing down Monroe Street.

Janet turned her attention toward numerous and colorful neon lights down the street advertising a variety of Greek restaurants. The surroundings gave the impression of the festive sights a person might experience visiting Disney World in Florida. They walked about halfway up the street and went into restaurant with a sign displaying a horse with wings. The hostess escorted them to a booth. A male waiter walked up to them.

"Can I get you folks a drink?"

The thought of ouzo made her cringe. "I'll have sweet tea."

"You mean a cup of tea with sugar?"

The server obviously didn't know what she meant. This was the North, not Florida or other southern states that drank sweet tea. "No. Instead, I'll have a Sprite."

"I'll have the same please." Simon then looked at Janet and grinned. "Nothing stronger?"

"Are you a mind reader, too? You're obviously referring to my ouzo incident a couple of years ago."

"I'm not a mind reader. When we were walking to our booth, I thought I smelled licorice. Then I heard you take a deep breath."

"Very observant, Simon."

"Thank you. I have a sensitive nose to certain aromas."

"Did Frank's super smell somehow transfer to you?"

"Oh no. I've always been this way. Some odors make me feel nauseated or lightheaded. I have an overactive olfactory nerve. It why I don't wear cologne or aftershave. And why I don't associate with women who splash on perfume."

"I don't use…wait a minute. It seems coincidental I don't use perfume. And since I'm suspicious of coincidence. You already knew I didn't use perfume when you chose me to assist you and your team. Am I right?"

Simon put out his hands in a gesture of being handcuffed. "Guilty as charged."

"What other idiosyncrasies do you know about me?"

"None that I can recollect."

"You now sound like a politician. Not committing yourself to an exact answer to a question."

"I guess I'll have to plea the Fifth." He grinned. "I'm kidding. I don't have any more personal information about you."

*I'm sure he knows what kind of toothpaste I use.* "We'll see." She liked Simon but didn't have a hundred percent trust in him. He presented himself as a conscientious and trustworthy individual, but so did her first husband, Rick Ridder, when she first met him. Since her divorce, she kept men at arm's-length, not letting them get the best of her or get emotionally close to her.

The waiter brought them their drinks. "Can I take your order?"

Simon ordered a chicken gyro platter with a Greek salad for them. Janet didn't want lamb, veal or squid, even though she had never tasted them before. She wanted to stick to her normal palate of chicken, beef or pork. After eating, Simon tried to pay for both their meals, but Janet insisted on paying for her own. He gave in and paid for his meal after she said they weren't on a date.

They left the restaurant and walked back toward their car.

As they were about to enter the parking structure, Janet had a sudden feeling of dread as a frigid sensation overwhelmed her. She stopped, causing Simon to stop.

"Something wrong?" Simon asked as he glanced straight ahead into the parking structure then back to Janet. "Are you having a premonition?"

"Yes. Not sure what. Something terrible is going happen," she answered. "You're not having a vision…are you?"

"No. At least not yet."

Janet didn't know what to do as she stood there, reluctant to move, afraid to move. What if her feelings are reflecting a bomb planted in or under the rental car? A loud crashing sound of metal against metal, followed by the reverberating sound of clanging metal came from beyond a pillar to their right. Numerous iron rods with a diameter of about six inches and a length of about six feet cascaded by them, stopping when they struck the parking structure wall to their left. She glanced at Simon and saw wide opened eyes with a slightly lowered jaw demonstrating a look of shock. They shuffled a few feet forward, stepping around the pillar. Janet hollered, "Oh my God."

In front of them, a car with a smashed passenger-side front end with steam billowing from the radiator was pressed against a parked pickup truck's right rear end. Their car was parked three car stalls in front of the crash.

A man in his forties got out of his car and kept yelling, "I couldn't stop. My brakes wouldn't work."

Simon hurried over to the man, avoiding the metal rods strewed over the concrete floor. "Are you hurt?"

The man didn't answer right away. He then reached up and rubbed the back of his neck. "I didn't have any brakes. My car then suddenly turned to the right. I didn't have any control of my car."

Simon repeated, "Are you hurt?"

"I don't think I am," answered the distraught man, as he moved his neck in a circular movement.

Janet called 911. She told the operator about the accident and that EMS was needed. The distraught victim in the accident appeared normal without any outward signs of an injury. From previous experiences, she understood an adrenaline surge could be blocking a serious internal injury. Janet walked over to their car as Simon tried to console the accident victim. An ominous thought crossed her mind. If she hadn't had the ominous premonition causing Simon and her to stop in front of the concrete pillar before the accident, they could've been struck by the metal bars, which surely would've injured or even killed one of them or both. She assumed the force of the brakeless car striking the rear end of the parked pickup truck caused the metal rods in the bed of the truck to be catapulted out and onto the concrete floor.

After EMS and the Detroit police officers arrived, Janet and Simon got into their car and drove out of the parking structure, heading toward the Wayne County Coroner's office.

Janet's cell phone rang. She removed it from her holder and glanced at the caller ID: Bill Matters. *He's probably checking up on me. I'm sure he feels I abandoned him.* "Hi, Bill. What's up?"

"Hey, partner. Having a good time in the Motor City?"

Janet picked up a hint of sarcasm in his voice. She didn't blame him for feeling left out the past couple of days on the investigation of Whispers Before Death. No way would she mention she and Simon a moment ago left Greek Town after delving into a delicious Greek cuisine lunch. "No. Not really. Although it has been rewarding. There's possibly a connection between the fourteen deaths in Ocala and the death of a security officer at a Ford dealership here two years ago. And we're going—"

"Don't you want to know why I called?" Bill interrupted.

"Ah. Of course." *He didn't let me complete my sentence, so it must be important.* "Did you find something out about the deaths?"

"Are you psychic or something? Or did someone call you from forensics about what they discovered?"

"No. I knew it had to be something important. You had excitement in your voice. Plus, you cut me short a moment ago."

"Sorry. Anyway. Forensics called me about ten minutes ago. They retrieved a video from a cell phone showing a close-up shot of Melody Richards saying something before collapsing on the steps in front of the high school. They can't make out the audio because of all the extraneous noises around her."

"You know what that means?"

"We need to find an expert lip reader."

## Chapter Twelve

"This is great bake lava," Keith Nelson said, as he put the last piece into his mouth.

Cary Gaines shook his head in a negative gesture. "Idiot. It's pronounced bak-la-va."

"It's good whatever it's called."

Cary peered at Detective Bennett and Doctor Woods driving out of the parking structure in front of them. When he and Keith saw the police and EMS drive into the three-storied parking lot about fifteen minutes ago they assumed the two of them were killed or injured. At least, that's what they hoped after taking control of the car coming down the ramp, hoping it would strike the detective and the doctor as they walked into the first level toward their car. It would've looked like an accident. From where they were parked on the street, they couldn't see when Janet and Simon had stopped next to a concrete pillar and avoided the collision of the disabled car and the parked pickup truck.

"Damn," Cary said. "Obviously our plan didn't work."

"Seth is going to be pissed off," Keith said scratching his head.

"We'll have other opportunities. We need to be patient. They still don't have any knowledge about our organization. The time will come when the whole world will know about The Circle. Be glad we're members."

"You mean we're field agents like the FBI and CIA. Like you told me two years ago when I became your partner. Right?"

"Yeah. Yeah. We're field agents." *Thank God you don't carry a gun. Otherwise I'd probably be shot accidentally by you.* He put their grey Ford Taurus in drive and began following Janet and Simon. Cary had initially planned to put a listening device in Dr. Woods' airport rental car but before he could install the listening bug in the doctor's vehicle carjackers in a black van stole the car. Cary couldn't believe the irony in the whole situation—two different criminal factions embarking on the same vehicle. They didn't put a listening bug in the doctor's second rental car. The lower level of the parking structure near the entranceway had security video cameras and the cameras would've shown him breaking into the doctor's car. Cameras on the second and third floors weren't working. Right now it was more important to follow them, since they didn't know if they were going to meet someone.

Cary's cell phone rang. He looked at the phone. It was Seth. He had talked with him earlier about the failed planning of a listening device in Simon Wood's second vehicle due to the security cameras on the first level of the parking structure. Seth had told him to stage an accident in the parking structure. He sighed as he pushed the talk icon. "The detective and the doctor are still alive. Somehow they avoided the planned accident."

"Don't worry about it. Plans…plans have changed. Continue to follow them. And make sure you avoid detection or suspicion. When you have the opportunity, place a listening bug in their vehicle."

"Yes, sir."

Cary knew not to question Seth's orders. Although, he wondered why his boss had changed his mind about the detective and the doctor. A year ago, Cary had the assignment of silencing a state senator by staging a suicide. He asked Seth why they wanted the senator dead. The response to his question nearly got him expelled from The Circle, which meant all memory after being selected as a member would be erased. In other words, he'd have no knowledge of the organization, or any knowledge of deeds he'd completed for The Circle. Cary knew there were people in high places, including corporations and governments, throughout the world that possessed controlling interests in the organization. He didn't know the names of people, their positions or whom they represented.

Keith gulped down a can of grape soda, then burped. "Was he mad at us?"

"No. We were lucky this time. Someone must be looking down on us."

Keith frowned, followed a moment later with a smirk. “I thought *he* was looking up at us?” He laughed.

Cary didn’t laugh. He couldn’t believe his partner’s dumb sense of humor. “Anyway, Seth wants us to follow them and at the appropriate time plant another listening bug under their dash.”

Cary followed Simon and Janet several car lengths away. The doctor slowed down and turned right into the parking lot of Wayne County Medical Examiner and Coroner’s Building.

~ * ~

“You can park over there,” Simon said, pointing to his right. “It’s closer to the entrance.”

“I presume you’ve been here before?”

“Yes. I did a two-month elective rotation in pathology my fourth year of medical school. I found it informative, but decided I’d rather work on live patients as a physician.”

They parked the car, went through the front entrance of the building and walked up to the reception desk. A woman in her late twenties sat behind a desk. “My name is Doctor Simon Woods, and this is Detective Bennett. We’d like to talk with Dr. Phillip Pearson.” Dr. Pearson was the chief medical examiner when he was doing his rotation here several years ago. Simon assumed the pathologist still held this position, since he would now be in his late fifties. He had told Simon that he planned on working here as the head pathologist until retirement.

“Do you have an appointment?”

“No. We’re from Ocala, Florida, Ms. Robins.” He had glanced down at her ID clipped to her collar. “We’re investigating a death.”

“Oh. So, you’re from the Horse Capital of the World? My sister lives in Ocala with her husband. I’ve never been there, but my sister says it’s a beautiful area.”

“Yes, it is.” Simon didn’t lie to the receptionist even though he was a resident of Atlanta, Georgia and working on a case in Ocala for the past few days. “Like the old saying goes, ‘it’s a small world.’”

“Isn’t that the truth.” The receptionist reached to her right, picked up a phone and dialed. A few seconds past. "This is Rhonda. I have a doctor and detective here to see you. They don't have an appointment. Dr. Woods said he knows you." A pause. "Yes, his first name is Simon." Another short pause. "I'll tell them." She set the desk phone down on its cradle, then looked up at them. "He'll be right here."

Simon and Janet walked over and sat on a cushioned bench to the right of the reception desk.

~ * ~

Frank Littlefield showed his FMI badge to Craig Davis, a Forensic Unit supervisor. "I'd like to examine the truck found behind the warehouse on Silver Springs Boulevard."

"We already thoroughly went through the truck for any forensic evidence. Nothing was found."

"I'm sure you and your associates did a thorough job. I'd like to take a moment and look around inside the truck's cab."

"What are you looking for?"

Frank knew he couldn't tell Davis the truth about his true intentions. That he wasn't looking for anything but wanted to use his super sense of smell to sniff around for any unusual—or even familiar—odors other Forensic Unit personnel may have encounter but were unable to smell it. "I need to get a sense of what the perpetrator saw from inside the truck."

"Like the agents in the human behavioral department of the FBI?"

"Yeah. Something like the TV series, *Criminal Minds*."

"Cool. I'll take you to the truck."

Frank sat inside the pickup truck and closed the driver side door. He closed his eyes, taking a slow and deep breath. The sensitized olfactory nerve endings inside his nose seized a variety of odors, compartmentalizing each of them. His sense of smell captured the odor of Old Spice aftershave or cologne. He leaned over until his nose was near the passenger seat, the odor: pepperoni, garlic. He then sniffed the back of the passenger seat. No distinct odor. Next, he sniffed the steering wheel. An odor of coconut. He got out of the pickup truck and sat in the passenger seat. Frank leaned over and sniffed the back of the driver seat. Coconut aroma flowed through his nostrils. He removed a small, hand-size CD recorder from his shirt pocket, turned it on and said: "Ford One-Fifty examined." He recorded his findings. "Conclusion: Perpetrator recently ate a pizza. Person likely a male since he uses Old Spice cologne or after shave. Uses Coconut shampoo and/or body wash. No odor of tobacco anywhere in the truck. Likely perp is nonsmoker." Frank paused the recorder, reached out and opened the glove compartment in front of him. Nothing present other than pickup truck booklet/manuals.

He leaned forward and breathed deeply through his nose. He turned the CD recorder back on and added: "The odor of a firearm present in the glove compartment…firearm had been fired at one time."

Frank thanked Craig and left the Forensic Unit's forensic garage. Once he got into his car, he dialed a number on his cell phone.

~ * ~

Simon's cell phone rang. He glanced at the caller's name: Frank Littlefield. "Hey, Frank. What's up?" Simon listened to what Frank had found out about the pickup truck involved in the intersection accident. "So, what you're saying is…we should be looking for a perpetrator who's a non-smoker, wears Old Spice cologne or aftershave, likes pizza, and uses coconut shampoo and/or a body wash."

"Yes. It's the logical conclusion to my evidence. All we have to do is find the person with these characteristics."

"That should be an easy task," Simon said with skepticism. "Don't you think?"

"Hum. It'll be like finding where Jimmy Hoffa is buried or where Amelia Earhart's plane crashed or—"

"I get it," Simon interrupted. "Highly unlikely we'll find the person." *Damn. He rambles like me.* Simon thanked Frank for the information. He then told Frank what they had found: Alexander Mendelson two years ago used the name Caleb Johnson and worked at the Ford dealership as an electronic technician. "Continue your computer search for any common denominators between the victims. By the way, how's Jean doing?"

"She hasn't found anything pertinent to the deaths so far. I'll tell Jean what you told me."

"Talk to you later."

Janet removed her cell phone and glanced down at it, apparently checking for any calls. "What did Frank have to say?"

Simon told her what he had said. And Janet agreed it would be difficult, if not impossible, to find the perpetrator with those characteristics and idiosyncrasies. "The next thing we have to do is—"

"Simon," said a man in his fifties walking toward him and Janet.

Simon turned, looked up and saw Phillip Pearson standing in front of them. He hadn't aged a year since their parting goodbyes eight years ago. He still displayed his beaming smile. "Dr. Pearson, it's great to see you again." Simon stood—along with Janet—and shook his hand.

"Call me Phillip. You're a doctor now, not a fourth-year medical student. What can I do for you?" He glanced at Janet.

"This is Detective Janet Bennett."

"Please to meet you, detective."

"The reason we're here, Janet and I are investigating the death of a security guard at a Ford Dealership on Woodward Avenue two years ago. His name was—"

"Walter Osborn," interrupted Phillip.

Simon frowned. He knew he didn't tell the receptionist the name of the deceased person they were inquiring about. *How did Phillip know his name*? *Mayb*e... "Did Detective Morse from the Detroit Police Department call you? I did mention to him we were coming here."

"No. Although, I do know Detective Morse. It was when you said a security guard's death two years ago…because I did the autopsy on him. Mr. Osborn is one of the few cases as a forensic pathologist that I had to write 'Death Undetermined' on the death certificate as cause of death. Why don't you two come to my office? I'll pull up his autopsy report."

"I'd appreciate it."

They stood in front of an elevator, waiting for it to arrive. Phillip said, "So, are you a forensic pathologist?"

"No. I work for the CDC. I'm an Internist. My team and I investigate unusual deaths."

"Like the ones the past few days in Ocala, Florida?"

"Yes. So obviously you know about Ocala's mysterious deaths."

"The deaths have been on all the major news stations."

"Detective Bennett is from the Marion County Sheriff's Department, Major Crime Unit. We're working together trying to solve these deaths."

Phillip said. "So, you're thinking there might be a link to Walter Osborn's death? There's one problem with connecting Ocala's deaths with Osborn's death. He died in the evening…not at 11:58 in the morning."

"We know. But a person who worked at the Ford dealership two years ago moved to Ocala shortly afterwards. It may be a coincidence."

"Sounds like it's more than a coincidence. More like a whodunit crime/mystery case."

"You're right. It's been a challenge."

On their way on the elevator up to Phillip's office, Simon called Frank and asked him to check the death records of all cities, county and state coroner or medical examiners' offices for a diagnosis of Death Undetermined occurring at 11:58 a.m. during Ocala's two days of mysterious deaths. It would be a monumental task, but it might lead them to the answer of these mysterious deaths in Ocala.

"I couldn't help in listening to your phone conversation," Phillip said. "So, you think there have been other death cases similar to the ones in Ocala and here?"

"It's speculation. No concrete evidence."

Phillip's sat behind his desk and brought up the patient's autopsy report on his computer. He motioned them to come around the desk. "Come here. The two of you can read the results of the autopsy report."

Simon began reading the report: *Walter Osborn, African-American, age forty-eight, seventy-two inches tall, weight one hundred and ninety pounds.* He skimmed over the weight and condition of Osborn's organs. All organs were normal without any disease or trauma. *No evidence of needle tracks or any skin punctures on body. No evidence of coronary disease, aneurysms, brain tumors or hemorrhages*. He skipped down to the Cause of Death. The words *Undetermined* stared back at him. The same conclusion of the fourteen deaths in Ocala. "You're right, Phillip. The autopsy didn't determine Osborn's cause of death. What was the toxicology report?"

Phillip moved the computer mouse's arrow and clicked an icon with the letters LAB. "Here's the report."

Simon scanned the computer-generated report. "All the blood work and his spinal fluid were normal. His toxicology screen doesn't show any illicit drugs or prescription medications in his system. I see you even checked for arsenic, propofol and antifreeze poisoning, including several other drugs and potentially poisonous compounds."

"When an autopsy is normal without any physical evidence of foul play or natural causes such as a stroke or heart attack, our policy is to look for uncommon causes. With the popularity of TV criminal programs, the public has been exposed to various means of killing people. It's the main reason why we updated our toxicology profile."

Simon didn't have the heart to tell Phillip that FMI routinely searched for those types of drugs and compounds. "Sounds like you're right on top of things here. But unfortunately, none of those things caused Walter Osborn's death. I presume since he didn't have a cause of death his case was put into the cold case files?"

"Matter of fact, yes, it is."

"We potentially have fourteen mysterious and undetermined deaths in Ocala," Janet said. "If we don't get a clue in solving those deaths..."

Simon walked back around to the front of Phillip's desk, as did Janet. "Could you do a favor for me, Phillip?"

"Sure. What is it?"

"Can you check and see if any other cases of undetermined death occurred in Detroit the same day as the security guard?"

"No problem. I'd be glad to check this out for you. I'll do anything to help in your investigation."

Four people with frightened faces standing in an elevator flashed across Simon's mind. All four people appeared to be in their late teens, two males and two females. The boys were wearing shirts with a logo of an overly muscular man with a large mustache in a fighting position and clothed in fighter's garb of the early twentieth century. The elevator panel illuminated the number thirteen. Also, a vision of two granite-appearing building busts of a WW I doughboy and an aviator. Simon gently tapped Janet's forearm with his elbow. "We better get going. We have an important appointment to make."

Janet looked at him with a puzzled expression. "Okay."

"You just got here," Phillip said, standing up. "Can't you stay a little while longer?"

"I'll give you a call later today. Maybe we can get a beer at Mickey's Sports Bar and Restaurant. Is it still on Woodward?"

"Yeah. It's still there. Sounds good. Give me a call later."

"By the way—" Simon described to Phillip the logo on the two teenagers.

"It's the logo for Mount Clemens High School. It's where I went to high school many years ago. Why do you ask?"

Simon couldn't tell him about his foreshadowing visions. "Curious. I noticed the logo on some kids earlier and meant to ask them what it stood for. It's sort of coincidental you happened to go to school there."

"Small world, isn't it?"

"Yeah. Small world. Call you later."

Simon told Janet about his vision after walking out of Phillip's office.

She nodded. "That's why you wanted to leave Dr. Pearson's office so abruptly. Right?"

"I did." He also told her about the stone heads. "There must be a connection with them, four teenagers and the elevator."

"The stone heads are probably on a building. You said your visions occur within a fifty-mile radius. So, we need to find a building with these stone heads. The first place to look will be the internet. Since the teenagers were in an elevator on the thirteenth floor of a building, we need to Google a building with at least thirteen floors in a fifty-mile radius from where we are now. The most logical place to start is Mount Clemens."

"Makes sense to me," Simon replied as they approached the reception desk. He walked in front of the receptionist desk, glanced down at Ms. Robins and said, "This may be an unusual request. Can we use your computer for a couple of minutes? We need to look some important information."

"Sure. I'll be glad to look it up for you, Dr. Woods. Tell me what you need to look up. I'll Google search it."

"We need to know if there's a thirteen-floor building in Mount Clemens, Michigan."

Ms. Robins typed: THIRTEEN FLOOR BUILDING IN MOUNT CLEMENS, MICHIGAN into Google search.

Simon sighed. Was there connection between the unsolved deaths in Ocala, the security guard in Detroit, and now his newest vision of four people in an elevator on the thirteenth floor of an unknown building? He glanced at Janet. She stood next to him with her normal stoic expression.

"I found something," Ms. Robins said as she turned the monitor around toward them.

## Chapter Thirteen

Simon stared at the computer screen. The monitor's screen displayed the photograph of a tall building with the name Old Macomb County building. He scanned over its description. It was a thirteen-story Art Deco building built in 1931. Near the top of the limestone-constructed buildings were eight granite heads: two Native Americans, two Revolutionary War soldiers, a sailor and a Marine, —his eye stopped at the names of the last two granite heads—an aviator and a World War I doughboy. Simon wanted to shout out, "That's them!" Instead, he said: "I believe this is the building we've been looking for. Can you print out the page for me?"

"Sure. Glad to."

When they got outside, Simon handed the printout to Janet. "This has to be where the four teenagers in the elevator were in my vision."

Janet glanced at the printout. "No doubt in my mind either. We'll need to investigate the building's elevator or elevators. Talk to employees and find out if there was a reason why teenagers would be at Macomb County building."

"In other words, we'll be following detective investigative procedures."

She grinned. "I couldn't have said it any better.

When they got into the car, Janet put the address of the county building into her cell phone's GPS. "We'll take I-94 north to exit 237 North River Road to downtown Mount Clemens. It's about twenty-six miles from here or about twenty-four minutes."

"Does it include pit stops?"

Janet chuckled. "I bet you were once a NASCAR driver."

"How'd you know? I quit the circuit to become a doctor."

They laughed, as Simon pulled onto Woodward Avenue.

A few minutes later, Janet stated, "The entrance to I-94 should be coming up to our right shortly."

~ * ~

Jean Cliftwood walked out of District 5 Medical Examiner's office in Leesburg, Florida after discussing the fourteen deaths with a forensic pathologist. There still wasn't any cause of death for any of the victims. It was a medical/forensic mystery. She got into her car and headed back to the hotel.

Jean parked her car in the front parking lot of the Holiday Inn hotel. A tourist bus was parked in front of the entrance. She knew the bus was there to take a group of retirees back to Sarasota, Florida. She had talked with a few of the senior citizens the past couple of days during the morning buffet breakfast adjacent to the lobby. The group was in Ocala for a three-day excursion including visits to Silver Springs State Park, Ocala National Forest and to a play at the Ocala Civic Theatre. Jean walked into the lobby. Most of the elderly were checking out of the hotel.

"Oh, my God!" Jean observed yellow glows around all the elderly people in the tourist group, including the bus driver.

A woman in her late sixties apparently heard her. "What's wrong?"

Jean knew she couldn't tell her the truth of her outburst. That in the next twenty-four hours all of them would die or be seriously injured. Her mind raced with the scenarios of ways the group could die. The most logical conclusion: there'd be a bus accident on the way back to Sarasota. How can she warn the group and the bus driver without revealing her paranormal ability? "I remembered something. I was supposed to call my Mom this morning. I forgot."

"Well, dear. Call her now. I'm sure she understands you have a busy schedule. I encounter the same thing with my kids. They have their own busy life. I'm retired so I don't have a working schedule and—"

"Thank you," Jean interrupted. "I'll run to my room and call my mother." She loved talking with retirees. Although, they do tend to talk a lot. Frank should be in his room. Maybe he'll have a solution in how the bus group could be delayed and possibly avoid a deadly accident.

"We'll be departing in about forty-five minutes, folks," announced the driver.

Frank opened his door. "Hey, little woman, what's up?"

Jean hated him calling her this derogatory name. But she knew it was said with endearment. Besides, she was five-foot two inches tall and he was six-foot four inches in stature. "I had a vision in the lobby."

"You saw someone with a yellow glow?"

"Not someone. It's more like…many someone*s*." Jean told him about the retirement group. "What do you think we can do to avoid a tragedy?"

Frank didn't say anything right away, as he sat in a swivel chair and faced Jean, who sat at the end of the bed. Behind him sat two computers on a desk next to the wall with the room's flat screen TV, dresser, small refrigerator and microwave. "I thought about quarantining them. Of course, it would be a lie. Plus, there wouldn't be a legitimate explanation for it. I could puncture one of the bus tires, so it would delay their departure. But likely I'd be seen doing it since there be a loud hissing noise, causing the bus to suddenly lean. We could tell them the truth, which of course we can't do. It leaves one feasible solution."

"What is it?"

"I'll hack into the hotel's computer at the front desk and temporarily crash it, so the checking out process would delay their departure for at least an hour. This should avoid the accident."

"I can't thank you enough." Jean removed her cell phone and called Simon.

The phone rang two times. "Hey, Jean. Good news or bad news?"

She put the phone on speaker. "Hopefully the reverse."

"What do you mean, the reverse?"

She told Simon about the senior citizen tourist group's yellow glow and what Frank plans on doing to try to terminate the ominous foreshadowing. "So, like I said a moment ago, I believe we'll be able to reverse a tragic incident."

"I pray to God this'll prevent a terrible tragedy." A brief pause. "To update what's been going on here with our investigation, Detective Bennett and I are following up on a vision I had about thirty minutes ago. We don't believe my vision is related to the fourteen deaths in Ocala or the one here in Detroit two years ago. Of course, we can't be sure about anything since starting our investigation three days ago. We're heading north of Detroit to a city called Mount Clemens. I'll let you and Frank know the outcome after our investigation. I assume you haven't learned anything new about the deaths?"

"No," answered Jean. "We're pretty much at a standstill here in Ocala."

"Not completely true," Frank said. "Let me talk with him."

"Wait a minute. Frank wants to talk with you." She handed him the cell phone.

"Hey, boss. I haven't told Jean yet about what I found out a little while ago after talking with you."

"What did you find out?"

"I found out two things. First, there weren't any other undetermined deaths occurring at or around 11:58 in the morning. The Ocala death victims were the only ones. Second, each of the Ocala victims had seen a dentist in the past two years."

"What's so strange about seeing a dentist? Most people in the United States probably have seen a dentist in the past two years."

"True. Although in this case, they all saw the same dentist."

"That's beyond coincidence. You may have found the common denominator among the fourteen victims. What significance this means regarding the deaths, we'll have to determine. Great work, Frank. Find out as much as you can about the dentist, then call me back."

"Sure will. Talk to you later." He handed the phone back to Jean.

She glanced at the phone. Simon had disconnected the call. "This sounds like the break we've been looking for. What can I do to help?"

"Nothing right now. I'll hack into the hotel's computer now and shut it down for about an hour. After I shut it down, I'll continue my computer search on our dentist, George Cassidy."

I wish I could do something to help."

"I'd say saving the lives of a bus load of senior citizens is a great accomplishment."

"Yeah, you're right. We'll know in about an hour if we changed their fate. Their yellow glows should be gone, meaning we, I mean you, prevented them from being involved in a deadly accident." *An hour from now will seem like an eternity.*

~ * ~

Simon turned onto Exit 237. In several minutes, they'd be pulling up in front of the Old Macomb County Building. Janet agreed with him regarding a definite connection with the dentist and the fourteen deaths in Ocala. Also, Janet suggested they find out if the security guard had seen a dentist in the past two years. She then had added: "Will it be the same dentist?" Simon had called Phillip Pearson and asked him if he could check Walter Osborn's medical pathology record and find out if there was any information on Osborn having any dental procedures and the name of the dentist. Simon told the forensic pathologist there might be a connection to his death. Phillip agreed to check Osborn's record, and if he didn't find anything, he'd call and ask family members.

North River Road meandered near Clinton River. Several minutes later Simon turned onto North Main Street and downtown Mount Clemens. A tall, gray limestone thirteen-story building came into view. Near the top of the building's facet and facing them were two granite busts, a sailor and a Marine. As they got closer and moved around toward the front entrance, the building's façade displayed a doughboy and an aviator peering outward toward the city—they were the two busts seen in Simon's vision. After parking the car in a nearby parking lot, they walked up to the front door of the Old Macomb County Building and went inside.

The lobby contained an electronic board showing the building's businesses along with their floor and room number. Simon scanned the board until he reached the thirteenth floor:

CIRCUIT COURT LAW LIBRARY

PUBLIC COMPUTER WORKSTATIONS FOR THE MICHIGAN LEGAL HELP

## SELF-HELP CENTER OF MACOMB COUNTY

"The four teenagers in my vision were on the thirteenth floor. Were they utilizing either of these services or both?"

"Not sure. But maybe they were utilizing the library and workstations for a term paper assignment?"

"That would make sense. And from what I saw in my vision, the four teenagers were either getting on or getting off the elevator. From my brief flash of them, they appeared to be standing against the wall with the elevator control board to their right with frightened faces. I can't guess why they were scared. Also, I couldn't tell if the elevator door was open or closed."

"Maybe the elevator was plunging uncontrollably to the bottom floor where it would crash, surely killing them. The floor numbers would be flashing rapidly as it made its deadly descent. At least, I think it would."

"I can't say, since I've never experienced being in a falling elevator," Simon said as they walked over to the elevator. "I've only seen it in movies." He pushed the number thirteen on the control panel. Ding! The elevator door opened, and they stepped into an empty elevator.

Simon pushed the number thirteen on the numerical control panel. Thirteen lit up, followed by the elevator door closing. As they made their ascent to the top floor, every slight mini-jolt movement of the elevator raised his eyebrows with the anticipation the elevator would suddenly fall. Simon was a rational person, but still experienced this irrational reaction. He glanced at Janet; she appeared calm and unaffected by their ascension to the thirteenth floor. *Man, am I a pansy or what*? He stared at the panel and watched the numbers rise until it reached "thirteen." The elevator stopped with a slight jerk. "We're here," Simon announced.

"I have a bad feeling," Janet said as a worried expression emerged.

The elevator's sliding doors parted.

No one stood in the hallway waiting to get onto the elevator. Across from the elevator on the wall were two metal name plates side by side. An arrow beneath Law Library directed them to the left. The public computers workstations' arrow directed them to the right. "Your ominous feeling didn't produce anything when the elevator door opened."

"True. But we haven't checked out the law library or the public computers workstations yet. My feeling might be referring to either of these."

Simon and Janet checked out the library. They talked with a woman who said four high school students were in the library for about two hours researching information regarding circuit court procedures in civil cases. They then left the library about thirty minutes ago. The librarian then told Simon and Janet, they probably had gone to the computer workstations down the hall where navigators, county personnel who assisted people at the facility, including high school and college students, on the use of their public computer workstations. Simon and Janet's earlier assumption of why the four students from Mount Clemens High School were on the thirteenth floor was correct. They were there doing research for a term paper.

They left the library and walked to the other end of the hallway. They stopped in front of a glass-windowed door with the long county name written across the top and middle area of the door. Underneath the name were the business hours: MONDAY AND FRIDAY 9AM TO 5PM. Simon glanced at his watch. They'd be closing in thirty minutes. He turned toward Janet. "Since you didn't have an ominous feeling in the law library, are you feeling anything now?"

"No. Only before the elevator door opened. This has never happened before. Normally something happens a few seconds later, like at the parking structure earlier today."

"Maybe it's an exception?" Simon opened the door and walked inside a large room with computers at workstations situated throughout the room. Across the room, about fifty feet away, four teenagers sat at workstations.

"Are those the teenagers you saw?"

"I think so. I need to get closer to look at their faces to be sure." The two teenage boys had the same type and color of shirts. He couldn't see if they had the logo of the prize fighter on the front of their shirts. The two girls were wearing the same apparel he saw in his vision. "If it's them, what are we going to say or ask them?" Simon said quietly.

"Nothing. We'll sit at the workstation next to them, so you can confirm if they're the teenagers in your vision. If it's them, we'll walk out of here with them whenever that happens in the next thirty minutes. I believe if something's going to happen to the teenagers…it'll happen in the elevator."

~*~

Jean stood behind Frank, as he did magic with his computers and restored the hotel's front desk computer. "The hotel's back online."

Jean was anxious to see if the delay in checking out process had changed the fate of retirement group. "I'm going to the lobby."

"I'll go with you. I want to see if we changed the horrible fate of this tourist group from Sarasota."

They left their room and walked down the first-floor hallway toward the lobby. Jean's heart raced and her palms perspired as they reached the area of the lobby. A line of at least twenty senior citizens had formed in front of the hotel's front desk. Jean sighed as she grabbed Frank's forearm. "It's gone!" The retiree's previous yellow glows no longer existed. They had changed their deadly fate. By delaying their departure, she had likely changed the timeline and prevented their bus from being involved in an accident.

Unbeknownst to Jean and Frank—and the bus group—about an hour ago a gasoline tanker had lost control, hit a guard rail, flipped over on its side and blocked three lanes on the Southbound I-75. The bus would've struck the tanker, causing it to explode, killing all the passengers and bus driver in a fiery, agonizing death. Thank God, this scenario didn't happen. The automobiles behind the accident were able to stop in time or swerve around the tanker. No one was injured or died.

Jean and Frank went back to the room. He continued his search of the personal and professional history of the dentist, including any associations. He'd also check what procedures were done on each of the fourteen victims. Jean called Simon.

~*~

Simon's cell phone rang. He answered on the second ring. "Hey, Jean."

"Good news. We avoided a bus tragedy with the tourist group."

"Great. Your gift saved many lives. I'm proud of you. Anything else new?"

"Not with me. Frank is busy on the computer in front of me, doing his computer stuff on the dentist."

A county employee stood up from her desk and announced, "We'll be closing in five minutes."

The four teenagers got up from their workstations. Simon had confirmed earlier to Janet the high school students he saw in his vision were the same students sitting at the workstation. "We've got to go, Jean. Talk to you later."

Simon and Janet had discussed what they'd do when the teenagers left the room. They would tell the teenagers the elevator wasn't working properly, and that they would need to take the stairway. This would eliminate any ominous event on the elevator Simon had visualized earlier.

The three teenagers were a few paces ahead of them, as they headed toward the elevator. Janet stopped them and informed them about the elevator not working properly. She showed her sheriff's badge, convincing them. As the five of them approached the elevator in the middle of the hallway with the stairwell at the end of the hallway, a "ding" sounded, announcing the elevator's arrival.

The male teenager with reddish hair said, "The elevator's working." The elevator's door slid open. Before Simon and Janet could say anything, the four high school students hurried inside an empty elevator.

Simon, along with Janet, quickly stepped in front of the opened elevator entranceway. He placed his hand on the recessed area to his right, preventing the door from closing. A few seconds past, the four high school students' jubilant facial expression suddenly changed to one of horror, as if pending doom stood in front of them. Simon saw their frightened faces, identical to their expression in his vision earlier today.

The terrified students weren't staring toward Simon and Janet…but what stood behind them.

## Chapter Fourteen

A man, who stood about six-feet, six inches tall and weighed about two hundred and forty pounds, with medium length black hair and a short-cut beard peered at the four high school students with piercing green eyes. Sweat cascaded from his forehead. He held a shiny, cylindrical object in his right hand. He shouted, "Get out of the elevator."

Janet turned and faced the intimidating stranger. The right side of her jacket flew open exposing her hand grasping the handle of her holstered Glock. "What's going on?" She glanced down at the shiny, silver-colored flashlight. *What's he doing with a flashlight?*

The man looked down toward Janet's right hand cuddling a Glock inside her belt holster. "No harm, ma'am. There's an electrical short somewhere in the elevator panel. I need to check it."

Janet released the grip on the gun, letting her hand dangle next to her. "By all means. We'll take the stairs." She turned around. "Okay, you guys. You heard the man. Off the elevator."

The students got off the elevator. Simon and Janet walked behind them as they headed toward the stairs at the end of the hallway. Janet turned around and saw the tall, burly man step into the elevator. Something silvery stuck out from the back of his trousers at the waistline. She couldn't make out what it was.

Several minutes elapsed before Janet and Simon reached the lobby. They were both slightly out of breath. The high school students had sped down the stairs, way ahead of them. Janet and Simon came up to the elevator doors to their right. There wasn't an OUT OF ORDER sign near the "up" and "down" buttons.

"Ding." The elevator door panels slid open and several people stepped out and into the lobby.

"The elevator guy must've fixed the electrical short in the elevator panel." Simon stated.

Janet's cell phone rang. She glanced at the caller's name. It was Bill Matters. "Hey, Bill. What's going on?"

"I found a lip reader." She heard excitement in his voice.

Janet turned to Simon. "Detective Matters found a lip reader." She walked over to a bench across from the elevator and sat down. Simon sat next to her.

"What did Melody Richards whisper before she died?" Janet's mind conjured up the vision of the teenager three days ago standing at the top of the high school's front entrance steps. Melody stared directly at them, as she and the FMI team rushed toward her at 11:58 a.m.

"As far as what the lip reader translated, he was sure the girl had said: 'What's that sound?' Apparently, she's hearing something. I wonder if other people around her heard the same sound?"

"So, Melody Richards whispered, 'What's that sound?' There's only one way to find out if someone else had heard the mysterious sound. Talk to the kids standing next to her. On my desk is a manila file. Inside are the names and phone numbers of all the kids standing near Melody when she collapsed. Also, you'll need to check with other detectives and find out if a strange sound occurred during the deaths of the other victims."

"I knew you were going to say something like that. Since you're in Michigan and I'm in Florida, it only leaves one person who can interview people who were standing around Melody at the time of her death…me."

"I don't mean to—"

"No worry," Bill interrupted. "I can handle it. I'll talk with the other detectives and the kids on your list. It's why they pay me the big money."

Janet chuckled. She now knew Bill wasn't upset with her for leaving the investigation in Ocala for him to handle. He'd be sarcastic if it bothered him, not make humorous remarks. She wanted to tell him about the four Mount Clemens High School students and the elevator but knew she couldn't divulge Simon's or the other two FMI's ESP gift. "I know you're the right man for this task."

"You mean, I'm the only guy for this task, since there isn't any other detective that I can pass it on to. I'll call you if I learn anything. By the way, when are you coming back to the horse capital of the world?"

"Not sure yet. Still tracing down a lead. I really appreciate you taking over the investigation while I'm gone. Talk to you later." She put her cell phone back into her jacket pocket. She turned to Simon. "So, what do you think about Melody Richards' whispering words?"

"I agree with your comment to Detective Matters regarding what to do. There are at least two possibilities regarding the sound mentioned by Melody Richards. The first, did other people hear the same sound she did. And secondly, no one around her had heard the sound. Which means what she heard came from inside her head. She imagined it. Or she had an episode of tinnitus."

Janet frowned. "Tinnitus?"

"Ringing, buzzing, whistling or the sound of rushing water emanating from the ears. It's a common medical condition. I'll call Frank and have him check the victim's medical records and see if any of them had tinnitus. Also, I'll have Frank check to see if any of the victims had psychiatric disorders."

Janet slightly leaned backwards and stretched out her arms attempting to loosen her tight shoulder muscles. "At least now we have some type of clues to follow."

"Amen." Simon removed his cell phone from his belt holster and dialed. A few seconds later, "Hey. Anything on the dentist?" A short pause. "Let me know if you find anything. I have something else I need you to do." He relayed the information about tinnitus to Frank. "Call me back after you check it out." He put his cell phone away. "No significant information about the dentist or the fourteen victims' dental visits yet. Frank is still working on it."

Janet glanced down at her watch. It was nearly five o'clock. There wasn't much they could do now until they heard back from Frank, Bill and Dr. Pearson. "Why don't we go to the car and—"

The front door of the Old Macomb County Building swung open and six Macomb County S.W.A.T. team deputies dressed in full gear rushed into the lobby. An officer with captain bars on his white shirt walked in behind them and announced: "We need everyone to please stay. There are questions we need to ask you before you can leave." Including Janet and Simon, there were nine people in the lobby to be questioned.

Janet stood, along with Simon, and walked up to the captain. She peered down at his name: J. Bowman. "I'm Detective Bennett from the Marion County Sherriff Department in Florida." She showed him her badge. "Doctor Woods and I are here investigating a case. What's going on?"

"An employee from the Circuit Court Library on the thirteenth floor called nine-one-one. She told the operator about a man who had pointed a gun at her through the partial glassed door."

The hairs on the back of her neck vibrated like a million icicles causing a chill cascading down her spine. "Was the guy tall with a beard?"

Captain Bowman frowned. "Yeah. Do you know the guy?"

Janet told him what they'd encountered at the elevator on the thirteenth floor. She now knew what the silvery object was stuck into the waistline of the perp's pants. A gun. Janet didn't tell the captain about the silvery object. Simon's vision about the students in the elevator was accurate. They'd altered the outcome by being there when the man showed up in front of the elevator. The crazed man may have injured or possibly killed them. The students' fate was changed. "I never suspected what this guy's real intentions were. Is he still on the thirteenth floor?"

"Don't know. Ms. Black locked herself in the law library's lavatory. We don't know his motive, which makes the situation even more dangerous. Our department personnel have been notifying every office in the building. And telling them about a potential shooter in the building. Since they're county employees, they've been trained and oriented in this scenario. So, they know what to do. Can you wait here in the lobby? We may need you to identify the perp."

Janet nodded. "Absolutely. We'll wait."

The captain barked out his orders to his officers. Two sets of three officers would split up. One team would start on the thirteenth floor and the other would start on the ground level. Both teams would search each floor, then move onto the next floor below or above them respectively. When they reached a locked room, they would shout out a code word. A county employee behind the locked door would respond with one of two words supplied to them when S.W.A.T. personnel called them on the phone. One word meant everything was good and the other word meant the perp was in the room with them. A S.W.A.T. team deputy would then mark a small letter on the door with a colored felt tip marker indicating room checked and no perp. The letter and color were chosen before they entered the building. preventing a perp from knowing what letter and color they were using that day. This prevented the perp from marking a door, so the officer wouldn't check it for occupancy.

Janet and Simon stood next to the captain as he explained this information to them. She was impressed with the S.W.A.T. team's stealthy and meticulous procedures.

Captain Bowman then added: "The Michigan State Police and the Mount Clemens Police Department officers have secured a one block perimeter around the Macomb County Building. They've been given the description of the tall and burly Caucasian man with a gun. Hopefully this guy hasn't already fled the building and immediate area making our search for him all for nothing."

Janet's cell phone rang. Bill calling her back crossed her mind. She peered down at the caller's name. Rick Ridder—her ex-husband. *You gotta be kidding me. Why in the hell is he calling me*? She pushed the talk icon on her cell phone, as she walked over to the bench across from the elevator and sat. "This is not a good time, Rick. I'm in the middle of something," she said firmly, staring down at the floor in front of her.

"I want to meet at our old restaurant, the one where we had our first date. There's something important I want to talk about."

*This guy never lets up. It seems like he calls me every couple months. I gotta tell him not to call me anymore*. "Rick. We're divorced. We have no children to discuss about. We had an amicable, uncontested divorce with an even split of property and assets. There is nothing more to discuss."

"Are you seeing someone? Is that why you don't want to see me?"

*He's not getting it. More than an asshole, he's a hopeless, pitiful human being*. "It wouldn't matter if I was or wasn't seeing someone. I don't want to talk to you or see you. Nor do I want any more text messages from you. We're done. We're finished. Get a life. Find someone else."

"Does that mean you don't want to meet at our old restaurant?"

"Exactly. Like I said, have a good life. Bye." Before he could reply, Janet put the cell phone back into her sports jacket's pocket ending their conversation. She looked up and saw Simon with pursed lips and raised eyebrows standing a few feet away to her left. Janet was sure he had heard most of what she'd said to her ex-husband by Simon's gestural expression. "Have you been married?"

"No. I haven't found the right woman yet."

"As you probably heard, I found the wrong man."

Shouting interrupted their conversation. The commotion was coming from the elevator across from them. A S.W.A. T. deputy stood in the opened doorway of the elevator with his left arm holding the sliding door open. His right hand held a gun pointing down at someone lying on the elevator floor. Captain Bowman rushed over to the officer with his gun drawn.

Janet got up and cautiously walked toward the elevator. A tall man with a full beard laid sprawled out on the elevator floor. It was the burly man she and Simon encountered on the thirteenth floor. There wasn't any movement or sound coming from the perp. A revolver was clutched in his right hand. She was now close enough to see the man was dead. Janet couldn't see any blood on the floor or any open gunshot wounds to his body. Had an officer shot him on one of the twelve floors and the perp managed to stumble into the elevator, dying on the way to the lobby floor? This scenario raced through her mind.

The captain radioed the S.W.A.T. deputies. "We have the suspect in the lobby. He's lying dead in the elevator. Did anyone encounter him?" The same answer came back from all the deputies: Negative.

Simon stood next to Janet. He glanced down at his watch. "It's not 11:58. If you know what I mean?"

"I do." Janet thought about telling the captain about the death cases in Ocala and the death of the Ford dealership security guard two years ago in Detroit. Was the death of this perp the same: death undetermined? She decided to wait until the autopsy report. Janet whispered her decision to Simon.

He nodded in agreement.

Before leaving the lobby of the Macomb County Building, Janet and Simon gave their statement to a deputy about their encounter with the tall, bearded, burly man on the thirteenth floor.

As they walked back to their car, a grey Ford Taurus with its motor running was parked in the street near the county building. Neither of them thought anything about it.

~ * ~

Cary Gaines sat in the driver seat of their grey Ford Taurus watching the detective and the doctor walk by him. Behind them about twenty paces was Keith. A moment later, he sat in the front passenger seat of the car.

"You won't believe what had happened. Some guy with a gun apparently was terrorizing people. That's why the S.W.A.T. guys were called."

"Did he kill anyone?"

"No. They found him dead in the elevator. They're not sure how he died."

"Humm. So, what were the detective and doctor doing in the county building?"

"Not sure. All I know is they went to the thirteenth floor. I overheard them when they were standing in front of the building's directory in the lobby. I waited a few minutes, then rode the elevator to the thirteenth floor. They were coming out of law library when I got to the floor. They headed to the other end of the hall to a public computer room. All they did was sit at a computer table. I left and waited in the lobby for them. About thirty minutes later, they came back down to the lobby. Each of them made cell phone calls. I couldn't hear what they were saying. Shortly afterwards, S.W.A.T. came." He paused. "I meant to ask you before I started to follow them into the building. Do you know if any of our people work inside the county building?"

"Not sure. I'll call Seth and ask him. He may have an answer to this question. Also, we'll need to tell him what has happened here." He looked to his right and saw Janet and Simon walk up to their car. "They got to be thinking, why does trouble follow them everywhere they go? At least, I would think that."

"Were you able to bug their car?"

"Yes. Maybe now we'll be able to hear why they came to the Macomb County Building?"

~ * ~

Janet turned to Simon as he began walking with her to the passenger side of the car. "I don't need your help to open my door. Thanks anyways. I can do it myself."

"I guess chivalry is dead in your eyes."

"I hope not. I'd rather do things on my own right now." She couldn't tell Simon that her feelings toward most men fringed on the verge of mistrust, especially those men whom presented flirtatious behavior. "But thanks for your chivalrous gesture." A few seconds later, a frigid wave overwhelmed her as she was about to open the passenger side door. She stopped and looked anxiously across the car toward Simon.

He peered back at Janet. "Is there something wrong? Did you get a premonition feeling?"

"I did. Not sure what it means, though. Other than, something could be wrong inside when I open the car door."

"Maybe a bomb was planted inside or outside the car? Or another listening device like the one planted under the dashboard in my other car?"

"I'll check beneath the car."

"I can check it."

"Huh. Really? You don't think I'm capable? Besides, have you ever seen an explosive device?"

"No. I haven't."

Janet laid on the ground and moved slightly under the car. She grunted as she slid from under the car and stood. "I don't see anything unusual."

"What you sensed is probably inside the car."

"Or under the hood in the engine compartment."

"I agree."

"Since someone may be watching us, we'll get into the car and pretend the car won't start. I'll then get out of the car and check underneath the hood."

"Sounds like a good plan."

They got into the car. "What's wrong with this car? It won't start."

"I'll check it out. Open up the hood." Janet got out of the car, opened the hood and peered meticulously over the engine. No foreign object or device lay anywhere in the engine compartment. She closed the hood. Anyone looking in their direction would think they were having car engine problems. She then got into the car. She looked at Simon.

He put his index finger against his lips in the gesture of quiet or don't say anything, then pointed down to an object lying in the palm of his hand.

Janet glanced down at a circular object about three inches in diameter in the palm of his hand. He then turned it over. It appeared to be the same type of listening device, with the manufacturer's name and model number obliterated on the back of it, planted underneath the other car dash two days ago. She pointed toward the dashboard.

Simon nodded, as he put the device back underneath the dashboard.

"So, I found a loose wire near the engine starter. I tightened it. We should be good, now."

"Great." Simon turned the ignition key. The car started right up. "We got power."

He pulled out of the parking space and turned onto Main Street. They created a fabricated story of why they went to the Old Macomb County Building, saying the lead given to them regarding the deaths in Ocala ended up not being irrelevant to their investigation. Janet stated their encounter with the dead man in the elevator but not why they were on the thirteenth floor.

Simon's cell phone rang. He glanced down at the caller ID, then handed the phone to Janet. "Answer the phone for me while I'm driving."

"Sure. No problem." She glanced down at the caller's name: Phillip Pearson. Had he discovered important information regarding the death of the security guard, Walter Osborn? "This is Janet Bennett. Simon asked me to take your call while he's driving the car." Janet didn't put the speaker phone on, not wanting whoever planted the listening bug to hear the conversation between her and Phillip.

"I talked with Osborn's sister. You won't believe what she told me."

## Chapter Fifteen

Janet listened to what Phillip had to say. "I'll let Simon know. We're leaving Mount Clemens now. We'll see you there." She disconnected the call and turned toward Simon. "He said he'll meet us at the restaurant on Woodward." Janet wanted to tell Simon what Phillip had to say, but it would have to wait until they got to the restaurant.

"The food is great there. Can't wait," Simon said, as he drove down Main Street, heading toward I-94.

What Phillip said to her on the phone ran through her mind. He didn't find any other undetermined deaths around the time of the security guard's death two years ago. The deceased security guard, Walter Osborn, had complained about ringing in his ears a few weeks prior to him dying two years ago at the Ford dealership. This was a major clue in their connection between the mysterious deaths in Ocala and Walter Osborn. How many other deaths of undetermined cause are associated with ringing in the ears, medically called tinnitus? Hopefully, Frank could do his computer magic and find other victims suffering from this medical condition.

If it wasn't for the Ford truck abandoned in Ocala and its VIN number leading them to Detroit and the mysterious death of Walter Osborn, who incidentally had tinnitus, a connection to Alexander Mendelson wouldn't have been discovered. Two more important questions whirled in Janet's mind as Simon merged onto I-94: Who was trying to listen in on their conversations in the car? And why? Another question crossed her mind. Was it a deliberate accident in the first level of parking structure near Greek Town? Or was it an unfortunate accident? There appeared to be a resistance by an unknown person, group or entity. And was the burly perpetrator on the thirteenth floor targeting her and Simon and not the four high school students? No way to know now, since a lifeless body can't answer.

Nothing significant was discussed as they headed toward Detroit. Only small talk transpired between them. About twenty-five minutes later, they exited at 215C and onto Woodward, heading east to Mickey's Sports Bar and Restaurant. Simon parked the car in the rear of the bar and restaurant. Once they got out of the car, Janet told him what Phillip had said on the phone as she glanced around to see if a vehicle had followed them into the parking lot. She only saw parked vehicles.

"This may be the link to these deaths," Simon concluded. "Although, tinnitus is a common medical condition, but people don't die from it. We'll continue our conversation inside."

Janet nodded. "I agree. Away from listening devices." Before Simon opened the entrance door for her, she turned around to see if any vehicle drove into the parking lot behind them. Again, she only saw parked vehicles.

The place was crowded with a mixture of conversations kept at a low murmur. Phillip waved his hand from a booth to the right of them.

~ * ~

Simon glanced around the room. Nothing had changed since the last time he ate and drank here, which would've been shortly after graduating from medical school. "Hey, Phillip. Everything looks the same here." Simon gestured for Janet to slide to the far end of the booth. He sat across from Phillip.

"Yep. It's the same place. I checked our records for any other undetermined deaths occurring the same day as Walter Osborn's death. He was the only one recorded that day."

"Thanks for checking it out for me."

"Glad to help out."

The waitress came over to the booth and took their order. All three of them ordered the Mickey Burger and fries along with a pitcher of light beer and three frosted mugs. Phillip reiterated his findings regarding Walter

Osborn's tinnitus. Simon knew there were several causes for this annoying medical condition, which he and Phillip laid out to Janet: *People sixty and older*. This couldn't be since three of the victims were teenagers and the rest of the people were under sixty years old. *Repeated exposure to loud sounds*. This could be a possibility but unlikely for all fifteen victims being exposed to loud repeated noises. *Ear wax*. Unlikely all the victims had impacted ear wax. *Head or neck trauma*. Another possibility. All the victims' medical records would have to be checked for that cause. *Acoustic neuroma*. For every victim to have a tumor on the cranial nerve between the brain and the inner ear structures would be statistically unfeasible. *Several blood vessel disorders*. Again, unfeasible for everyone to have one of these disorders. And *several medications* can cause tinnitus. Both agreed, for all the victims to take any of these drugs and all of them developing tinnitus would be highly improbable.

The waitress brought the pitcher of beer and set it on the table along with the mugs. Janet poured the beer in her mug before Phillip or Simon could do the honor. Simon raised his eyebrows and grinned. Phillip reciprocated with a shrug. After filling their mugs with beer, Phillip gave a toast: "To friendship." Their mugs met in the middle of the table with a soft "click."

Simon gulped down some of his beer, then thought about another cause of tinnitus. *All the victims saw the same dentist.* "There's another cause for tinnitus. TMJ or temporomandibular joint disorder." He turned his head toward Janet. "It's the area of the upper jawbone adjacent to the ear."

"I'm not an idiot. I know what you're talking about."

Simon grimaced. "I wasn't sure. Sorry. Anyway, all the victims saw the same dentist. And TMJ is normally treated by a dentist."

"Can TMJ cause a person to die?" Janet questioned.

"No, it can't." Phillip answered. "It only causes pain and of course sometimes ringing in the ear on the affected side."

Simon told him about what Melody Richards had whispered before dying. "We suspect all the victims in Ocala had tinnitus along with your findings about the security guard. Not sure what it has to do with their deaths. The dentist who treated them may have the answer."

Phillip put down his mug of beer. “Haven’t you talked with him?”

“No. One of my associates is checking into the dentist’s background. Also, he’s trying to find out what their dental appointments were about. And what procedures were done on them.”

“That would be normal investigative procedures,” added Janet. “We’d need evidence to tie him to their deaths. And if he was responsible, we don’t want to alert him and subsequently have him destroy evidence.”

“Makes sense to me, Detective Bennett.”

For the next hour Simon and Phillip talked about what each had done, interesting medical cases, the professional sports team in Detroit and Auburn Hills. Janet sat there not saying much. It was the two doctors’ hour of camaraderie.

After they finished eating and emptying the pitcher of beer, Simon was about to thank him for helping in their investigation when he had a vision of a person wearing a black hooded jacket and brandishing a gun. The man was pointing the weapon at a clean-shaven, mid-twenties Hispanic man wearing a navy-blue shirt and sitting at a table with three other people; two were females, one blonde and the other a redhead, and a young black male. All four people were shot by the assailant.

“Something wrong, Simon?” Phillip asked. “You look like you saw something horrible.”

“Oh, no. I was thinking about all those people dying in Ocala. Sorry.” What else could he say to him? Obviously, he couldn’t tell him the truth.

“I gotta get going,” Phillip said. “If you need assistance on any other case, please give me a call. I’d be glad to help you and Detective Bennett. Like I said earlier, I envy you traveling all over the country solving medical cases.” He glanced at Janet. “Nice meeting you, detective.”

“You too, Dr. Pearson.”

Simon stood and gave Phillip a hug. He then sat back down and watched Phillip walk toward the back entrance of the restaurant. Two couples sitting at a table to his right caught his attention. “Oh, my God. They’re here!”

“Who’s here?” Janet asked.

“I had another vision.”

"Before Phillip questioned your ominous expression?"

"Yes." Simon told her what he had seen in his vision. He then turned his head and stared at the people in his vision. "The four people are sitting over there."

She turned her attention to the table of four people Simon was staring at. "They definitely fit your description. We'll need to warn them before the gunman gets here."

"Or intercept the guy outside before he comes into the restaurant."

Janet grunted, nodded. "I like your idea better than mine. You're thinking like a sheriff detective."

Simon paid the bill, including Phillip and Janet's meal. Janet left the tip.

Once outside, they concluded the gunman could only come through the back door or parking lot side of the one-story building. The front door facing Woodward was an emergency door. No access from the outside. They thought about calling Detective Morse and informing him of a potential shooter. But that would reveal Simon's ESP gift. Not a good idea. Besides, if they did tell him about Simon's vision, he most likely couldn't do anything since he would need solid, realistic evidence of a potential crime. Detective Morse would have to follow standard police protocol and procedures.

There was an empty parking space about twenty feet from the entrance door. Simon backed up the car into the space. It was an ideal position to identify the hooded, lethal perpetrator. Janet stared down at the dashboard. "The food was great. I'm glad we came here to eat."

Simon turned the radio on to a classical music station. "Do you like this music?"

"If I was sitting on a Victorian-styled couch in a royal palace sitting room with the queen and king of England it would be appropriate music, but not in a car."

"What kind of music do you like?"

"Right now? None. My mind's concentrating on what we talked about earlier. Any other time, I like country-western songs."

*I guess she told me*. He reached out and turned off the radio.

A car drove into the parking lot. Only one person in the car. He appeared to be in his mid to late twenties. Simon never saw the face of the gunman, but the gunman was wearing a hooded jacket similar to the one in his foreshadowing vision. A warm rush encompassed his entire body for a few seconds. He had a feeling this hooded man was the shooter. The man parked his car, got out and started walking toward the restaurant door. "This may be the guy."

"You stay here," Janet said, removing her Glock from the holster. "I don't want you to get hurt."

"I can handle myself. I'll be your backup. I'm trained in firearm scenarios. Besides, when he sees two of us, he may back down from any aggression he's feeling."

"All right. Stand behind me."

When the suspect was about twenty feet from them, he reached into his jacket pocket. Simon's muscles stiffened as his heart began to race. Every breath searched for air. He was sure the suspect was about to pull out a gun.

The restaurant's back door burst open to their left. Screams of panic rang out from inside, as people ran through the opened doorway and into the parking lot. Inside the restaurant shouts of "He's got a gun" could be heard. Simon glanced to his right at their suspect, he pulled out a cell phone from his jacket pocket, not a gun. Simon barked: "The gunman's inside."

"You're right," agreed Janet. She ran inside, followed by Simon.

The hooded man stood next to a table with a gun pointed at the Hispanic man in the blue shirt, as the other three potential victims at the table squirmed in their chairs. The Hispanic man in the blue shirt cried, "Put the gun away. We can settle this. Don't shoot, homie."

"I'm not your homie, asshole."

Janet now stood a few feet behind the gunman and shouted: "I'm Detective Bennett. Drop your gun. Don't make me shoot you. No one's been hurt yet. So, lay your gun on the floor." Her austere voice barked out the standard law enforcement commands.

The hooded man slowly turned around, holding the gun in his right hand. He pushed the hood off his head. He had the facial looks of a teenager. Simon recognized him. He was the bus boy who cleared the tables after the patrons left. A fearful expression projected from the young face, not the expression of a cold-blooded killer. Perspiration saturated his forehead and cheeks. The gun quivered in his hand.

"He killed my brother, Fernando."

"Did you see him do it?" Janet asked.

"No. But I know he did."

"Did the police question him?"

"Yes. The Detroit police told me there wasn't any evidence he did it. My brother was afraid of him. Telling me if he was killed, Garcia would've done it. The police didn't believe me."

"Killing him will put you in prison, maybe for the rest of your life. It's not worth it. And if what you say is true," she glanced toward Garcia, "let the justice system sort it out, not you."

"I have to avenge my big brother's death." Tears began to flow, mixing with his facial sweat.

Simon stepped around Janet. "Like the detective said to you, 'It's not worth getting killed.' You have a whole life ahead of you. Don't waste it in prison. I'm sure your brother, Fernando, wouldn't want you to do this." Sincerity and compassion filled Simon's words. "We'll talk with the detective in charge of your brother's death. We'll do everything we can to help you. Please hand us your gun or put it on the floor. Don't make this situation worse than what it is. What's your name?"

"Ernesto Benavides."

"Ernesto, please let us help you. But you must hand over your gun, first."

Ernesto glared down at the floor. Tears cascaded down his cheeks. He then bent over and laid the gun on the floor in front of him. Janet quickly bent down and picked up the gun. The sound of police sirens flooded around the building outside. Janet put handcuffs on him.

Detroit Police officers rushed through the restaurant's back door. Their guns were drawn and pointed toward them.

"Please stand down. I'm Detective Bennett." Janet presented her detective badge to the officers. "Everything is under control. This is Ernesto Benavides, the young man with the gun. No one was shot or injured." She handed the gun to one of the officers, turned around and pointed to the threatened victims. "These are the people Mr. Benavides confronted with his gun."

Janet and Simon gave their statements to an officer. Another officer obtained statements from the four threatened people at the table. Simon periodically glanced over toward Garcia. He sat erect with his head slightly cocked along with an arrogant smirk, his demeanor and features portraying a tough guy. When Benavides' gun was pointed down at his head, he portrayed a scared human being. *What a pompous despicable punk.* Simon walked a few steps to his right, stood in front of Garcia, peered down at him and said: "This must be your lucky day?" Simon never wanted malevolence toward anybody. Including unscrupulous individuals with questionable morals.

Before Garcia could respond to the incisive statement, Simon turned abruptly around and left the restaurant with Janet by his side. A moment later, they stopped in the parking lot beside their car.

Simon looked around then said: "We better not mention anything relevant regarding our meeting with Phillip or anything important regarding our investigation in our bugged car."

"I agree. I got to say one thing about you, Simon, there doesn't seem to be a dull moment with you. Especially today, saving eight people, four in an elevator and now four people in the restaurant. Do you ever have uneventful and boring days?"

"Yes, to answer your question. Although, I've had more foreshadowing visions than usual." A grin appeared. "Maybe your presence helps proliferate my visions?"

"God, I hope not. I don't think my heart can take all this excitement. I'm a simple girl who likes boredom occasionally."

Simon chuckled. "I can understand what you're saying. But I don't have any control of these visions. I can go a week without having a vision. All I can say is, I don't live a boring life."

"That's an understatement."

"We still don't know the cause of the gunman's death on the Macomb County Building's elevator floor. If his death is undetermined, then he may be relevant to the security guard's death and our victims in Ocala. If he died of a known cause, then his case will be closed in our books. Phillip said he'd let us know the results of the man's autopsy as soon as he gets it. We probably won't know the results until sometime tomorrow morning or afternoon."

"Of course, we still haven't a clue why someone is bugging our vehicles, staging an accident on our way to the high school in Ocala and preventing us from talking with Melody Richards. The question is, why are they trying to hinder our investigation?"

"I agree someone doesn't want us to solve these deaths. If we don't get any answers tomorrow, we'll head back to Ocala tomorrow evening. Of course, I'm hoping we'll get a clue that'll lead us in solving all these deaths."

Janet nodded in agreement. "We also have the relevance of the dentist in our fourteen victims in Ocala."

The Hispanic man in the blue shirt came out with his three companions. He glanced at Janet and Simon with a sneer. Simon had the urge to reciprocate with a vulgar gesture but decided to keep his feelings toward the punk and his friends to himself. "What do think about Ernesto Benavides accusing this guy of murdering his brother?"

"As a detective, I'd need concrete evidence he had something to do with the murder. As a woman with intuition, he's guilty as sin."

"My same sentiments. I think we should notify the detective in charge of his brother's death. I did tell Ernesto we'd talk with the detective in charge. Don't you think?"

"Yeah. We don't want to break a promise. I'll call Detective Morse. He'll be able to put us in contact with the detective covering Fernando's murder. I'll call him from inside our car. It'll give our listeners something to digest."

After Janet talked with the detective in charge of Fernando's murder, they went to a hotel along the riverfront in Detroit. Simon had made reservation for two adjoining rooms from the plane before landing in Detroit earlier this morning. They placed overnight luggage in their rooms. Each of them checked their rooms for listening devices. Not that they were paranoid, but only being precautious. They both knew someone, or some entity was listening and probably watching every move they made. Simon and Janet went to the hotel's lounge on the first floor to talk. Janet ordered a soda. Simon ordered Captain Morgan with a Coke.

Simon sipped his drink. His cell phone rang. He glanced at the caller ID. The LED displayed Frank's name. "Hey Frank. Good news I hope?"

"I'd say relevant and interesting."

## Chapter Sixteen

Cary Gaines and Keith Nelson sat at a table about ten feet away from Dr. Woods and Detective Bennett. There were at least twenty people in the lounge creating a low, mixed murmur of voices. Cary squinted and cocked his head, trying to hear what Brian and Janet were talking about. He whispered to Keith, "Can you hear what they're saying?"

"Only bits and pieces," he whispered, adjusting his blue cap. "Nothing making any sense to me."

"Yeah. I agree. Can't believe they didn't say anything important in their car. Still don't know if they're getting close to understanding what's going on with the deaths in Ocala."

"They did find the security guard killed two years ago at the car lot and..."

"That was the stupidity of Fred," Cary interrupted. "Leaving the pickup truck behind an empty building in Ocala. I can't believe he left the truck there for the police to find and connect it to the thefts of the other vehicles two years ago. We'll never know why he left it there since he died getting killed crossing the road in front of the building. The police were too stupid to connect him with the abandoned pickup. What else were you going to say?"

"Oh, yeah. They probably know about Alex working at the Ford dealership in Detroit two years ago. Don't you think?"

"More than likely. This detective is pretty smart…besides being good looking."

Keith snickered. "What? You want to date her?"

Cary glanced at Janet. "Of course not. Are you crazy? She's our enemy." He couldn't tell his partner the truth, that in fact, she did turn him on. He liked mentally strong women, especially cute ones. His partner had a different view about women and marriage. Cary now looked at Keith. Cary could still hear Keith saying a few times over the past three years, "If you want a happy life, make an ugly broad your wife." Of course, he screwed up the saying. What else did he expect from a mind like Keith's?

Cary had called Seth on the way back from Mount Clemens and explained to him what had happened at the Macomb County Building. Seth knew nothing about the dead man found in the elevator. He called a member of The Circle working inside the Macomb County Building. Seth then called Cary back and told him the member was in her office on the tenth floor when the perpetrator with a gun showed up and terrorized a woman on the thirteenth floor.

The Circle had nothing to do with this gunman. Neither Cary nor Keith knew why Janet and Simon went to Mount Clemens and rode the elevator to the thirteenth floor. They assumed the doctor and the detective met someone who had information about the death of the security guard? But they would probably never know since it wasn't talked about in Dr. Wood's car on their way back to Detroit.

Seth told Cary for Dr. Simon and Detective Bennett not to discuss why they went to the county building or any other pertinent information about their investigation, they must've found the listening device underneath the car's dashboard. It was the only thing which made sense to him. Cary agreed with him.

Cary called Seth again after leaving Mickey's Sport's Bar and Restaurant. He told Seth what had happened. His boss told him it seemed like trouble followed the doctor and detective on a regular basis. Of course, Cary agreed with Seth. Neither of them had an explanation of why they kept encountering deadly incidents.

Keith glanced over toward Simon and Janet. "So, the only thing we can do is continue following them and hope they say something crucial about their investigation."

"It's all we can do at this point." He sipped some of his bourbon and coke. "And it's the same thing Seth told us to do."

~ * ~

Simon switched his cell phone to his other hand, then glanced at Janet. "So, Frank, what do you mean by relevant and interesting? Are you referring to the dentist and the victims?"

"Yes. I crossed referenced the fourteen victims and the dentist. All the victims had dental bridges. The bridges were removable dental prostheses, mostly in different areas. And all of them were done within the last two years."

"Hum. What's so shocking about that? Maybe coincidental?"

"I first thought the same thing…coincidental. But when I searched further into this dental procedure and crossed referenced their medical records, each victim periodically complained of earaches. The cause was attributed to the dental work. The pain was resolved with ibuprofen or acetaminophen. The earache was diagnosed as referred dental pain. Not sure what referred dental pain means."

"The nerves to the upper and lower mandible or jaw and the teeth have a common nerve called the trigeminal nerve which goes to the brain. The nerve courses around the ear, and when a person has lower teeth or jaw pain, the pain can travel backwards toward the ear, causing the sensation of an earache." It didn't seem feasible all the victims would have earaches due to them having bridge work done, thought Simon. For a hundred percent symptom of referred ear pain to occur from this type of dental procedure was too coincidental. "The bridge work somehow eventually triggered the tinnitus and possibly the victims' deaths."

"Holy cow! Remind me not to have any dental work done soon."

Simon wanted to chuckle but refrained himself. He should be used to Frank's comic statements during serious issues. "So, none of them had TMJ problems?"

"No. There wasn't any record of temporomandibular joint pain in the dental or medical files of the victims."

"Wow. I'm impressed by your pronunciation of TMJ."

"Thanks. I also checked all the other causes of tinnitus and didn't find anything else that could've caused this condition. What's our next step with this information?"

"This likely rules out tinnitus caused from TMJ or any other common cause." Simon looked at Janet and shook his head back and forth in reflection of his conclusion. "So, now we must focus on the victims' tinnitus and the bridge work each of the victims had. There's somehow a connection. You and Jean need to call District Five Medical Examiner's office tomorrow morning and have them examine each of the victims' bridge composition."

"I agree. Did the security guard have bridge work done?"

"Don't know yet. I'll be calling the ME in charge of his autopsy"

"Oh. So, you don't need me to check it out."

"No. Won't be necessary."

"Are you coming back to Ocala soon?"

"Yes. The way it looks now, we'll probably be flying back to Ocala tomorrow afternoon. We're waiting on an autopsy report."

"Was there another suspicious death besides the security guard?"

Simon told Frank about their encounter with the Macomb County Building crazed gunman. "That's the autopsy report we're waiting on." He didn't tell Frank about his vision of the restaurant gunman and its resolution, since it wasn't related to their investigation. "Talk to you later. Bye." Simon summarized to Janet what Frank found out regarding the dental bridge work.

"I agree with you. Somehow the dental bridge work on the victims is related to their deaths. We'll need the medical examiner to remove the bridge work and examine them. Not sure what they'll find. This seems to be the clue we've been looking for. Don't you think?"

"I do…finally. I'll call Phillip and let him know what we discovered. He'll need to check the security guard's pathology report for medical and dental records regarding previous bridge work."

"Good idea. You know, if wasn't for you and your associates, I'd likely have fourteen mysterious deaths without a clue."

Simon wanted to tell her, "Yes. You're probably right. You'd be at a complete standstill." Instead, he answered, "I'm sure you would've uncovered evidence leading to an answer to those deaths."

"Hmm. You don't lie very good."

Simon didn't know what to say. Janet seemed to know when a

person lied to her. She was a student of body language, that's all. Nothing more than that. "I'm not telling you a lie. There's the possibility you would've uncovered these clues."

Janet raised her eyebrows and smirked. "Okay. Thank you for the compliment, Simon."

"I'm glad we were here to assist you in this investigation." He removed his cell phone and called Phillip's cell phone number.

Phillip answered on the second ring. "Hi, Simon. What's up?"

Simon told him what they discovered regarding the Ocala victims all having bridge work done by the same dentist over the past two years.

"I can't remember if Walter Osborn had a dental bridge," Phillip said. "I'll check the autopsy record first thing tomorrow morning." A short pause. "What are you specifically looking for?"

"Not sure. It all seems too coincidental."

"Yeah. It does. Doesn't it? As soon as I find out if Osborn had dental bridge work, I'll call you right away. I should also have the autopsy report on the Macomb County Building gunman."

"I appreciate it. Have a good evening." Simon didn't tell Phillip about the incident in the restaurant. Knowing Phillip's inquisitiveness, he'd wonder why trouble seemed to encounter them everywhere they went.

~ * ~

Janet gulped down the last of her soda. Her cell phone rang. She glanced at the caller ID name: Bill Matters. He must have news about whether other students heard a noise around Melody Richards before she collapsed. "Hey. Bill. What'd you find out?"

"I called everyone on the list of students near Ms. Richards. I even called the students in the high school cafeteria sitting around Pam Whittaker, Allen Murdock sitting at his desk in history class and finally John Mitchell's friend, Derrick Olson. No one heard any unusual sounds."

"This only leaves one conclusion now. Most likely all fourteen victims experienced tinnitus."

"It sure sounds like it to me, too."

Janet went into details regarding the victim's dental bridges. She explained to Bill that Frank and Jean from the CDC would be investigating the dental findings, along with him. She gave Frank's cell phone number to Bill, then asked him to call Frank and set up a time for them to meet tomorrow morning. "The three of you go to District Five ME's office tomorrow morning and have the ME remove the bridges and analyze each fitting for anything unusual."

"Sounds like a good plan to me. I'll call you when we find something out."

"Talk to you tomorrow." Janet put her cell phone away. She then looked at Simon and said, "That's taken care of. We should have answers one way or another tomorrow of how the victims died."

"I sure hope so. These have been the most mysterious death cases I've ever encountered. Especially when someone is trying to record our conversations in two different cars. If we didn't have our special capabilities, we'd never know we were being recorded. Still don't know for what purpose."

"Like we'd mentioned before, Simon, they may be tied into these deaths. But we may never know since we can't trace the bugging devices back to anyone."

The sound of glass breaking across the room caused her—and Simon—to glance at the noise. A man in his early thirties wearing a blue cap sat at a table with another man at least ten years older. They both glanced in their direction, not sure if they were peering at them or at the bartender standing at the bar. The older man, holding a glass in his hand, peered down at the floor where a broken glass with its liquid content lay next to his companion. He shook his head, apparently in dismay. The bartender walked from behind the bar with a broom and dustpan, along with a bar towel. A moment later, the area on the floor next to the table was clean and dry.

Janet chuckled. An embarrassing moment a few years ago crossed her mind.

"What's so funny?"

Janet told Simon about an incident where she sat in a restaurant at a table with white table linen during a dinner hour meeting with detectives in her department. She had knocked over a decanter of red wine on the white table linen and onto the floor. She had felt terrible at the time, and unfortunately the detectives brought up humorous comments about the red wine incident over the next few weeks. "Of course, now I can chuckle about it. So, I can relate to the man with the blue cap spilling his drink. He'll probably look back at it in the future and laugh about this embarrassing moment in his life."

"Not me," Simon said frowning. "I'd blame the person sitting next to me for spilling my drink. People around you would then stare and blame them for spilling your drink."

Janet sat up; her shoulders pressed against the cushioned back of the chair. She couldn't believe what he said. "Are you serious?"

Simon smiled. "No. I wanted to see your reaction to my outlandish comment. But I know now not to spill a drink around you or any other detective after your story."

They both laughed. Janet then turned her head to the right. The man with the blue cap and his friend were gone. After saying their goodnights in the hallway, outside each of their hotel room door, Janet went inside her room. Several minutes later, she lay on a queen-size bed. The room was quiet and dark. She sighed as a feeling of loneliness overcame her. *What's wrong with me? I like living by myself. I only have to worry about me. No one else.* She then thought about Simon. A good-looking and intelligent man. A warm sensation moved over her entire body. The day's events with him drifted slowly across her mind.

Soon sleep overtook her conscious thoughts.

~ * ~

Simon sat in the room's desk chair typing on his laptop computer. A lamp on top of a rectangular table serving as computer desk lit up the surrounding area, including the two queen-size beds behind him. The window curtain was fully drawn, blocking out a full moon and the city lights of Windsor across the Detroit River. At the end of each day during any of his FMI cases, he'd write about the events and any evidence of his investigation. He would also mention the ESP events experienced by him and his associates, Frank and Jean. Simon also included Janet's premonition feelings, since she agreed to assist him and the other two Federal Medical Investigators three days ago.

Simon stopped typing, sat back in his chair, closed his eyes and thought about Janet. A pretty and smart woman. He chuckled. And obstinate at times. She greatly contributed to their investigation, along with her partner, Detective Matters. Simon knew about her past: what high school she graduated from, an associate degree in criminal law, divorced due to incompatibility, Marion County Sheriff commendations, and an older brother, Michael Bennett, M.D. She occasionally drank alcohol. He chuckled, remembering what she told him about her ouzo incident at a Greek wedding.

Simon closed his laptop, walked over and sat on the bed. Leaning toward the nightstand, he set an alarm clock for six-thirty a.m.

A knock on the front door startled him. He glanced down at the nightstand clock: 9:35 p.m. *Who'd be knocking on my door this time of the night?*

## Chapter Seventeen

Simon walked over to the door and peered through the peephole. A man with a blue cap stood in the hallway, staring back at him. *It's the guy who spilled his drink in the lounge. What's he doing here?* Without hesitation, Simon opened the door. "Can I help you?"

Keith Nelson, who stood about three inches taller and at least thirty pounds heavier than Simon, answered, "I have some information about your investigation regarding the death of the security guard and the fourteen people in Ocala."

Simon frowned in bewilderment. "Do I know you?"

"No. You don't." Keith looked to the left and right down the hallway, then added: "But I'm sure you'd want to hear what I have to say. Can I come in your room and talked to you about it?"

Simon's mind focused on his gun laying on the nightstand. This guy could be a foe, wanting to injure or even kill him, or this guy could be a helpful contributor to FMI's investigation. *Which one is he*? There weren't any weapons in the guy's hands. "Wait here for a moment." He hurried to his gun and stuck it behind him into his pants' waistband. Simon walked back to the door. The man stood outside the door looking up and down the hallway, then toward Simon with an apprehensive expression. "Come on in." After the man stepped into the room, Simon gazed up and down the hotel's corridor. It was empty. He then closed the door.

Keith stood in front of the TV, which sat on a lowboy dresser. "I don't have much time, Dr. Woods. My partner, Cary Gaines, thinks I went to our car in the parking lot to shut off the recorder. I purposely left it on, hoping I'd have the opportunity to talk with you or Detective Bennett."

"Who are you? What do you want to tell me?" Simon felt like he was in a James Bond movie filled with suspense, intrigue and danger. And when the mysterious man had said the word, *recorder*, Simon knew who he was dealing with: the people whom had planted the listening device in his car. He reached around and felt the security of his gun.

"My name is Keith Nelson. I work for an organization called The Circle. They're plotting to take control of all the governments throughout the world. When I first joined them two years ago, I had hated and resented our government, wanting to get even for everything it stole from me."

"What did it take from you?"

Keith walked over and sat at the end of the bed across from the desk. "I was fired from my government job as a maintenance engineer in the Federal Senate Building in Washington D.C. I was accused of sexual harassment in the workplace several years ago. I wasn't given the opportunity of defending myself or even given due process of law. Because of it, my wife divorced me, I lost my house and couldn't find another job due to the stigma placed on me by our government." He glanced down at his watch. "I better get to the point. I came to the realization the past several weeks, this organization called The Circle will destroy the free will of people all over the world, making people live in a robotic society. It's much worse than what our government did to me with their false allegations. I don't know much about this organization other than they plan to take over the world governments by implanting their people in positions of power. Fear is one of their tactics, such as people suddenly dying for no apparent reason. I don't know how it's done. Most of us are only given specific task without questioning their reason. We're not sure how much you know about these deaths in Ocala or the death of the security guard at the Ford dealership. Also, how does trouble seem to follow you and Detective Bennett?"

Simon wasn't sure if Keith had told the truth or if Keith wanted to know what he and Janet knew about these deaths. And once he told this guy about their investigation and their ESP powers, he and Janet would suddenly die. He couldn't take the chance. "I appreciate what you told me about this organization. First, to answer your questions, we don't know how these people died." Which of course was the truth, pending the outcome of the analysis of the dental bridge work on the fourteen victims in Ocala.

"And second, Detective Bennett and I don't know why trouble seems to follow us. It's happenchance, I guess. To ask you a question: Where is The Circle organization located? And who're the leaders of it?"

Keith's cell phone rang. He fumbled for it in his pants pocket. "Hey, Cary. Turned off the recorder." A short pause. "Sorry, I stopped to have a cigarette outside. Be right up." He put the phone back into his pocket. "Gotta go. Don't know where The Circle's main location is or who the leaders are, other than a man called Seth, who we get orders from. He's located at the Perfect Flower Shop in Ocala. That's all I know. I may not get another chance to talk with you. Please do what you can with the information I've given to you. This plot to destroy world order and people's freewill through fear, intimidation and selective death must be stopped."

"You've given me a lot of disturbing information. I'll do what I can. If what you told me is true, the world is in deep trouble."

"I'm afraid it's all true." Keith hurried out of the room.

Simon wrote down the main points of what Keith Nelson told him, including pertinent names: Cary Gaines, The Circle, Seth and Perfect Flower Shop. This organization wouldn't have any trepidation about getting rid of him or Janet if they felt threatened with being exposed. Simon believed what Keith had told him. Now what was he going to do with this information? The logical thing to do was to tell Janet, then call Frank and have him do a computer search of the information. One problem. What if their cell phones were bugged? Simon doubted it, since Keith didn't mention it during their conversation. Besides, he had talked with Frank on their cell phones regarding how the victims' bridge work might be tied to their deaths. The four of them would probably be dead by now if The Circle knew they were about to solve the 11:58 A.M. Deaths. Simon called Janet and asked her to come to his room to discuss some revolutionary information he received a few minutes ago. He unlocked his side of the room's adjoining door.

A few minutes later, Janet unlocked her side of the adjoining door and walked through the doorway into Simon's room. "What's so important it couldn't wait until tomorrow morning?"

He told her what Keith had said to him. "This is why I didn't want to wait until tomorrow morning to tell you."

"I'm glad you woke me. Are you sure this guy named Keith Nelson wasn't playing you and what he told you was all a lie? And his only purpose was to find out if we were close to solving these murders?"

"I thought the same thing. No way to know until we follow up in what he said."

"The problem with waiting to verify his information, we may be dead before tomorrow morning if what this man, Keith Nelson, said was all a scam. And the organization called The Circle was a figment of his imagination in order to gain knowledge on what we know about the 11:58 A.M. Deaths. I think we should stay together tonight."

"Great idea." A grin appeared. "Your room or mine?"

Janet shook her head and raised her eyebrows. "Is that all men think about? Even in a time of crisis?"

"No, of course not. We also think about: Does she know how to cook?"

Laughter filled the room.

While Janet went back to her room to retrieve a few things, such as her gun, Simon called Frank informing him what had transpired in his motel room with Keith Nelson. Simon asked him to check the names the informant mentioned and find out all the information about them. "This may turn out to be a ruse by this Nelson guy."

Janet came back into the room.

"We won't know until I find out. I'll get on it right away," Frank said eagerly.

"You can wait 'till tomorrow morning."

"No problem. I don't normally go to sleep until about one in the morning. As long as I get six to seven hours of sleep, I'm okay."

"So be it. It's up to you. Hopefully this isn't all a con by this guy."

"We'll soon find out. I'll call you back after I look into it."

Simon put his cell phone on the nightstand, then sat on the bed. "I'm too anxious to go to sleep right now. Do you wanna play some cards?"

Janet frowned. "What kind of cards?"

He grinned. "Not the kind of cards you're thinking of." *Obvious she's thinking of strip poker*. "I was thinking about the card game called George. A smart lady like you, it'll take five minutes to explain. Before you ask me, I carry playing cards in my overnight satchel. To pass away the time during a lull in our FMI investigations, Frank, Jean and I play this card game."

For the next hour and a half, they sat at the side of bed playing George. Like anyone playing a game they never played before, Janet won over seventy-five percent of the games. Simon stared into Janet's eyes and said, "I'm glad we're not playing for money."

A smile appeared. "If that were the case, I would've probably won all the games."

He chuckled as he picked up the cards. "I wouldn't doubt it." Simon's cell phone rang. He quickly picked it off the top of the bed. It had to be Frank calling him back. The caller ID displayed Frank's name. Simon anxiously asked, "What did you find out?" He put his phone on speaker, so Janet can hear what Frank found out.

"Everything Keith Nelson told you about himself had happened regarding being fired for sexual harassment, divorced, and losing all his worldly possessions. He and Cary Gaines are listed as security employees for a multinational company called The Circle. They're listed on the New York Stock Exchange as an investment company with holdings all over the world in real estate properties, manufacturing businesses, pharmaceuticals, medical and dental supply/manufacturing and communications to mention a few of them. A Seth Appleton also is employed by The Circle as Chief of Security for North Central Florida. As for the Perfect Flower Shop, I spent a while trying to trace ownership. I finally connected the flower shop as a subsidiary of The Circle. There are numerous Perfect Flower Shops all over the United States."

Simon smirked and nodded. "I'd say we found our criminal adversary. At least now we know who we're dealing with regarding being bugged and followed. And if Keith was correct about The Circle being the responsible party for the death of fourteen people in Ocala and the security guard, all we have to do now is to prove it."

Janet stood and peered down at the floor. "Even if what Keith had said about The Circle wanting to control governments and people of the world is true, why kill innocent people?" A disgusting look appeared, as she shook her head. "We're dealing with pure evil."

"Pure evil definitely describes The Circle," Frank said, "an evil entity wanting world dominance. If I can tie in the dental bridges to one of their companies, and if the bridges are somehow the catalyst causing the death of these people, we'll then have solid evidence on them in a court of law."

"You're absolutely right. The medical examiner should have the answer tomorrow." He glanced at his watch. "I mean today…since it's almost twelve-thirty in the morning. I appreciate your computer wizardry. Talk to you later." He stood, reached over and laid his cell phone on the nightstand. "Well, detective. I think we should go to bed?"

Janet grinned. "Is that an offer?"

A warm sensation burst across his blushed face. "I mean…"

"Just kidding. You're right. It's getting late." She laid her Glock on the nightstand between the queen-size beds. She walked over to the open door between their adjoining rooms, closed and locked it. She then went to the bed of her right and laid down on top of the covers. "Thanks for teaching me the card game George. It was fun."

"You welcome. You're now part of the FMI's official George card group."

She smiled. "Goodnight, Simon." She then rolled on her left side, facing away from him. "If someone knocks on the door again. Don't answer it. I'll go and see who it is."

Simon wanted to say, "*I can handle myself in a perilous situation*." Instead, he replied, "Thanks." He reached over and turned the lamp off on the table between the beds. Darkness engulfed the room. He enjoyed her company and small talk conversation they shared for the past hour and a half, something he hadn't experienced for a few years. Of course, there were Frank and Jean and other colleagues over the years, but not a woman who made him feel good inside, and who he looked forward to being with the next day. Like what he said to himself the first day they spent together investigating the Whispers before Death case, *Janet was special, pretty and bright*. Amorous feelings were now part of his attraction toward her. He didn't want to jeopardize and complicate their professional relationship.

Simon lay on his back, on top of the covers, staring up at the room's dark ceiling His mind raced over all the events of the day. He couldn't remember ever having so many traumatic, hair-raising incidents in a twenty-four-hour period. His inner voice asked: *What will tomorrow bring me?*

## Chapter Eighteen

Simon's watch alarm sounded, waking him up. It was seven-fifteen. He rolled over and faced Janet's bed. Daylight sneaked around the window drapes, dimly lighting the room. Janet wasn't lying in her bed. He sat up. The adjoining door was open. *I know it was closed when we went to sleep.* Janet's room light was on. He reached to his left and turned the lamp on. The room lit up.

"Good morning, Simon," Janet's voice bellowed from her hotel room.

Simon stretched out his arms, awakening his upper body muscles. "Morning, Janet."

She walked into the room and stopped a foot beyond the doorway holding a paper cup. She wore a different outfit from yesterday, other than her blue blazer.

"I see you're already dressed."

"I am. But not until I enjoyed a pleasant, warm shower. I made a cup of java from the room's coffee maker." She took a sip, and then grimaced. "If this was the last coffee I could ever drink again, I'd pour it down the toilet. After you get ready, maybe we can go downstairs to the restaurant and get a real cup of coffee?"

"Sounds like a good plan to me."

"After you shower and get dressed, come over to my room." She walked back into her hotel room.

About twenty minutes later, they went downstairs to the hotel's restaurant. Simon looked around for Keith Nelson and/or Cary Gaines. He had a good idea what Cary looked like from the incident with Keith spilling his drink. Simon didn't see them among the twenty or more people sitting by themselves or sitting with one, two or three people at tables throughout the room. He and Janet sat at a table in the far corner of the dining room with a view of everyone in the room and whoever walked into the restaurant. The waitress walked up to their table. They gave the waitress their breakfast order.

A few minutes later, Janet sipped her decaffeinated coffee, then asked: "Do you think the medical examiner will find something inside the dental bridges?"

"I hope so. I can't even speculate what they'll find." He glanced at a couple in their seventies who walked into the restaurant. "It would have to be something that caused each of the victims' death at 11:58 a.m., two mornings in a row. We know there weren't any unusual or illicit substances found in their blood toxicology report, eliminating the diagnosis of death by poisoning. It's a medical mystery. I hope the bridge work in each of the victims will answer…solve the reason why they suddenly died."

"If the bridge work is normal, this investigation will be at a standstill. There wouldn't be any evidence for prosecution against The Circle. It would be the word of one man against an army of attorneys representing The Circle."

"Unfortunately, your assessment would be right."

The waitress brought their breakfast. After eating, the waitress came over and gave them a warmup on their coffee. Simon's cell phone rang. He glanced at the caller ID. "It's Dr. Pearson. I'll put him on speaker. Morning, Phillip."

"Good morning." He cleared his throat. "I have the results on the two things your wanted me to check out. First, there wasn't any evidence of bridge work on my autopsy report of Walter Osborn. And second, regarding the gunman at the county building, he died of a massive cerebral hemorrhage, killing him instantly."

That eliminated the county building gunman being connected to the security guard's death or the deaths in Ocala, thought Simon. "Thanks for—"

"There's more about this crazy guy," Phillip interrupted. "His name is, or should I say was, Richmond Stark. He was hired by a jealous teenager to shoot the three teenagers at the county building. The teenager came from a wealthy family in Mount Clemens. The disgruntled teenager was arrested for three counts of conspiracy to commit murder. There wasn't any explanation why Mr. Stark brandished his gun at the lady in the circuit court library."

"Thanks, Phillip. You've been a great help."

"Anything new on your investigation?"

Simon knew he still couldn't divulge any information about FMI's supernatural abilities, including Janet's premonition feelings. Since Walter Osborn didn't have any bridges or dental procedures the past ten years, he no longer was part of their investigation. "No. We're pretty much at a standstill, a lull in our investigation. At least until the medical examiner in Florida examines the dental bridges of the fourteen victims in Ocala. Detective Bennett and I will be heading back to Ocala in a couple of hours. Our investigation here in Detroit and in Mount Clemens is completed. Again, Phillip, I really appreciate your help in this investigation. Plus, it was great seeing you and talking about the past. It brought back a lot of good memories."

"I agree. It was great seeing you again after all these years. Good luck in your investigation…and future investigations. Keep in touch."

"Shall do. Bye." Simon put his cell phone away.

He and Janet checked out of the hotel. Simon called the pilot earlier about them leaving. The pilot had already filed their fight plan back to Ocala with the airport. Simon drove to westbound I-94 and headed for the airport. Traffic was moderate going out of Detroit with the eastbound traffic extremely heavy. "So, what do you think about the city that was my home during medical school?"

"I'd say from what I saw, the people were friendly. A great city to visit with all its historical sites. And if you like casino gambling, this would be the place for you. Although, I like the small-city living Ocala has to offer with fewer people and less traffic. Plus, I'm not a fan of snow, sleet and freezing temperatures. I'm a southern girl with thin skin, who craves warm weather and sunshine."

Simon chuckled. "A real southern belle, huh?"

"And proud of it, Dr. Simon Woods." A grin appeared, erasing her previous sullen affect.

Within an hour they were seated in the plane and buckled up, waiting for the plane to taxi onto the runway. Simon looked over at Janet sitting across the plane's aisle to his right. She stared down at her small notebook containing the events and her observations of the past two days. Simon knew this because she had shared her notes with him on the way to the airport. They concluded their trip to Detroit and subsequently Mount Clemens didn't evolve into anything significant. If Keith hadn't stepped in and told Simon about the clandestine organization called The Circle and what their ultimate goal and intentions were, he and Janet would've drawn a dead end in Detroit. Simon also learned that The Circle attempted to listen in on his and Janet's conversations, including following them around, observing their movements, all in an attempt to gain any information on their investigation of the fourteen victims in Ocala. As far as Simon knew, The Circle didn't know FMI was on the trail of a potential major piece in this puzzling investigation: the victims' removable dental bridges had something to do with each of the victims' deaths.

Simon's cell phone rang. It was Frank. He turned toward Janet. "It's Frank. I'll put him on speaker."

"Thanks. I'm anxious to hear what he has to say about the dentures and their connection to the mysterious deaths."

"Good morning, Frank. Have you guys gone to the medical examiner's morgue yet?"

"It was a good morning when I woke up. And yes, Detective Matters, Jean and I went to District Five's morgue. Matter of fact, we're standing in the morgue now. It's not a good morning."

"Why isn't it a good morning?"

"All the dental bridges were removed from the corpses."

"Great. What did the medical examiners find?"

"Nothing. Because all the removable dental prostheses were taken from all the victims' mouths before the ME could remove them this morning. Someone apparently broke into the morgue late last night and removed all of them from the bodies of the fourteen victims."

"You gotta be kidding me!"

"I wish I was. Detective Matters at first felt an employee had to be involved in these thefts because there wasn't any evidence of a break-in. It would only take one person to remove the dental bridges from our victims, since each of the bridges were easily removable."

"Does the morgue have security cameras?" A thought flashed across his mind. "Don't tell me the surveillance cameras weren't working last night."

"You're right. The cameras were down, like during the accident with the pickup truck the other day."

"Unbelievable." The Circle must've infiltrated Division Five Medical Examiner's medical staff. Or at least an employee was coerced into letting someone come into the morgue and remove the dental bridges. "Did Detective Matters talk with staff members working at the morgue last night?"

"Yes. And that's another interesting development."

"What do you mean?"

"There were two employees working in the morgue. A morgue technician who'd accept corpses from an on-call medical examiner at a crime scene and a security guard. Both stated to Detective Matters they lost consciousness between midnight and three a.m. this morning. Neither said anything to one another, thinking they had fallen asleep for a few hours. They didn't want to jeopardize their jobs."

Simon sighed, then grunted. *Either they were both lying, or in fact they were telling the truth.* "This wasn't the news I'd expected."

"The two employees agreed to take a lie detector test per Detective Matters suggestion. Also, the two employees were sent to the hospital's emergency room for a full examination, including a panel of blood work and a complete drug toxicology panel. I'm going to guess their exams and blood work will be normal, along with negative lie detector tests."

"I'm afraid you're going to be right in your assumptions. From what we've learned in Detroit from Keith Nelson recently, I'd say The Circle was responsible for the missing dental bridges." But there was one thing puzzling Simon: he never told Nelson about their investigation of the fourteen victims' bridges and its possible connection to their deaths. Someone had to tip off The Circle. Or a member or an informant of The Circle overheard their conversation regarding the dental bridges.

"You're probably right about The Circle being responsible for the removal of the bridges. All three of us here agree to this assumption. So, Simon, where do we go from here?"

"Don't know. We'll be landing in Ocala in about two hours, around two o'clock. Pick us up at the airport. Did you tell Detective Matters about The Circle?"

"Yes. Weren't we supposed to?"

"No problem. He's now part of our investigative team. Although, at this time don't you or Jean mention to him about our special powers."

"We won't."

"I'll call you in about thirty minutes before we land. Talk to you all then." Simon turned to Janet, who had put her notebook in her lap. She stared at him with sagging eyebrows, tightened lips while shaking her head in a gesture of disappointment. "Can you believe this crap? The Circle had obviously had something to do with this. Don't you think?"

"I do. It's now for sure the dental bridges had something to do with the death of our victims."

She thought a moment. "We have another option regarding bridges."

"What's that?"

"We need to find a living patient of the dentist, George Cassidy, who had bridge work done in the past two years. There may be other patients who had the same dental procedure as our victims."

Simon reached down to his right, picked up a cardboard cup filled with coffee from a circular holder in the arm rest and took a drink. He then set the cup back down. "Or the fourteen victims are the only patients the dentist targeted for his special, deadly removable bridges."

"Possible. One way to find out. We'll need a list of all the patients he inserted bridges on excluding our victims."

"I'll have Frank bring up the list of Dr. Cassidy's patients with dental bridges over the past few years. We need to find someone to prove our assumption. I thought of something. What about getting a search warrant for the dentist office to confiscate all the dental bridges?"

"One problem with your idea: no judge will give us a search warrant without concrete evidence demonstrating the dental bridges caused the deaths of fourteen people. The only evidence we have is the coincidence of all the victims seeing the same dentist and having bridge work done by him. Plus, there'd be no way we could prove The Circle was behind all these deaths. We're only relying on Keith Nelson's testimony, an unscrupulous person with a vendetta against the government."

Simon nodded. "You make a lot of logical sense. That's why you're a sheriff's detective and I'm a medical doctor. You have detective experience and I have medical experience."

"Although, with you, Frank and Jean combined with my expertise, we make a good investigative team."

"I can't dispute your statement about us being a great team because it's absolutely true. We need your legal and detective prowess." Simon wanted to tell her, he liked her as a person, a beautiful sensuous woman he felt comfortable being with and sharing their ideas and beliefs.

"Is there something else you want to say to me?"

*Does she read minds*? A warm wave encompassed his entire body. "Ah. Ah." *She caught me off guard. What should I say to her?* "I'd add, hopefully we'd be friends. I mean…hopefully we are friends."

She smiled. "I'd say we're friends."

Simon nodded and smiled. The rest of the flight was uneventful, regarding their investigation. He learned a lot about Janet's childhood, high school years and her associate degree in police science, followed by a bachelor's degree in criminal justice. She loved dogs but didn't have one for the past five years due to her long and unpredictable hours as a detective. Janet only briefly mentioned her marriage to Rick Ridder. Simon basically talked about interesting medical cases he had encountered since medical school. He did tell Janet that he was an only child—a spoiled only child. Janet asked him why he never got married. Many people had asked him the same question, so he had a patented answer used by a high percentage of unmarried men: "Never found the right woman." Being an agent for the clandestine FMI team made it more difficult to find a woman with the amount of time spent away from a house in the suburbs. In fact, Simon lived in the suburbs, but lived alone in a two-bedroom condominium without any commitments to a female. Besides being an only child, he only had adoptive parents; he had never known who his biological parents were or anything about his true bloodline.

The plane landed at Ocala International Airport/Jim Taylor Field. Frank, Jean and Bill Matters greeted them once they were inside the SUV. "How's everyone doing?" Janet asked as she got into the backseat next to her detective partner. They answered from "okay" to "had better days." Frank uttered the latter response.

Simon, who sat in the front passenger seat of the SUV, asked Frank: "Did you complete the list of dental patients who had removable dental bridges put in by Dr. George Cassidy?"

"I did. The list with the patients' street addresses and phone numbers is sitting on the console."

"Great." Simon reached down and picked up the list.

"Eight patients saw Dr. Cassidy and had bridge work done by him in the past two years, excluding the already dead fourteen victims. This time of the day most of them are probably at work. We should call them first and see if they're at home or work. Don't tell them what you specifically want from them. Say you're doing a medical investigation for CDC and need to talk with them in person."

"Good idea. Between the four of us, we should be able to check these dental patients out and ask them questions about tinnitus and referred ear pain after their dental procedure. But…what we really need from them is to have their removable bridge work examined by a dentist. There's no way we could get a court order to confiscate them. Since we're only speculating the partial bridges were involved with the fourteen victims' deaths."

~ * ~

A small jet engine plane had landed a several minutes before the FMI's plane landed at Ocala International Airport.

"That was an uneventful trip in Michigan the past two days," Cary Gaines said as he and Keith got into their vehicle, a white, unmarked van.

"Yeah. It was like a mini vacation for us." Keith played dumb, an act he'd been portraying for the past two years. He thought The Circle would feel sorry for him and support his anger and hurt toward the government if he had a dull-witted persona. It worked. They teamed him up with Cary, who supposed to be the "brains" of their stealthy partnership. He did some bad things for The Circle, which he now regretted. He felt some redemption after speaking to Dr. Woods about the plans of The Circle. If they found out what he did, he knew a speedy death would shortly follow. "There's the SUV Seth told us about that would pick up the detective and the doctor." The SUV was leaving the pickup area in front of the entrance to the airport's terminal.

"I see it. Do you think I'm blind?"

"No. Of course not. You wouldn't be able to drive the car if you were."

Cary shook his head in disgust. "Idiot," he whispered.

"There are five people in the SUV. Wonder where they're going?"

"My guess would be Dr. Woods and his associates' hotel."

"Makes sense to me." Keith wanted to say, "Probably our office at the flower shop to talk with Seth about The Circle."

~ * ~

Simon peered at the front passenger side view mirror. Ten minutes ago, a white van left the airport with them. *I wonder if people from The Circle are inside of it and are following us?* He turned his head toward Frank and said: "We'll go the hotel and get our vehicles. We'll split up in two pairs: Janet and I will be team one. Jean and Frank will be team two. Detective Matters will be on standby in case we need a search warrant from a circuit judge."

They all agreed to Simon's plan.

Janet added, "When we interview these people, we don't want to cause panic or fear in them. No way do we want to tell them about a possible correlation between their removable dental bridges and the death of the fourteen victims. We need to tell them we're investigating faulty bridges which may contain mercury…a toxic chemical which could do harm to their body. If they are skeptical about your credentials, have them call the sheriff department's major crime unit and ask for Detective Bill Matters. They must volunteer their bridges for evaluation by forensic specialist. The bridges will be returned to them in a day or two. With this presentation, I don't think we'll have any problems."

Simon periodically glanced into the side view mirror. The white van stayed about ten car-lengths behind them. The Holliday Inn came into view. The van pulled into a gas station to the right. Frank pulled into the Holliday Inn's parking lot.

Frank dropped off Bill Matters. He then drove about fifty more feet where Simon's car was parked. "I checked your car again for any bugging devices. Your car is clean."

"Thanks." Simon peered at the side view mirror. He didn't see the white van pull into the parking lot.

Jean, who sat in the driver's side backseat, put her hands to her mouth, "Oh, my God!"

"What's wrong?" Janet asked.

"I see a yellow glow around Simon!"

# Chapter Nineteen

Janet sighed. Simon was too young to have a heart attack or stroke. From her previous conversations with him, he enjoyed excellent health. He didn't smoke tobacco, or did he drink alcohol to excess. His six-foot tall frame complimented his one-hundred-and-eighty-pound weight. It only left a couple of ominous possibilities for his yellow glow: accidental or intentional injury or death. The Circle flashed across her mind. If true, why only him? Why not all the FMI team agents, which now included her? Janet passed her thoughts to everyone in the car.

"I agree, Janet, about your assumption regarding my general health. What's relevant about me having this glow is I must be careful of the next twenty-four hours. Look both ways at intersections, not walk under ladders and look over my shoulder periodically. We all know by changing events or a person's timeline, death or injury can be avoided. Right, Jean?"

"Yes. You're right. Sort of."

"What do you mean, sort of?" Simon asked.

"You can change the events leading up to accidental injury or death. But you can't change someone intentionally trying to kill you. Unless you know the person or persons plotting your demise."

"Like The Circle," Janet stated.

Jean nodded. "Yes. Like them."

Simon cleared his throat. "We can't let this deter us from our investigation."

Frank rubbed his forehead. "You'll have to be more focused about your surroundings." He grinned. "Especially someone holding a knife or gun."

Simon rolled his eyes and smirked. "Thanks for the advice."

Janet reached for the inside door handle. "Let's get going, Simon, and check out these dental patients on our list."

"I agree. I'm ready." He looked at Frank, then Jean. "Talk to you guys later."

Simon pulled out of the parking lot and headed for the first name on their list. The first two people on their list no longer had their removable bridges, which were ordered one and a half years ago by the dentist, George Cassidy. Both had dental implants the past year. Neither of them had their old bridges. They were thrown away. The next patient, Barbara Russet, threw away her removable bridge about a year ago because it was too loose to wear. She never went back to see Dr. Cassidy.

Simon and Janet weren't the first people to ask their first three dental patients about the removable dental bridges. A man and woman from the Marion County Health Department had visited them yesterday evening and asked them about their removable dental bridges. Janet called the health department and was told no one from their department was investigating people with defective dental bridges. In fact, the health department didn't have any knowledge of a problem with dental bridges. Somehow The Circle knew about their investigation of the fourteen victims' dental bridges.

Janet glanced down at the next name on the list. "So far, we're batting zero on obtaining a dental bridge. Plus, we're one step behind The Circle. The next person is Mary Larson." She looked up. "Make a left at the traffic light ahead."

"Give Frank a call and see how they're doing. And if a couple from the Health Department had already visited the people on their list. Hopefully they hadn't gotten away with one or more of the removable dental bridges."

Janet called Frank's cell phone. "Hi, Frank. I have you on speaker phone. Simon's here with me. So, what did you find out?"

"I was about to call you guys. Bad news. Two of the patients on our list died within the past twelve months. Each died of chronic illnesses. Both were cremated. The third patient has been out of the country for the past several months according to a neighbor. No family to contact. His cell phone number is not available, so there's no way to get a hold of him. The fourth person, Emily Brewster, lost her removable bridge a few months ago. I almost burst out laughing when she said her pet pot-bellied pig may have swallowed it. But then she said her pig suddenly died a few days ago."

"Don't tell me the pig died around noon three days ago?"

"Yes. It did. And unfortunately for us, Ms. Brewster had her pig cremated. Its ashes were in a wooden box in her living room. What is it, with so many people having their loved ones cremated? But what's strange about the people on the list—"

Janet interrupted: "The Health Department had already been there before you, inquiring about their dental bridges."

"Yeah. How'd you know?"

She told Frank what she found out after calling the Health Department. And that she and Simon didn't have any luck with their first three people on their list.

Simon added: "Frank, you and Jean go back to the hotel. We'll meet you there after we interview our last person on the list."

Janet put her cell phone away, then said: "Turn right at the next street."

A moment later, Simon turned right.

"The house of the next person, Mary Larson, should be up ahead to our right."

"Oh, my God!"

"What's wrong? Simon."

"The white van parked in the street three houses up to our right looks like the one that followed us from the airport earlier."

Janet looked at the address of the house they were looking for. The white van was parked in front of Mary Larson's house. Could it be a coincidence? "Pull up behind the van." She reached down to her right and felt the handle of her gun. Hopefully she wouldn't have to use it. Janet glanced at Simon, who also felt for his gun sitting snuggly in his left shoulder holster. If The Circle people owned the van, what were they doing here? Was Simon going to face death or serious bodily injury inside the house as predicted by Jean's yellow glow vision around her boss? Janet felt her pulse increase as she and Simon got out of the truck and walked up to the front door.

Simon rang the doorbell.

A sudden chill engulfed Janet. Danger stood behind the front door. A woman's scream vibrated from inside the house. She removed her gun from the belt holster, unlocked the safety switch and placed the gun in her left hand. "Stand back!" Simon stepped to his left, allowing Janet complete access to the front door. She threw open the front storm door and grabbed the inside front doorknob. It was locked. She raised her right shoulder, stepped back a couple feet, then lunged forward, slamming her shoulder against the wooden door.

The door swung open.

In front of Janet, about twelve feet away, stood a petite woman in her sixties; she was being held around the chest from behind by a medium-built man. It was the same man she had seen in the hotel's restaurant in Detroit. Another man held a gun in his right hand; the gun was pointing toward her. It was the same man who had dropped his drink in the Detroit restaurant. She shouted, "Drop your gun."

Keith's gun hand slightly shook. A frightened expression stared back at Janet. He then peered at Cary as if to say *What should I do?*

"Shoot the bitch!" Cary ordered.

"Drop the gun, Keith," stated Simon, as he came from behind Janet.

"How does he know your name?" Cary questioned Keith angrily.

Keith shrugged his shoulders as he raised his eyebrows. "I…I…don't know." He then looked toward Simon.

Janet answered, "We know quite a bit about the both of you."

Cary released the terrified woman, then struck her with the butt of his gun, causing her to fall to the right onto the hardwood floor with a thud. He raised his gun and fired two shots toward Janet and Simon.

Janet fired three shots at Cary. He stumbled forward and collapsed to the floor. Keith dropped his gun. She didn't feel pain anywhere in her body. Her thoughts jumped to Simon, as she turned toward him. He wasn't standing next to her but lay on the floor face down. He wasn't moving. "Simon!" Her panicky voice filled the living room. Jean's foreshadowing had come true. Simon was dead.

"Oh, my God. The doctor's dead," Keith proclaimed, as he brought both of his hands up to the lower aspect of his face.

Janet hurried toward Keith and picked up the gun off the floor. She quickly handcuffed him and had him sit on the couch. She then turned around and walked over to Cary. She bent down and turned Cary over on his back. Dead eyes peered up at her. Janet stood, stepped to her right a couple steps, bent down to evaluate the unconscious woman, who lay on her right side. Janet checked for Mary Larson's pulse, then observed for any breathing. Both were present. A moaning sound came from behind Janet. She turned around and saw Simon move his hands. "He's alive." She stood, hurried over to him and rolled him on his side. Two bullet holes penetrated the front right side of his buttoned sports coat without any signs of blood.

He opened his eyes and said, "Are we dead and in heaven?"

Two tears cascaded down onto her cheeks. "No. You're alive."

"Thank God I wore my bulletproof vest. I forgot to tell you I put the vest on before the plane landed at the airport. It's so light and non-bulky, you don't realize you're wearing it."

"I thought you were dead."

"The bullets striking me took my breath away causing me to fall and lose consciousness for a minute or two." He sat up and looked down at the two bullet holes in his sport coat. He stood and unbuttoned the coat. Two flattened bullets fell to the living room floor. "Thank the Lord for armor technology."

"Jean's vision would've come true about you, Simon, if you hadn't worn your protective vest."

"Amen." Simon peered down at Cary, who lay on his back with three bloody bullet holes on the left side of his chest and obviously dead. "I assume those bullet holes in his chest are from your gun. Remind me never to have a shootout with you." He then looked to his left at a cuffed Keith Nelson.

Mary Larson began to move; she was regaining consciousness.

A scenario flashed through Janet's mind. Keith had no intention on shooting either her or Simon a few minutes ago. Cary was dead. Would he be willing to work undercover from FMI? If The Circle infiltrated and influenced governments, corporations and God knows what else throughout the world, it would be advantageous to their investigation of the fourteen deaths here in Ocala. "Mr. Nelson come with me into the kitchen." He stood and followed Janet. She said to Simon, "He may be helpful to our investigation."

"I agree. I think I know what you're about to ask him, which I support." Simon then walked over to assist Ms. Larson, who still lay on the living room floor, semi-conscious.

~*~

About ten minutes later, Simon heard a vehicle's engine starting up in front of the house as he now sat at the kitchen table next to Ms. Larson, who held a plastic bag of ice against the back of her head. A minute passed when Janet came through the front door, walked through the living room and into the kitchen. She nodded toward him, acknowledging Keith Nelson had accepted her proposal of him being an informant for them. Simon had heard a good percentage of what she had asked Keith in the kitchen. Keith had agreed to be an informant for her and Simon. The Circle wanted the removable bridge from Ms. Larson, which she hadn't used for the past month due to its irritation on her gum. Unbeknownst to her, that had saved her life. Plus, she had stayed at her daughter's house all day yesterday and didn't get home until about an hour before Keith and Cary knocked on her front door. Keith had stated they were about to obtain the whereabouts of the bridge when he and Janet rushed into the living room.

"I called Detective Matters. He'll notify the Forensic Unit and the ME. I also called EMS for Ms. Larson. How's she doing?"

"Dazed. She has a concussion. With the type of blow she had to the back of her head and loss of consciousness, she'll need a CT brain scan and a twenty-four-hour observation at the hospital."

"I gotta call my daughter."

"Once the sheriff deputies get here, they'll call your daughter. You'll need to go with the paramedics when they get here. They'll take you to the hospital."

"I have bingo tonight."

"You'll have to miss bingo. The doctor at the hospital will have to check out your head for any serious injury."

"Can't remember what happened. Did I trip and fall in the kitchen?"

"No. You fell in the living room. What was the last thing you remember before you were knocked out?"

"Someone rang the front doorbell. I can't remember who it was. Was it you?"

"No. You'll eventually remember. It's common after a severe blow to the head. We call it post-traumatic amnesia."

The sound of sirens got closer and closer.

"Ms. Larson, I noticed when I was checking your mouth, you have a large gap between your lower teeth on the right side. Do you wear a removable partial bridge? If you do, where is it?"

She frowned. "Why do you want to know if I have a bridge?"

"There might be a flaw in them. Plus, they may contain mercury. Something you shouldn't have in your mouth."

"Hum. Maybe that's why my partial bridge didn't fit right?"

"Where's your bridge?"

"Oh yeah. You'll find the bridge in a plastic container. The container is in my jewelry box on the dresser in the bedroom."

Janet left the kitchen and headed to the bedroom.

Simon didn't ask her why she'd put them in a jewelry box. The front door opened. Sherriff deputies entered the living room followed by EMS first responders with a stretcher.

Janet came back into the kitchen holding a white plastic container. A smile lit up her face. "We got it. Once we're done here, we'll take the bridge to the ME."

Paramedics placed Ms. Larson on a stretcher after they did their preliminary assessment and vital signs. They blocked her view of the bullet-ridden body lying in her living room. Detective Matters arrived. Janet walked him to the end of the hallway leading to the bedrooms. She told him the full story of what had happened without anyone in the living room hearing her summation of events leading to and including the shootout with Cary Gaines. The investigative report would state Cary Gaines had perpetrated a home invasion and was shot by Detective Janet Bennett when Mr. Gaines opened fire at her and Dr. Woods, striking Simon's bulletproof vest with two bullets and knocking him to the living room floor. She and Simon came to the house to question Mary Larson regarding the deaths of Ocala's fourteen victims. As far as Keith Nelson, whose name wouldn't be mentioned in the sheriff's report, a second person escaped and drove away in a white van. Janet was unable to get a license plate number or identify the perpetrator since the person apparently hid in the kitchen during the altercation in the living room. Right after the shooting, the gunman's partner apparently exited the side door of the kitchen and ran to the parked van on the street in front of the house.

Since Ms. Larson had post-traumatic amnesia with no recollection of what had happened in the living room, Janet and Simon's official version would prevail. Janet relinquished her gun to Bill pending investigation of the shooting incident by the sheriff's department's Internal Affairs.

Simon came down the hallway and stood next to Janet. Simon told Detective Matters the death of Cary Gaines by Janet was definitely a justified shooting. And if Janet hadn't intervened as quick as she did, he might have taken a bullet to the head or neck, vital areas not protected by his bulletproof vest.

Bill nodded. "I agree with you, Dr. Woods. But like I said, it'll be up to Internal Affairs officials." He then wrote Simon's statement regarding the shooting down in a notebook. Simon's statement matched Janet's descriptive narrative of the event in the living room.

The Crime Scene Investigation team arrived. Janet, Simon and Bill went into the living room. "I'll finish up here," Bill stated. "Since I'm the lead detective in this home invasion incident, I'll direct the crime scene investigators during their forensic investigation."

"You're right. You're in charge here."

Bill said to a Forensic Unit investigator, "Please give me a bag to put this gun in." A man in his late twenties wearing a Forensic Unit investigator's jacket handed him an evidence bag. Bill turned to Janet. "Let me know what the ME says about Mary Larson's bridge."

"I definitely will, Bill." Janet answered, touching his right forearm. "Talk to you later."

Simon started the car. "Do you think Keith Nelson will cooperate with us and be an informant?"

"I'm usually a good judge of character. And if someone is truthful.

I believe we can trust him."

"Good. I sort of like the guy. He seemed to be honest with me." *Thank God I've been honest with her.* He put the car in drive and headed to Leesburg and District Five's medical examiner's office.

Janet looked down at the plastic container. "If this dental bridge turns out to be the cause of the 11:58 A.M. Deaths, we'll then focus on The Circle's involvement with the help of Keith Nelson."

Simon's cell phone rang. He pulled over, parked the car at the curb and removed the cell phone from his shirt pocket. Frank's name displayed across the phone's LED screen. He put him on speaker phone, so Janet could hear their conversation. "Hi, Frank. Good news, we're going to the ME's office with a dental bridge to be examined."

"Great. But the reason I called was to tell you some conflicting information about the security guard, Walter Osborne and—"

"What about the security guard?"

"You told me Mr. Osborne didn't have a removable dental bridge according to Dr. Pearson. Well…he did have a removable bridge. According to dental records I obtained from his dentist in Detroit, the bridge was inserted two months before he died. The bridge was made by a subsidiary of The Circle."

"Not sure what this means, Frank." Simon couldn't understand why Phillip would lie to him. Maybe his previous mentor didn't record Osborne's dental bridge due to an oversight during the autopsy? Or Osborne didn't wear his bridge the night he died? What other reason could there be? Two words flashed across his mind: The Circle! No way Phillip was involved with this stealthy, evil organization. Or was he? "Frank. Right now, are number one priority is to find out if the fourteen victims' bridges had contributed to their deaths."

"You're right," agreed Frank. "And I found something else out about the dentist, George Cassidy."

"What did you find out about him?"

"He's dead. The dentist died when his car went out of control and crashed head on into a bridge embankment. The initial police report stated it was an apparent accident."

"You gotta be kidding? An accident? I have a feeling The Circle had something to do with this so-called accident."

"Kind of coincidental when we're about to tie him in with the dental bridges and the fourteen deaths here in Ocala."

"Yeah. Another coincidence. Talk you later." He glanced at Janet and shook his head with disgust.

"If this accident was at the hands of The Circle, I'm sure they've already destroyed or altered his office records, making it more difficult for us to tie them to the dentist. We'll have to wait and see." Janet held up Ms. Larson's dental bridge. "Right now, let's have the medical examiner checkout this bridge."

Simon put the car in drive, pulled away from the curb and headed to the ME's office. A thought flashed through his mind: *The only person other than Janet, Frank, Jean and me who knew about the dental bridges was Phillip. And he was told late yesterday afternoon/early evening. Yesterday evening was when The Circle members impersonating county health personnel visited the individuals on Frank's list. Was it coincidental that after telling Phillip about the dental bridges, The Circle people showed up a couple of hours later at the dental patients' doorsteps in Ocala?*

## Chapter Twenty

Simon pulled into the parking lot of District Five Medical Examiner's building. Janet had called ahead and talked with James Scott, M.D., one of the medical examiners, and told him what they were bringing in for a forensic analysis. She didn't tell him that it might be related to the fourteen deaths in Ocala. Janet had dealings with the ME on several death cases over the past couple of years.

Janet and Simon walked into the autopsy room. Dr. Scott, who appeared to be in his early fifties, removed his blue latex examining gloves and placed them along with his paper gown into a metal receptacle. A male cadaver lay on a silver-colored metal gurney. A young man in his mid-twenties wearing green surgical scrubs leaned over the deceased male body on the gurney and zipped up a white, plastic shroud. Janet grimaced as the distinct pungent odor of an autopsy room saturated her olfactory nerves inside her nose. "I'll never get used to this smell, Dr. Scott."

He turned around and faced them. "Oh. Detective Bennett. What smell?" A frown appeared. "I only smell the pleasant aroma of my working environment."

"I guess smell is in the nose of the beholder?"

"An astute assessment," Dr. Scott answered with a grin. "So, you have something to show me? A removable dental bridge?"

"Yes." Janet handed him the evidence bag.

He opened the bag, removed the bridge and stared down at it, turning the bridge three hundred and sixty degrees. "It appears to be like any other dental bridge, including the weight. I'll start by doing an x-ray." Dr. Scott looked over to his assistant putting the recent autopsy body from the gurney and into a morgue drawer. He then pushed the drawer into a refrigerated wall compartment at the far end of the room. "Elliot. Bring me the portable x-ray machine."

James placed the dental bridge under a small digital plate, positioned the cone-shaped scanner and started taking x-rays at different angles, front and back. A computer screen attached to the x-ray machine displayed the images. The three of them leaned toward the screen. James said: "There's something inside the false tooth. Not sure what it is. I'll make the anterior posterior image larger." He slid his finger at the bottom of the screen, enlarging the x-ray.

Simon squinted, moved a little closer to the screen and questioned. "It looks like a microchip."

"This isn't a small microchip compared to chips that are seven nanometers wide," James said.

"I read something about nanometers," Janet interrupted. "But how small is seven nanometers?"

"About one ten-thousands the width of a human hair. So, this chip is half the width of a molar tooth. In other words, this chip is the size of a luxury liner compared to seven nanometers or the size of a rubber ducky floating on top of bathtub water. Since around the mid-seventies, microchips have continued to get smaller."

"We need to retrieve this chip," ordered Janet. She knew somehow this chip caused our victims' deaths.

"I don't have any instrument small enough to cut the tooth without damaging the microchip. I'll call Dr. Stanley Stone, a forensic odontologist. He'll have the right instruments to get to the chip without damaging it." He put the dental bridge into the plastic container.

"Great," Janet said.

Dr. Scott removed his cell phone from a belt holster, walked away from them and called Dr. Stone.

Simon said to Janet, "We'll need someone to analyze the chip after Dr. Stone retrieves it from the bridge tooth."

Janet sighed. "I never needed a microchip analysis during any of my investigation. Only the whole computer by our computer forensic personnel. I'm not sure they have the capability for this type of analysis."

"The only person I know who'd have this information or knowledge of analyzing microchips is Frank. I'll give him a call."

"Hi, Frank. You won't believe what we found." Simon told Frank him what the x-ray showed. "So. Do you know anyone who can analyze a microchip?" A short pause. "Perfect. I knew you would know. I'll call you when we leave the ME's office. Talk to you soon. Bye."

"I assume Frank knows where to take the microchip for analysis?"

"Yes. A computer geek friend of his knows a person in Ocala who has the equipment and knowhow to tell us what's on the chip."

"It sounds like Frank belongs to a network of computer geeks?"

"I'd say your assumption is spot on. Frank is an irreplaceable FMI agent on our team." *And so are you as far as I'm concerned.* "We'll meet him back at the hotel, then drive to the guy who'll analyze the microchip."

"Damn," she whispered. "I'm anxious to find out how this microchip caused all these deaths."

Dr. Scott walked back toward them as he put the cell phone back into his belt holster. "Dr. Stone will be here in fifteen minutes. Can I get you two something to drink?"

"Sure. Sounds good," Janet answered. Simon nodded.

Janet and Simon sat in Dr. Scott's office adjacent to the morgue.

"Do you two know why this microchip is in this dental bridge tooth?" Dr. Scott asked, leaning back in his leather-covered swivel desk chair.

A chill streaked up Janet's spine to the back of her head. *What caused that? I've never experienced this feeling in this type of setting. The phone hasn't rung, or no one was about to come through the door. Maybe Dr. Scott's question triggered my premonition sensation.*

Simon glanced at Janet's ominous demeanor. "Not sure."

Janet didn't want to answer truthfully. If Simon's previous pathology preceptor, Phillip Pearson, was possibly connected with The Circle, maybe this ME is also connected? If Simon answered "not sure" then he likely felt not to give out any information in case The Circle influenced this medical examiner's office. *My God. We're becoming paranoid.* "Dr. Woods is right in what he answered. We don't know for sure. Since we don't know what caused the fourteen deaths in Ocala, we're checking everything. It looks like it'll be an unsolved medical mystery."

James grinned. "Oh. You're on a fishing expedition?"

"You could say it that way." If Dr. Scott was part of The Circle, he'd already know the microchip had to do something with the fourteen deaths and would've insisted on trying to open the bridge tooth and somehow destroy it accidentally. More she thought about it, he likely had nothing to do with The Circle.

A male with a deep voice behind her announced: "Good afternoon. So, you need my dental expertise?"

"Yes. We do," James answered. "Dr. Stone, I'd like you to meet Detective Bennett and Dr. Woods."

Janet and Simon were already standing and facing the forensic deontologist. They shook hands with a tall, slim man in his early sixties. Several minutes later, Dr. Stone meticulously began to cut away the top of the tooth, away from the microchip. The whining sound of a cutting instrument piercing the tooth's crown echoed throughout the morgue room's confined space. About five minutes later, the forensic dentist removed a metal microchip from inside the tooth with forceps. "Here it is lady and gentlemen. I have to say this is the first time in my thirty plus years I've removed a microchip from inside a tooth."

It may not be the last one, thought Janet. "I appreciate you coming in and doing this for us."

"You're welcome, Detective Bennett."

Janet and Simon thanked everyone, put the microchip into an envelope and left the autopsy room. The microchip's chain of custody had been consistent and unbroken so far. Janet knew if they were able to prove, then prosecute the entity responsible for the microchip's creation, chain of custody would have to be flawless without any doubt in the eyes of the judicial court systems, the prosecution or the defense attorneys,

Simon stopped the car in front of the hotel's covered front entrance. Frank left the front lobby and a moment later, got into the backseat of the car, behind Janet. Simon turned and looked at Frank. "This should be near the final puzzle piece that'll hopefully solve our mysterious deaths."

"Amen," Frank interjected.

"Where's Jean?"

"She'll be right here. She had to get her cell phone from the room."

Jean hurried through the hotel's front entrance and sat in the backseat behind Simon. "My God, Simon," Jean exclaimed. "You still have the glow. Your fate hasn't changed…even after being shot twice today. Some other deadly or ominous event awaits you in less than twenty-four hours."

Simon shrugged his shoulders. "Like I said earlier today, I'll have to be careful." He glanced to his right toward the front passenger seat. "And make sure Janet is standing or sitting next to me with her Glock."

Janet smirked. "You handled yourself fine today."

"Yeah. Right. I make a good backstop for bullets. You fired two shots before I could remove my gun. My reflexes were practically nil…nonexistent."

Frank directed Simon from his cell phone's GPS on how to get to Danny Emerick, the computer geek with a microchip analysis machine. On the way to Danny's house, Janet and Simon discussed the future steps of their investigation once it was determined the microchip caused the 11:58 A.M. Deaths. A subpoena would be issued by a judge to search the company's files and the manufacturing sites of the dental bridges and microchips. If Keith Nelson's claims were true about The Circle's diabolical plan of wanting to control all governments of the world and its people, a microchip planted in a tooth or any other place in the human body would be the ideal means for world control.

"But first things first," Janet stated, "let's see what's on this microchip that's possibly capable of causing the deaths in Ocala."

Frank glanced at his cell phone's GPS, then said: "It's the blue house on the right."

The houses on the blacktop road were far apart, about fifty-acre plots separating each homestead. Simon saw the light-blue painted house and turned right onto a gravel driveway. A two-hundred-foot driveway led to the front of the house. Pine and elm trees were scattered throughout the estate. As the car got closer to the house, a two-car garage stood to the right side of the house near the back yard.

Simon parked the car in front of the house on a circle drive. The FMI team got out of the car and walked up to a covered front porch running the full width of a two-story farmhouse, which needed a fresh coat of paint.

Frank reached out toward the center of a solid wooden door where a brass door knocker was attached. No other means of announcing their presence, such as a doorbell, could be seen.

The door suddenly opened, startling everyone on the porch.

A clean-shaven young man with short red hair in his late twenties and about five-foot-five inches stood inside the doorway. A smile lit up his face. "Frank Littlefield," he then glanced at everyone else on the porch, "and associates. Please come in. My name is Danny Emerick."

"Please to meet you," Frank said.

Once inside, Janet quickly scanned the foyer. A small crystal globe hung from the ceiling. A polished wooden floor shone up at her. A few steps forward, she looked to her left at a furnished living room with Victorian furniture sitting on a large area rug along with accessories complementing the room's décor. Stairs with an elaborately carved mahogany banister to her right led up to the second floor. Danny led them up a long hallway in front of them. In the middle of the hallway to their right they walked into a room containing electronic devices and computers. Janet thought she had walked through a time portal and into the year 2120. There were electronic devices with different colored lights, some blinking, others displaying wavy horizontal or vertical lines. The room's walls and ceiling presented with sterile-white paint. A white tiled floor gave the illusion of a sterile research room.

"Are you from this century or the next century?" Janet asked as she gazed around the room.

Danny grinned. "This century, Detective Bennett."

Janet frowned. She didn't tell him her name. Or did she hear Frank when he talked to Danny earlier on his cell phone mention her name or anybody else, except his own name. Maybe this guy possessed telepathic capabilities?

"If you're wondering detective how I knew your name, it's because I've been monitoring the news and computer social news sites regarding Ocala's fourteen mysterious deaths and saw your photograph standing on the steps in front of North Marion High school at the time Melody Richards' death. I also recognize Dr. Simon Woods, Jean Cliftwood, and of course, Frank, who are agents of the CDC's FMI division."

"I guess you don't miss anything?"

"Not true," Danny answered, as he walked over to an electronic circuit panel. "I do miss things…if they're not in the computer." He chuckled then placed the microchip into a slot in the circuit panel, then typed something on a computer keyboard. A computer screen above and next to the circuit panel displayed numbers and letters rapidly changing. The screen went black. A second or two later, words then sentences appeared across a white screen:

RECEIVER MICROCHIP PROGRAMMED TO TRANSMIT A BURST OF THREE HUNDRED DECIBELS.

"What does this mean in laymen's language?" Janet asked.

"Standing near a NASA rocket launch at the Cape generates around 180 decibels. At about 194 decibels sound waves become shock waves. The chip must receive a signal from an outside source. Like a cell phone, radio transmitter—"

"Or a satellite signal," Frank interrupted.

"Yes," Danny answered. "A satellite could've sent out a signal to this microchip and trigger the chip to emit a high frequency impulse."

"It's all making sense now," Simon said, rubbing his chin. "Melody Richards had whispered: 'What's that sound?' She was referring to the high pitch sound being transmitted from the dental microchip. Somehow this high-pitched frequency triggered their death."

"You're saying something in their ear or near their ear caused their death?" Janet asked.

"Yes. Something near the inner ear." Simon paused, momentarily looking away as if collecting his thoughts. "What's in the area of the inner ear?" He looked at Danny. "Can you bring up a graphic diagram of the middle/inner ear on one of your computers?"

"Sure. No problem," Danny answered. He moved to another computer, next to the electronic computer panel and sat on a high-back stool on wheels. Simon, Jean, Frank and Janet moved to their right and stood behind the computer geek. Danny's fingers moved quickly over the keyboard. A few seconds later, the screen displayed a multi-colored middle/inner ear structure. “Here it is.”

Simon leaned forward over Danny’s right shoulder and appeared to focus on an area adjacent to the ear configuration. “It has to be the tenth cranial nerve, the vagus nerve, that caused the victims’ deaths.”

“How did this nerve cause their deaths?” Janet asked.

“The vagus nerve is a major cranial nerve and influences the heart and other major organs in the human body. The nerve originates in the brain near the inner ear. Branches of this nerve are part of the inner ear’s functions. The electronic microchip inside the tooth sent out the high frequency impulse along the mandible nerve to the inner ear, then to the vagus nerve. The impulse traveled down the vagus nerve to the heart, causing the overstimulation of the nerves to the cardiac muscles…cardiac standstill and finally death.”

“Quite an ingenious way to kill people,” Jean said.

“And who has a satellite communication system…The Circle,” Janet declared. “The problem now will be to prove their responsible for these fourteen deaths. And likely the security guard in Detroit.”

“There could be other deaths caused by these microchips we don’t even know about,” Frank added.

“We could be talking about hundreds, if not thousands of people that could’ve died due to these demonic microchips,” Jean said, shaking her head in dismay.

“You both could be right,” Janet said. “I thought of something. How did the pet pig die from swallowing the dental bridge?”

Simon answered: “The vagus nerve branches off into the stomach. The stomach is near the heart. The phrase ‘heart burn’ doesn’t mean the heart is burning. It’s the stomach causing the burning sensation, which is relieved by antacids or a stomach medication, not cardiac medication. The high frequency impulse triggered the microchip, sending an impulse through the stomach nerves to the vagus nerve and back to the heart muscles, causing cardiac arrest and death.”

Janet stepped a couple paces backwards. “Now that we got proof of how these deaths occurred and who likely caused their deaths, it’s now a matter of the district attorney obtaining subpoenas on The Circle and its subsidiary, Century Dental Prosthesis Company. Although, I don’t know if the DA won't need more evidence to prove their case against these two entities." Her cell phone rang. She glanced at the caller's name: Preston Davis. It was Keith Nelson's alias, a name she gave him in the kitchen of Mary Larson's house. Janet didn't want to use his real name in case someone from The Circle stood nearby when she talked to him either on a phone or in person. "Hi, Preston. What's up?"

"All of you are in danger. The Circle knows you have possession of the dental microchip, and who's analyzing it. The house you're in right now is going to be blown up any minute."

Janet shoved her cell phone into her jacket pocket, then shouted: "This house will be blown up any minute. We gotta get out now. We need the microchip, Danny."

"They might be waiting for us outside," Jean said.

Danny ran over and grabbed the microchip from the electronic circuit panel. He pushed a button on a small black device attached to his belt. The floor vibrated. In the far corner of the room a six-foot by four-foot section trapdoor in the floor swung upward, revealing a staircase descending downward beneath the house. "Everyone, hurry down the stairs. We'll be safe down there."

No one hesitated. Jean descended first, then Frank, then Simon, then Danny followed by Janet. She heard a high-pitched whirling noise outside. It was getting louder and closer as she placed her right foot on the first step. Would she be killed instantly from the explosion as she was swept away by the forceful blast? She heard Simon yell, "Hurry." As her head cleared the level of the floor, the trapdoor completely closed.

A thunderous explosion shook the house.

## Chapter Twenty-one

Simon stood in a concrete walled room about ten-foot square and a concrete ceiling containing the metal rectangular trapdoor and a steel staircase descending from it to the floor of the shelter. LED lights on two walls illuminated the room. Three computers with widescreen monitors along with keyboards and various other electronic machines sat on rectangular tables forming an L-shaped workstation against two walls in the room. None of the computers or machines were turned on. A twin-size bed, a refrigerator, a small oven/stove and a porcelain toilet lined up against one of the walls. A metal door about five feet high by three feet wide outlined the fourth wall. Huddled in the middle of the room stood Janet, Frank, Jean and Danny. Simon stood about three feet away from them. "Are you guys okay?"

Everyone nodded.

Jean stared at Simon and said, "You haven't lost the glow."

Danny frowned, apparently not understanding the comment. "What does that supposed to mean?"

"It has to do with his enlightened concern about us," answered Jean. Before he could respond to her odd answer, she added: "The first thing I thought about when we first stood together after climbing down the latter was how the air down here didn't have a musty or stale quality."

Frank raised his head and breathed deeply through his nose. "I agree with Jean. I don't smell anything but pure oxygenated air. Other than Danny's leather belt, which I assume is new."

Danny wrinkled his forehead. "Unbelievable. You're right about my new belt." He looked toward an air vent on the wall to his right. "As for the pure air down here, it originates from the outside air. The air is vented through an air purification system and into the shelter."

Janet scanned the room in all directions. "Are we in a hurricane and tornado shelter?"

"Yes," replied Danny. "It can also withstand a nuclear explosion…and now a conventional bombing."

"If whoever bombed us doesn't know about this shelter, they'll assume we all been killed," Simon stated.

"Probably," Danny answered as he walked over to a small metal box about six inches square attached to the wall above one of the computers. He opened the box and pushed a red button. Several seconds later, the computer screens lit up. "I'll check outside. I have security cameras around my property and yard." Everyone walked over and stood behind Danny.

"So, you saw us drive up your driveway earlier?"

"Yep. I did."

An ominous thought flashed across Simon's mind. Would the camera recordings be blank like the one at their intersection accident with the pickup truck? And like the blank recording two years ago during the theft of the vehicles at the Ford dealership and the security guard's death? The Circle may have known about Danny's security cameras surrounding his property and house. "Is it possible they may have hacked into your computers and shut down your security cameras?"

"Highly unlikely. I have a failsafe system. If someone tries to hack in my computers, an alarm signal is sent to my cell phone, warning me." A moment later, the computer screen in front of him displayed a front yard image of the house. Or where the house once stood. Two outside walls, the front and back wall, and the roof had collapsed onto the first level of the house. Only the end walls stood partially erect. The Circle obviously didn't know about the security cameras, thought Simon.

"Unbelievable," Jean exclaimed. "We all would've been killed if it wasn't for us being here in the shelter."

"You're absolutely right," Simon said. The screen switched to another camera view. But this view showed a front view of a dark-blue panel van with tinted windows making it difficult to see its occupants. The van drove slowly down the gravel driveway as it approached the road.

Simon didn't see any distinguishable markings on the vehicle. "Can you show when the perp got here?"

"Sure. I have a duplicate recording machine down here in case something goes wrong with the one in my computer room in the house. It runs twenty-four/seven like the other one. Or should I say the CD recorder that used to be in my computer room above us." Danny brought up the CD's video recordings, fast forwarding Frank and the rest of FMI's team's arrival. The next scene on the computer monitor showed the dark-blue van drive up the driveway toward the house.

"Stop it there," Janet requested, leaning over Danny's head and staring at the back of the van displayed on the computer's monitor. "Can you get a closer look at the license plate."

"I can."

A close up came into view. The license plate letters and numbers were obscured due to a black veil covering. Simon grunted. "Damn. This eliminates any identification of the perps."

"Even if we could see the license plate's letters and numbers, the plate could've been stolen," Janet stated, leaning back to an erect posture. "I've seen it many times, including the fake license plates Frank identified a couple of days ago."

The video continued: The van slowed down about fifty yards from the house and turned around by driving over the grass. The rear of the van faced the house. A moment later, a small projectile with a vapor trail burst from the back of the van. The house exploded, sending pieces of wood, glass and shingles in every direction. The two-story country farmhouse no longer existed. Simon's car was covered with house debris. Danny switched to a camera's view on the house facing outward toward the driveway and fast forwarded the CD to where the van had turned around. The van's rear door opened. A man dressed in black garb with a hood got out and slightly crouched. He held a missile launcher and fired. The missile streaked toward the house followed by smoke then a white screen.

"Man, thank God for my shelter," Danny said. "I'll make a CD copy."

"Good idea," Janet said, reaching down and briefly touching Danny's shoulder, apparently acknowledging his suggestion. "It'll be vital evidence in this missile attack against us."

He put a blank CD in a recorder machine and recorded the dark-blue van along with the perp launching the missile. He then handed Janet the CD. The computer screen now showed a live view of the driveway, a smoldering and demolished house and Simon's debris-covered car.

Janet reached over and rubbed her right elbow. She had bumped it against the stairs as she descended into the shelter earlier. "Unfortunately, there isn't any incriminating evidence pointing toward the people who are responsible for this military-like act. Even though we're sure it's The Circle organization responsible for it." She grabbed her cell phone. "I'll call Bill Matters and let him know what has happened here and a description of the dark-blue van."

Simon turned to Danny. "If the electric power line to the house was severed, where do you get the power source for the computers, lights and appliances down here?"

"The computers, electronic equipment and lights' power come from solar batteries stored in a small room beyond the metal door." Danny pointed at the metal door across the room, then returned his attention back to Simon. "In the back yard about fifty feet from the house are solar panels beneath the ground. You'd never know the solar panels where there because weeds and grass cover it." He reached over the computer monitor in front of him and put his finger on a green button, next to the red button. "When I push this green button, large metal paneled doors open outward and the solar panels rise above the ground, exposing them to sunlight. The refrigerator and stove run off propane. A commercial-size propane tank is also buried in the ground. There's enough propane to last over two years. I also have a water storage tank below ground, supplying water to drink and flush the toilet. I have enough food in my storage room beyond the metal door to feed four people for over two years."

Simon looked up at the staircase and trapdoor leading to Danny's computer room in the house. "What if there's debris on top of the staircase hatch? And we're unable to raise the trapdoor?"

"No problem." Danny turned and pointed toward the metal door on the far wall. "Beyond the door, there's a tunnel running under the right side of the house to about twenty-five feet outside. At the end of the tunnel is a ladder. It'll take you up to a metal hatch, leading you to the outside."

"As much as I've seen and what you told me, you've thought of everything to survive a catastrophic event, either manmade or by an act of God."

"Thanks. I believe I have all the bases covered to survive down here comfortably in my shelter for a while."

Janet walked over to them and announced: "I talked with Detective Matters. He put out an APB on the dark-blue van. The fire department should be here shortly. Bill will be showing up along with the FBI, since a handheld missile launcher with a missile was used in this attack. The FBI will likely be the lead investigators in this assault."

Danny sighed, letting it out quickly. "Let's see if the trapdoor opens." He walked over to the wall near the stairs and pushed a green button on the wall. A creaking noise screamed down from the ceiling. No movement from the trap door. Debris on top of door obviously prevented it from opening. "We go to plan B now."

Simon glanced at the metal door to his right. "Through the tunnel?"

"Yes. Through the tunnel."

Danny opened the metal door and bent forward, low enough to walk through the doorway and into the five-foot high by three-foot wide concrete rectangular tunnel. Everyone else followed him bent over and slightly bent at the knees. Jean bent her neck a little since she was only five-foot, one-inch tall. Six-inch diameter LED lights spaced ten feet apart along the tunnel lit up about twenty feet of the tunnel ahead of them. Simon turned his head to the right toward an opened doorway. A room to their right contained hundreds of can products and other various food and paper products. A minute or two later, they reached the ladder at the end of the tunnel.

"I'll go up and open the hatch," Danny said.

He climbed a ten-foot-high ladder extending through a tubular hatchway. Once he reached the top, he raised his arms above his head and slid a lever at the center of a round, metal hatch. A clank echoed downward through the vertical hatchway to the tunnel below. Bright daylight burst through the opening. Janet was the last one to climb out to the afternoon Florida sunshine. The odor of burning wood permeated the air.

The sound of unsynchronized sirens captured the air seemingly in all directions around them. Janet again rubbed her right elbow, probably aggravated from climbing the ladder. "Sounds like help is on the way."

"I'm thankful no one was injured," Simon said, then glanced down at Janet's right elbow. "That's the second time you rubbed your elbow."

"Oh. You look at me that often?"

A sudden warm sensation flashed across his face. *My God. I think I'm blushing*. He did look at Janet often because of his amorous attraction toward her, but he didn't think his glances were so obvious. "Often enough to notice you must've injured your right elbow coming down the stairs."

Janet grinned. "Huh. Good answer. I did bruise it coming down the shelter's stairs earlier and must've aggravated it climbing up the exit stairs.

"I'll be glad to look at your elbow," Simon suggested, as he stared down at her right elbow.

"It'll be fine. Thanks anyway." She turned and looked toward the front of house. "Why don't we check out the car and see if it's drivable?"

They spent a few minutes removing the debris from on top of the car. Everyone helped. Overall there were several dents on the hood, trunk and on top of the car's roof, but the windshield, back and side windows were intact, and the tires were unaffected. Simon got into the car behind the steering wheel. He reached out, put the key into the ignition switch and it started right up. Simon drove the car about thirty yards on the grass to the right of the driveway, allowing enough space for when the emergency vehicles arrive. A short time later, fire trucks, EMS, sheriff department's deputies and the Marion County's Crime Unit investigators drove up the driveway toward the house. And a minute or two later, two FBI agents, Williams and Carpenter, arrived in their vehicle. They got out of their car and walked up to them.

Janet introduced Danny, Frank and Jean to the FBI agents. "We have a CD showing at least one perpetrator holding a missile launcher and firing it. We also have their vehicle on the CD." She handed the CD to Agent Carpenter.

"Thanks. Do you know why this house and its occupants were targeted for this terrorist-like attack?"

Janet wasn't sure if she should give them the information about The

Circle and probable involvement in the fourteen deaths in Ocala with a microchip made by one of their subsidiaries? This was FMI's investigation. They've put in a lot of time and effort in this case. Why should she and the FMI team hand everything they know and suspect about The Circle over to the FBI. "Not sure. Other than we suspect someone doesn't want us to solve the fourteen victims' mysterious deaths in Ocala." She purposely omitted the reason for visiting Danny Emerick's house—to evaluate a microchip found inside an artificial tooth which was part of Mary Larson's dental bridge.

"I see," Agent Carpenter said nodding. "If we can piece together the missile used along with the CD video of the missile launcher, we might be able to narrow it down to the manufacturer. Only the military has authorized access to this weapon. We'll also have to check to see if any handheld missile launchers and missiles have been reported stolen from our military."

Agent Williams stared at Danny Emerick's smoldering house. "You still haven't answered why you were here at Mr. Emerick's house?" His eyes now peered at Janet, who stood between Danny and Frank.

"Mr. Emerick is a friend of one of my agents, Frank Littlefield." She acknowledged Frank by turning her head toward him. "We needed Danny's help in analyzing a computer microchip."

"What did you find out?"

She didn't want to lie to the FBI agent. "It's a chip programmed to receive a signal, then send out a sound wave." She sighed then thought, *Will this agent ask me another question about this chip?*"

"Oh. Computer geek stuff."

Janet brushed the hair from the lower forehead away from her eyes to the right. She nodded, then answered, "That's what it was. Computer geek jargon that's way out of my league."

Agent Williams glanced down at the ground and frowned, as if collecting his thoughts, then added, "What does this chip—"

Agent Carpenter interrupted, "Let's talk with the Forensic Unit people and make sure they search for the pieces of the missile."

*Saved by the missile*, Janet thought shifting her attention toward Carpenter. "I'll let you know how our investigation goes."

"Okay," Williams said, as he and his partner walked away toward the Forensic Unit van that had arrived a moment ago on the scene.

Simon pushed a smoldering piece of wood siding away from where they were standing. "So, Danny, what are going to do about your house?"

He looked up at the partially standing side of his house. "Rebuild another house. Of course, it won't be as well-made as this one. You figured the original house owner back in nineteen-thirties probably paid a couple of thousand dollars to have it built. My insurance should be enough to build a three-bedroom colonial-styled house. I'll live in my shelter while it's being built."

Frank walked up to them, after returning from retrieving his cell phone from Simon's car. "I'm really sorry about your house. I would've never got you involved if I knew someone wanted us dead."

"Don't worry about it, Frank. I haven't had this much excitement since…since. I've never had this type of hair-raising experience in my entire life. I'm normally sitting behind the computers in the quiet and mundane environment of my computer room. And what's important, none of us got hurt."

"I don't mean to be nosy," Janet said in an almost apologetic manner. "How can you afford a beautifully furnished home with sophisticated, expensive electronic equipment, computers and a survival shelter? Are you living off an inheritance or a trust fund?"

Danny chuckled. "No. Not an inheritance or trust fund. And not because of a lucrative business in computers. I won the Florida Lottery. About three years ago, my lucky numbers one, four, seven, thirteen, seventeen and twenty-three came in. The rest is history as the saying goes. Since then I've been helping people solve problems through the computer."

"A wealthy computer geek helping people," Janet commented. "Quite admirable. We sure do thank you for your help deciphering the microchip."

"Glad to help."

The fire department sprayed water on areas of the house that were smoldering, preventing flare ups of potential fire hot spots. The two FBI agents were talking with the Marion County Sheriff's department Forensic Unit investigators. Janet looked up the driveway and saw a familiar car coming down the driveway. It was Bill Matters.

Janet brought her partner up to date regarding the two FBI agents questioning the reason she and the FMI agents were visiting Danny Emerick.

"I'll be assisting Agents Williams and Carpenter in this bombing incident since you and the others were targeted victims of the crime. Thank God you all had a safe place to go prior to the missile attack."

Janet nodded. "We're going to head back to the hotel. We'll talk later."

Janet sat in the front passenger seat; Frank and Jean sat in the back seat as Simon started the car. Janet saw a blank stare fall upon his face as his body went motionless like a window mannequin. *He must be having a vision!*

## Chapter Twenty-two

Simon's visual premonition showed Keith Nelson talking, or more like pleading, with a man in his fifties. The man pointed a gun at Keith. A variety of floral arrangements surrounded them.

"Simon. Are you all right?" Janet asked, reaching over and touching his forearm.

The vision disappeared. "Yes. I'm okay, other than I had another vision."

"I thought so." She removed her hand from his forearm. "What did you see?"

Simon told them what he had seen. "Keith is obviously in danger. We must get to the flower shop before we have another death on our hands." Everyone agreed.

A small bell attached to the top of Perfect Flower Shop's front door rang out as Janet and Simon walked through the doorway. Frank and Jean waited in the car that was parked on the street in front of the flower shop. The fresh, fragrant aroma of flowers entered through Simon's nose on each breath. Beautiful arrangements of flowers filled glass door coolers on walls to his and Janet's right and left. How could the pleasant environment of flower shop harbor evil?

A woman in her thirties stood behind a register; the register sat on a small glass counter. "Can I help you, folks?"

"We're here to pick out some flowers for our wedding," Janet answered, followed with a smile.

Simon's jaw dropped in disbelief. He didn't expect her answer. They didn't discuss in the car what she would say when they walked into the flower shop.

"Great. Do you know what you want?"

"Sort of. We'd like to look—"

"No," shouted a man who interrupted her conversation. The commotion came from the direction behind the counter beyond a closed door. "What's going on in there?"

"I…I don't know." The woman appeared nervous, as if she was hiding something.

Janet removed a Glock from her holster. Since Bill Matters had confiscated her gun at Danny Emerick's house, Jean gave her Glock to Janet in the car on their way to the flower shop. The shouting increased in intensity. She glanced at Simon. "Stay behind me. Someone could be in danger."

"I agree." Simon knew they had probable cause to investigate under the law when imminent danger existed.

Janet turned the doorknob and pushed the door. She grasped her gun with two hands, pointing the Glock straight out in front of her as she stepped into the room and stopped.

Simon peered over Janet's right shoulder. In front of them stood the backside of a man, who appeared to be Keith Nelson from his long blond hair and six-foot three stature from what he remembered when he talked with him in the Detroit hotel room yesterday, and from his visual premonition less than thirty minutes ago. A man in his mid-fifties, sitting at a desk, pointed a revolver at Keith. His face showed no emotions other than an apathetic expression.

"I'm Detective Bennett. Put your gun down," commanded Janet. "Let's not escalate this situation more than a disagreement between the two of you."

"No problem, detective," replied Seth, as he placed the gun down on the desk in front of him.

"Why were you pointing a gun at this man?" Janet asked as she stepped forward and picked up the gun off the desk.

"I wasn't going to shoot Keith, only scare him," pleaded Seth. "He's an employee of mine."

Simon knew Janet couldn't tell Seth the truth of why they came to the flower shop. Although, Simon speculated Seth would wonder how by chance a detective and a doctor from CDC's FMI happened to be in the flower shop during his altercation with Keith. Janet had already lied to the woman at the register about picking out wedding flowers. Seth would figure out he and Janet are on to him and who he works for: The Circle.

"Do you treat all your employees this way? With threats?"

The door behind them closed. A chill engulfed Simon's entire body as he stood next to Janet. It had to be the woman at the register. He slowly reached for his gun.

"Both of you drop your guns," demanded the woman. "I have a .38 pointed at you. I'm not afraid of using it."

"I'll take my gun and yours, detective," Seth said standing, reaching out and taking both guns from her.

Simon had only one chance to react. He knew they would be killed once he relinquished his weapon. He glanced at Keith, who appeared concerned either about himself or him and Janet. He hoped for the latter. Simon nodded as did Keith. Almost simultaneously, Keith pulled out his gun from a shoulder holster, pointed it at Seth. Seth turned toward Keith and fired one shot, striking Keith in the chest. Keith fired: the bullet struck Seth in the forehead. Seth immediately slumped forward—dead. This incident had momentarily distracted the woman's attention in the doorway. Simon spun around with a gun in his right hand and fired two shots at the woman, striking the left side of her chest wall. Her mouth gaped open and her eyes rolled back as she dropped to the floor like a rag doll.

The door behind them swung open. Frank stood in the doorway, gun drawn and pointing toward them. He glanced at the man slumped in a chair behind the desk, then down at the woman lying face down on the floor in front of him. "Holy crap. I guess talking with them didn't work out? We saw the woman flip the closed sign on the front door. Jean and I knew there was a problem inside the flower shop. I was sure I'd find you and Detective Bennett lying dead on the floor when I heard the gun shots."

"We didn't have any other choice," Janet said. "It would've been us lying dead on the floor if we didn't shoot first. Or should I say Simon and Keith. I was a bystander when it came to the shooting."

Simon looked at Keith. He still held his gun which was still pointed at Seth. A half dollar size blood spot appeared on the left side of Keith's shirt near his heart. He stood there with an impending doom across his face.

Keith looked down at his chest. "I've been shot. But I don't feel anything." Keith's legs buckled as he slowly collapsed.

Simon rushed over to Keith, easing him to the floor. Simon put his arm around Keith's back for support; he then pressed his hand against the bullet wound and the oozing blood.

Janet leaned down and gently removed Keith's gun from his clutched right hand. "We'll need your gun for the forensic people when they get here. And I want to thank you. I owe you my life."

Keith pressed his lips together and nodded. His upper eye lids sagged. He then said: "I couldn't see the two of you killed. You're on the side of righteousness…they represent evil."

"You did good, Keith. You're a hero."

Keith smiled. "I finally did something worthwhile in my life. You know…it feels really good." He closed his eyes.

"Try to keep your eyes open," Simon pleaded. "Paramedics will be here soon." Keith's chest wall no longer heaved against Simon's hand. Keith's stopped breathing. Simon felt for a carotid pulse on his neck. Absent. Simon sighed then looked up at Janet. "He's gone."

"What a shame. Keith was finally turning his life around."

Simon lowered Keith's head to the floor then stood up.

Janet turned toward Simon. "I guess you do know how to handle a gun. Your quick reaction also saved our lives."

"I guess we can call things even now regarding pulling our guns at a gunfight. You did it first. And now I did it."

She grinned. "We're now indebted to each other for life."

Her enduring eyes met his as a warm sensation overwhelmed him. He was beginning to love this woman, something he hadn't felt in a long time. Or maybe it was only infatuation? Whatever it was, he liked the feeling. He winked at her. She reciprocated with a wink. "Sounds good to me." Simon stepped forward a couple of feet and placed his gun on the desk about two feet away from the other gun. "You know, I'm starting to get a complex. This is the second shooting we've been involved in today. Then there was the potential killing of three people at the restaurant yesterday in Detroit. Oh yeah. I forgot about the dead guy in the elevator. Trouble seems to follow us."

"Hopefully this'll be our last gunfight," Janet replied, as she glanced down at Keith, a true hero.

Jean, who'd been standing a few feet behind Frank, came through the doorway. She walked up to Simon, peered up at him with a bright smile and announced, "You lost your glow."

Simon sighed. He'd dodged the grim reaper, avoiding the sharp blade of his deadly scythe. "Great news for a change." He knew Keith played a role in eliminating his ominous yellow glow.

"You know if Keith had survived his gunshot," Janet said, "his safety would've been in jeopardy. The Circle wouldn't believe he avoided detection and capture in two separate shooting incidents with the death of three of their employees. We probably would've put him in the FBI's witness protection program or at least in a safehouse until we could get solid evidence of The Circle's involvement of the fourteen 11:58 A.M. Deaths."

Simon added, "I'm not so sure The Circle wouldn't have found Keith and killed him."

"Unfortunately, I think you're right about The Circle's capabilities," Janet replied. "I'll call this shooting in and talk with sheriff's deputies and the detective who'll be in charge with these two justified shootings and Keith's death." She removed her cell phone and made the call.

Frank began to sniff periodically throughout the room. The room probably measured out to be about forty feet long by thirty feet wide. There were two long metal tables containing bundles of flowers, various colored ribbons and glass vases of differing sizes. Many of the flowers were wilted, indicating they'd been lying on the tables for a few days.

Simon asked Frank, "Do you smell something unusual?"

"Yeah." He slightly lifted his head upward and sniffed. "Old Spice and coconut shampoo."

Simon frowned. "Why do these two things sound so familiar?"

"It was the odor inside the dark-blue pickup involved in our intersection accident." He walked over to an open door to the right that led upstairs to the second level. "The odor is stronger here."

"We need to check upstairs," Janet said. "Remove your gun. Hand it to me. There might be someone waiting to shoot us."

"That's encouraging," Frank said, handing his Glock to Janet.

Janet led the way as she and Frank slowly walked up the stairs, creaking sound of their footsteps was accentuated by the tunnel-like stairwell. As they reached the top of the stairs, a dimly lit hallway lay before them. Janet opened the first door on the left: a bathroom with a shower.

Frank stepped around her. "The smell of Old Spice and coconut shampoo."

Janet walked down the hallway to a partially opened door. She stepped into a bedroom, followed by Frank. Female attire hung in a closet.

Frank picked up a bottle of perfume and sniffed. "It's the same perfume used by the dead woman lying on the floor downstairs."

Janet nodded. "I'd say that would be a good assumption."

The next room was a kitchen containing a refrigerator, electric range, microwave and cupboards. A small, square wooden table with four chairs stood at the end of the room near a curtained window.

They left the kitchen and walked down the hallway to the next room on their left. "The odor of cologne and shampoo is getting much stronger," Frank said as Janet slowly opened the closed door. No occupant, only an unmade bed. Frank walked over to a dresser. On top of the dresser were a bottle of Old Spice aftershave and a plastic bottle of coconut shampoo. "We found our pickup driver's bedroom."

Janet picked up credit card receipts on an end table next to a single bed. She glanced at the name on the receipts. "The guy's name is Fredrick Jones. You'll need to do your computer magic and see if we can find this perpetrator and find out as much as you can about him."

"So far, we've found two people living up here. We still have one more room to look at."

"Yes, we do. I'll lead the way."

Frank grinned. "By all means. You're the one with a gun."

They left the bedroom. The sound of sirens outside became louder as they headed to the last room at the end of the hallway. Janet turned the doorknob. "The door's locked."

"I can handle this. Step aside." Frank lunged forward against the door. The door opened with the cracking sound of wood.

They took two steps into the room and stopped. Three computers and monitors were lined up along the wall to their right. None of them were turned on. A large commercial shredder stood on the opposite wall. Multi-shredded paper overflowed four plastic containers. "It looks like someone was quite busy in here," Janet said.

"Maybe they were destroying some evidence?"

"Could be," she answered looking around the room for anything suspicious or out of place. "It'll be impossible for anyone to tape the paper back. I'll have the Marion County Sheriff Department's computer forensic people check out the computers for any incriminating evidence, hopefully tying The Circle to the deaths in Ocala. Nothing more we can do up here. Let's head back downstairs."

Janet walked up to Simon, who stood next to Keith's body, and told him what she and Frank found upstairs. "If we can find and interrogate Fredrick Jones, we may be able to find collaborating evidence regarding the microchip, dental bridges and the fourteen deaths."

"That would be great. As far as I can see, this cell of The Circle has been shut down."

The medical examiner's investigators arrived as did the Marion County Sheriff's deputies since the flower shop was outside Ocala city limits. Statements from Janet and the Federal Medical Investigators on what happened in the flower shop were taken by sheriff's detectives. The story everyone told stated that they were investigating the fourteen deaths in Ocala and believed Seth Thompson and Karen Cunningham (they had obtained her name from ID in her purse) had something to do with the deaths. And Keith Nelson was an informant for Janet, who got shot trying to defend her and Simon Woods. No one mentioned the name The Circle since they didn't have solid evidence against them. They also didn't mention the microchip.

Simon got behind the wheel, Janet sat in the front passenger seat and Frank and Jean sat in the back seat. He started the car, then said, "It's getting late. I'll take you guys back to the hotel where you can get something to eat and relax the rest of the day and evening."

Frank reached around the driver seat and patted Simon on the shoulder "We love you, boss. You sure treat us good."

Simon shook his head, raised his eyebrows and chuckled. "Don't mention it. It's been a tough day for all of us. We'll start fresh tomorrow morning."

A crowd of people stood on the sidewalk in front of the flower shop. A person with a hooded shirt and wearing jeans watched Simon, Janet and the rest of the FMI team agents get into their car and driveway from the cluster of gawking bystanders. The person pushed back the hood. Alexander Mendelson or his alias, Caleb Johnson, removed a cell phone from his pants pocket. Alex smirked as he pushed speed-dial on his cell phone.

## Chapter Twenty-three

Alex waited as the phone at the other end of his call rang three times. A male answered, "What did you find out?"

"According to one of the sheriff's deputies, I heard Karen was shot and killed by Dr. Woods. Seth and Keith shot and killed each other. Like I said earlier, Detective Bennett and the CDC people are awful lucky. I can't see how they survived the missile attack and now a shootout at the flower shop."

"At this point it doesn't matter. Matter of fact, it's better none of them were killed. Their investigation has no place to go. All the computer and paper records at the dentist office regarding the dental bridges no longer exist. No way they'll now tie us to the fourteen deaths in Ocala. Plus, the microchip will never lead to The Circle. Your work is done in Ocala. I'll see you back here in Detroit."

~ * ~

Simon dropped off Frank and Jean at the front entrance to their hotel. He turned toward Janet. "I'll take you to your car." Her car was about fifty yards away at the far end of the parking lot.

"Do you want to get a drink? I'm not ready to go back to my place. I'd like to talk a bit and unwind from a crazy day."

"Sounds like a good plan to me. And crazy is a good word to describe our day." Simon parked the car. They walked through the hotel's front entrance and headed toward the lounge.

A waitress walked up to them. "What can I get you folks?"

"Yes. We're not eating. We're only having drinks this evening,"

Janet said. She glanced at Simon. "Sorry. Maybe you want something to eat?"

"No. I'm too wound up to eat anything," he replied with a grin. *Touché, as the saying goes.* Janet smirked back at him, acknowledging his pointed comment. *Besides, she's a take-charge person in most situations we've been involved in. I can handle that.*

For about thirty minutes they sat discussing the events of the day intermixed with personal information about each other. Such as, Simon being petrified of spiders with no rhyme or reason of why he possessed this phobia. Janet stated that since she was a teenager, she was afraid of heights and avoided ever getting on a ladder.

As Simon ordered a second round of drinks, Frank walked into the lounge with Jean. "Hey, guys. I'd thought you'd be down here since you didn't answer my knock on your room door. Although I wasn't expecting Janet to be with you. Anyway, I got information about Fredrick Jones."

"I thought I told you to relax this evening."

"You know me, relaxing is sitting in front of my computer."

"I can vouch for him," Jean said. "It takes everything to have him play George or Yahtzee with me."

Frank sat down at the table—as did Jean.

"So, what about Fredrick Jones?" Simon asked.

"He was killed crossing a street a few days ago."

Simon shook his head with disappointment. "We've reached the point in our investigation when all of our suspects likely tied or responsible for the 11:58 A.M. Deaths are dead."

"I guess the old adage: 'We've reached a dead end' holds true in our case," Frank said.

Simon sighed. "As for living suspects, we have Caleb…that is, Alex Mendelson, and the person or people in the missile van at Emerick's house. The person holding the missile launcher could've been Mendelson. If his habits are the same as when he was at the dealership in Detroit, or when he was a fugitive in Germany, he might be in another state or another country by now."

"You're right," Janet said. "We don't have any legal grounds and concrete evidence to pursue and subpoena The Circle's organization. We only have a theory. And our theories won't stand up for a request for a subpoena by a judge."

"There's something I found out about Seth Thompson and Karen Cunningham. They were the couple representing the Marion County Health Department when they visited the people on my list of Dr. Cassidy's patients with removable dental bridges."

Janet sipped some of her strawberry daiquiri. "We've now come full circle in this investigation. All we know is that the fourteen deaths won't have resolution. I don't believe we'll see a cluster of similar deaths. I believe The Circle used the microchip in the dental bridge as a preliminary test. I don't think they expected someone to find the microchip. Thanks to all of you, we solved these deaths in Ocala. The problem is we can't tell anyone what we discovered because we don't have prosecutable evidence against The Circle."

Simon added: "I'm sure we haven't heard the last of The Circle. What Keith Nelson proclaimed to me, this may only be the beginning of their goal of eventual world dominance. There something else I want to say." He peered into Janet's eyes. "I think we need a permanent law enforcement person by our side." Simon then glanced at Frank and Jean. They both nodded in agreement. He again stared at Janet. "So, what do you think, Detective Bennett? Will you join our FMI team?"

A tear cascaded down the right side of her face. "I don't know what to say. I'd say we all work great together. And I enjoyed every minute being with you, guys." She briefly stared down at the table, apparently taking in Simon's offer. She raised her head and peered into Simon's eyes. "Can I think about it for a minute or two?"

*She didn't immediately decline my offer*, thought Simon. *A good sign. At least, I think it is*? "Sure, by all means, take your time."

Frank and Jean ordered a drink from the waitress.

A few minutes later, Janet picked up her daiquiri glass and looked into Simon's eyes. "I'd like to make a toast." Everyone picked up their glass, presenting them to the center of the table. "Here's to the fourth FMI agent…me." Their glasses clinked fusing her acceptance to the team.

Janet reached over and touched Simon's hand.

Simon's cell phone rang. He glanced at the caller. "It's the CDC.

I'll put it on speaker." He pushed the green phone symbol on his phone, then said, "I was about to call you. We'll be leaving Ocala tomorrow afternoon. We don't have enough evidence for the district attorney to prosecute the responsible party for the deaths."

"Sorry to hear that," said a man calmly. "I have another assignment for you and the FMI team. There are six unexplained deaths in Chambersburg, Pennsylvania. I sent Frank an email attachment regarding this next case. Send me all the information and findings on the Whispers Before Death case. And by the way…we look forward, Detective Bennett, to you being the fourth FMI agent."

Janet appeared surprised by his comment, as her lower jaw fell. "Ah. Glad to be a part of your team."

"Talk to you all later." A dial tone sounded, ending the call.

"How did he know I accepted your offer?"

Simon shrugged his shoulders. "I really don't know. I'm as surprised as you are." He glanced at Frank, then Jean; both shrugged their shoulders.

"I assume the caller is your boss?"

"Yes. His name is Brian Littlefield. He's the director of FMI"

"Littlefield?" Janet looked at Frank.

"Brian is my older brother. And if you're wondering, he doesn't have any special powers."

"You're right, the thought crossed my mind." Janet sipped the last of her daiquiri, then looked at Simon. "Do I have to fill out an application for FMI?"

Simon chuckled to himself. They had enough personal and public information on Janet to complete a three-page job application. "No. All you have to do is recite a F.M.I. oath, which will be recorded. You can do the oath before we land in Chambersburg."

~ * ~

Before leaving the hotel's lounge, Janet called her brother and said she'd be stopping by his house. There was something important to discuss with him and Crystal.

"Hey, sis, what's so important you couldn't tell me on the phone?" Michael asked as Janet stepped through the front door doorway. Crystal stood next to Michael.

''Why don't we all sit?" Janet suggested.

"Wow. Must be important." He glanced down at her mid-section. "Are you pregnant?"

She laughed. "Heavens no, I'm not pregnant."

Michael and Crystal sat on the couch. Janet sat in a cushioned chair across from them. Their two children were in their bedrooms. "Too bad, I'd like to have a nephew or niece."

Janet told them what had happened the past couple of days, assisting a branch of the CDC's investigative team in trying to solve the fourteen deaths in Ocala. She didn't go into any details or names. "So, the investigation has ended without any cause of the victims' deaths."

"At least, that's what you're telling me. Right, Sis?"

Michael could always tell when Janet hadn't completely told the truth. "It's the only truth I can tell you. Me talking about the investigation isn't the reason I came over."

"I didn't think it was. So, why the visit?"

"I've resigned from my detective position. I've taken a position with a branch of CDC that investigates suspicious illnesses and deaths throughout the United States. I'll be leaving Ocala early tomorrow afternoon and flying to another case. I'll keep my townhouse and return periodically. Our home office is in Atlanta, Georgia. We'll keep in touch. You have my cell phone number." Janet stayed for a while before leaving.

The following morning, she went back to her office and said goodbye to Bill Matters. He congratulated her on the new position. He told her the two FBI agents didn't find any evidence of the missile being stolen from military installations. There weren't any recognizable markings on the missile to trace it to the manufacturer. The case would remain open until further evidence comes forward. Bill gave Janet's Glock back to her after it had been checked by forensics. The shooting was declared justifiable.

Janet stepped onto FMI's passenger jet about two o'clock and put two small suitcases in the overhead bin. Frank and Jean were already seated. They both welcomed her. She found a seat near a window.

Simon walked through the cabin's doorway. "Hey, you guys. A new day. A new unsolved mystery. Are we ready for this?"

Frank and Jean each raised an arm and said, "We're ready." Jean then went back to reading a magazine. Frank resumed typing on his laptop.

Janet assumed Simon did this pep talk prior to each case by the reaction of her fellow agents. Not to break tradition, she raised her arm and said, "I'm ready." Everyone laughed. Janet frowned. "What's going on?"

Simon answered, "There was a bet between Frank and Jean if you'd raise your arm."

Frank looked across the aisle toward Jean. "You owe me the next drink."

"So, do you do this scenario before your investigations?"

Simon put his luggage into a bin. "No, we don't. It would be kind of corny. Like a 'B' movie."

Janet normally anticipated or recognized prankster scenarios after going through them by her fellow detectives at the sheriff's department. She thought about her reaction to Simon and her cohorts. A smile appeared. *If I wasn't the targeted victim, I'd be laughing too.*

They fastened their seatbelts. A moment later, the jet sped down the runway, then lifted off. Destination: Chambersburg, Pennsylvania.

# About the Author

Greg graduated from Wayne State University with a secondary education degree in Unified Science and a minor in English. He then graduated from University of Detroit-Mercy with a Physician Assistant degree. He had previous published four medical mystery novels by Rogue Phoenix Press, *Frozen Death* (2009), *Sudden Blindness* (2014), *Strange Appearance* (2016) and Strange (2018). Greg lives in Florida with his wife, Holly.

## Also by G. L. Didaleusky
at
Rogue Phoenix Press

### *Strange*

Frightening dreams night after night are afflicting the chief of pediatrics, Adam Stafford, at Ocala Regional Medical Center. Will there be a conclusion of his dreams or will he succumb to a death spiral before he can awake? At ORMC, Adam attempts to understand why deathbed children on the pediatric floor at ORMC awakened cured without any medical explanation? In a near-by town, an archeologist, Lisa Douglas, is searching for the meaning of ancient hieroglyphs on various Mayan relics recently discovered in a cave along Mexico's Yucatan peninsula. There seems to be a possibility that all these scenarios are intertwined with a twelve-year-old male patient, Arius Turner, at Ocala Regional Medical Center.

### Chapter One

*A soft glowing ivory light is illuminating from the entire ceiling of this cube-shaped sterile-white room. Each of the room's dimensions, width, length, and height, appears to be about twelve feet. Where are the windows to let in the sunshine, the celestial light? Light that has been present since the first organism and plant needed its nurturing power of life? Absent on the walls are pictures, shelves and electrical outlets. There's a faint outline of a sliding door on one of the walls. Is this the way out of the tomb-like room?*

*In the center of the room is a white, square stone table supported by four round stone legs resting on a white glossy marble floor. On top of the table is a pastel blue, oval-shaped object resembling a football in size and shape. A hammock-shaped silvery metal apparatus is cradling the object. What's this bluish object?*

*Wait a minute. The room is getting brighter. Even with my eyes closed, the piercing light is burning my eyes. The light is becoming brighter and brighter and brighter....*

Adam Stafford's upper eyelids snapped open to the morning sun's rays piercing through his bedroom window. He rolled over to his right side. The thirty-nine-year old squinted at a digital clock sitting on the night table next to the bed. In less than a minute, the alarm would be going off at 6 a.m. He reached over and turned off the alarm. This morning, an unusually vivid dream, a nightmare, awakened him. He rolled onto his back and stared up toward a white stucco ceiling, focusing on the day lying ahead of him: the monthly pediatric meeting this morning at eight o'clock. One of the residents will present a difficult pediatric case, leading to an open discussion and a diagnosis.

After completing his pediatric residency program eight years ago, he thought his long marathon hours as a resident had ended. He had been fooling himself. Two years later, he accepted the responsibilities and duties as Chief of Pediatric at Ocala Regional Medical Center. Adam soon found out the prestigious position demanded more of his time and energy than the residency program.

"I better get up," he whispered

Adam began his morning ritual of showering with his favorite soap, Irish Spring, and shaving with an electric razor. He put his work clothes on; white dress shirt with a Mickey Mouse blue tie, dark-blue slacks and white tennis shoes. He went to the kitchen and poured himself a cup of coffee, retrieved a bowl and a box of cereal from the cupboard, milk from the refrigerator and sat down to enjoy his usual morning nourishment.

Adam's mind pondered on Arius Turner, a twelve-year-old patient who was admitted by one of his pediatric residents three days earlier through the emergency room. The patient had a three-week history of a persistently elevated temperature. His parents, Howard and Patricia Turner, told the resident their son's temperature had ranged from one-hundred and one to a hundred and three degrees Fahrenheit for three weeks. Arius didn't have any medical complaints. All preliminary testing had been normal. Adam had a "gut" feeling Arius had something unusual, a rare medical illness causing his fever.

During Adam's residency at the University of Florida Pediatric Residency Program, he had the reputation of looking further into symptoms and signs of an illness. When a patient's medical condition appeared to be a clear and common diagnosis to his colleagues and mentors, he would prove them wrong by diagnosing an unexpected, and sometimes rare, medical condition or disease. The other doctors had been listening for the common gallop of a horse, but Adam had heard the rare hoof sounds of a Zebra.

He looked at the digital watch on his right wrist: 6:45 A.M. It was time to leave for the hospital. He walked into the living room of his two-bedroom ranch condominium. The house was meticulously neat and clean—not the typical condition of a bachelor's residence.

After about thirty minutes of driving, he pulled off I-75 and turned east onto 200$^{th}$ Street. Several minutes later, the hospital came into view to his right. The hospital's tall, white, U-shaped structure towered majestically above the moderately treed surroundings.

After parking in the hospital's parking structure, he entered the hospital and stepped into the elevator. He rode the elevator to the sixth floor. The elevator door opened and Adam stepped out onto the pediatric floor. Physician Assistant Scott Templeton stood behind the nursing station, looking down at a chart.

"Hi, Scott. I'm sure all the residents are waiting for us in the conference room."

He glanced up. "Good morning. You're right. We don't want to keep them waiting."

A few moments later, Adam opened the conference room door. In front of him in the center of the room was a long, rectangular, highly glossed, mahogany table. On each side of the table were three pediatric residents sitting in their cushioned captain chairs. The chairs were spaced far enough apart allowing its occupants plenty of elbowroom. At each end of the table was an unoccupied chair, the chair to the left was Adam's, the other chair was for Scott.

Two of the three residents on the left side of the table, who were first-year residents, had solemn appearing expressions. The residents on the right side of the table and the one sitting next to the two first-year residents, smirked at Adam.

Adam stood in the doorway shaking his head back and forth. A serious expression emerged across his face. Looking straight across the table, he glared back and forth at the two first-year residents. "What a motley appearing group we have at this table. I hope you all brought your questions for this important staff meeting. I wouldn't want to expel anyone from the residency program."

The first-year residents looked at each other baffled by Adam's austere statement. "No one told us about having questions to ask," said one of them. "What were we…?"

"Loosen up," interrupted Adam. "I'm kidding."

The other residents laughed, causing the two, naive, first-year residents to roll their eyes upward in embarrassment.

The meeting lasted about an hour. Adam pushed his chair back, stood up and said in a firm, authoritative voice, "Our monthly medical meeting is now adjourned."

His cell phone went off, indicating there was a text message He removed the cell phone from a holster attached to his belt. Adam retrieved the message.

URGENT...REGARDS TO ARIUS TURNER...DR. WALKER.

Dr. Walker was the hospital's chief hematologist.

Adam told Scott to start the pediatric rounds with the residents and that he'd catch up with them later.

Adam walked into the hematology lab. His vision encountered several apparatuses. Some of them were blinking an array of white, green and red lights, other computer machines displayed a series of changing numbers. Several monitors displayed wavy or pointed lines in a graphic pattern. Lab technicians sat in front of sterile-white countertops with their eyes pressed against the lens of a microscope. In his mind, Adam visualized the technicians were viewing a world of bizarre looking microscopic organisms and structures. The sounds heard inside the room were the mixture of various hums and whining sounds coming from the laboratory apparatuses. Turning his head to the left he saw Dr. Walker, who was about twenty feet away, standing next to a blood analysis machine. The machine had three small computer screens; the screens were about six inches square and displayed a series of constant changing numbers. The middle-aged hematologist was wearing a long, white lab coat, the coat hung neatly on his short and overweight stature. His sideward profile accentuated a long, broad nose and an extra fold of skin below his chin. Streaks of grey hair highlighted his temples, as a six-inch ponytail hung down passed his shoulders.

"Good morning, Dr. Walker."

"Dr. Stafford. I'm glad you received my message. There's something astonishing I found on your patient, Arius Turner. Something unheard of in medical science." There was excitement in his voice. "This young boy has immunity to HIV. His CD4 count is twenty-two hundred. Normal high is fifteen hundred. His HIV viral load is undetectable. He either has natural immunity or received a vaccine. But that's not all. He has immunity to Hepatitis C. His viral load is undetectable and there isn't evidence of any active disease. So, Arius Turner either has natural immunity or was given a vaccine. I also did an assay on several other deadly diseases and found the patient had an immunity to each of the diseases. All this indicates our patient has a supercharged immune system. From what I can see from all of this, he'd be able to resist any deadly virulent viral, fungal and bacterial pathogens."

Adam stood there in complete awe. He felt like his body had walked out of a walk-in freezer. He reached up and rubbed the back of his neck, bringing warmth back into his psychologically frozen body. "Are you sure of the results? Maybe there was an error in your blood analysis?"

"I've rechecked every test, making make sure there wasn't an error in the technique. There are no doubts in the results of the blood tests."

"How can his immune system resist all of those devastating pathogens?"

"We may be seeing a genetic aberration. I can't say with any certainty this is what we're seeing with your patient. We'll need to look at his DNA for the possible answer to his unnatural immunity."

"I'll call Dr. Frank in the genetics department," said Adam.

"If you like. You can use the phone in my office to call him?"

"Thank you very much. But I don't want to take you away from what you were doing."

“No problem. I’m anxious to know what this twelve-year-old boy’s genetic make-up is all about.”

Adam followed Dr. Walker into his office and called Dr. Sidney Frank. Adam gave the geneticist a detailed scenario of Arius Turner and the results of his lab test.

“Yes, Dr. Frank, I can have his chart sent up to you with all the blood results.” He looked at his watch. “That’ll be okay with me. I’ll see you round three o’clock.” Adam hung up the phone.

“It’ll be important to check the parents’ blood,” said Dr. Walker. “They also may have a similar immunity system?”

“I’ll be sure to discuss this matter with them today.” He shook Dr. Walker’s hand, then walked briskly out of the department.

Adam glanced down at his watch: 11:30 A.M. It was almost lunchtime for the patients on the pediatric floor. Howard and Patricia Turner will probably be in Arius’s room. This would be the ideal time to question them.

As the elevated reached the sixth floor, he heard muffled voices. The elevator door opened.

No one was there.

## Also by the Author
at
Rogue Phoenix Press

### *Frozen Death*

Something is causing people to freeze to death in Florida during ninety-degree weather. Ancient Indian lore holds the answer to these mysterious medical aberrations. A newly constructed Florida male prison sits on ancient hallowed grounds called Forbidden Hill. Soon after the prison opens, two male inmates freeze to death without exposure to frigid temperatures. John Randall, a widowed prison doctor, meets Lena Windmaker, a single, off-duty sheriff detective at a local library. Their initial plutonic relationship soon kindles into a more amorous one. They hide a personal secret that could bring them together or destroy them. They uncover articles in local, post-Civil war newspapers describing residence succumbing to Frozen Death. John and Lena race to discover a cause before it chooses other victims.

### *Sudden Blindness*

People in Ocala, a small city in Florida, face an epidemic of sudden blindness. The head of Ocala Regional Medical Center's emergency room, David Belmont, and his wife, Sarah, a high school science teacher, seek answers to what is causing the blindness, where did the blindness originate and why did it suddenly afflict people and animals without warning or other symptoms? Their son, a high school senior, is one of the victims. These questions are baffling an experienced investigative medical team from

CDC whom arrive later in the day from Atlanta, Georgia. Unbeknownst to David, Sarah and the leader of the CDC's team, Russell Patton, has a mutual amorous secret.

## *Strange Appearance*

Two hairless teenage bodies are found dead with ritual-type death masks on their faces in Ocala National Forest. Robert Jenson, a fourth-year medical student and Cynthia Davidson, a pathologist's assistant, join together to solve these unexplained mysterious deaths. Clandestine members of a secluded satanic cult adjacent to the national forest cross their paths. Shortly afterwards, Robert and Cynthia face deadly situations jeopardizing their own lives as they soon discover someone doesn't want them to know the truth behind the teenagers' deaths. Robert and Cynthia's initial platonic relationship evolves to amorous feelings and needs complicating their investigation. Evil touches the two medical sleuths. And they don't realize it until it's almost too late.

## *The Strange Horizon*

The Strange Horizon ranges from stories less than a hundred words to over four thousand words. There isn't any profanity, gore or sexual innuendo in any of the short stories. The genre varies from mystery, suspense, contemporary, horror, science fiction and fantasy. You may smile, chuckle, express a tear or two, feel a sudden chill or feel warmth at the end of the story. Emotions are in the mind of the reader and the heart cuddles or rejects those emotions.

www.ingramcontent.com/pod-product-compliance
Lightning Source LLC
Chambersburg PA
CBHW051951220626
47052CB00004B/891
*9781624204432*